MORE *than* THIS

ALSO BY JAY MCLEAN

Where the Road Takes Me (2015)
Combative (2015)

THE MORE THAN SERIES

More Than Her
More Than Him
More Than Forever

MORE *than* THIS

MORE THAN SERIES
- BOOK ONE -

JAY McLEAN

SKYSCAPE

Text copyright © 2014 Jay McLean
All rights reserved.

Published by Skyscape, New York

www.apub.com

Amazon, the Amazon logo, and Skyscape are trademarks of Amazon.com, Inc., or its affiliates.

ISBN-13: 9781477820384
ISBN-10: 1477820388

Front cover design by Ari at Cover it! Designs.
Spine and back cover by Inkd.

Library of Congress Control Number: 2014913353

Printed in the United States of America

To my very own knight in shining armor and our two little princes. Thank you for making me your queen, and giving me my own happily-ever-after.

PROLOGUE

MIKAYLA

He was right. It made no difference whether it was six months or six years.

I couldn't undo what had been done. I couldn't change the future. I couldn't even predict it.

It was one night.

One night when everything changed.

It was so much more than just the betrayal.

It was the tragedy.

The deaths.

The murders.

But it was also that feeling . . .

That feeling of falling.

ONE

MIKAYLA

I finish getting ready with fifteen minutes to spare. I look in the mirror to make sure everything's in place. I'm nothing special to look at. I'm definitely no Megan (my best friend). I have naturally olive skin and slightly almond-shaped eyes from being a quarter Filipino on my mom's side. My dad's Irish/Scottish and six feet tall, and my mom's a tiny five-foot-nothing. Luckily, I'm a good in-between.

I'm not naive enough to think I'm popular based on looks or extracurricular activities. I'm book smart, but not so much that I'm socially awkward. I've made the popular list by association. My best friend is the head cheerleader, and my hot boyfriend James is captain of our basketball team.

I take one more look in the mirror. I'm ready for prom.

I open my bedroom door and almost run into my parents, who are standing in the hall. They have that look on their face, like whatever they're about to say has to be taken seriously. My dad's arm is wrapped around Mom's shoulders. Emily, my nine-year-old sister, is nowhere to be seen. They step forward, united, causing me to take a step back.

I'm officially worried.

They keep walking forward until I'm forced to sit on the edge of my bed. Only when I look up do they finally let go of each other and sit on either side of me.

Dad exhales loudly and shakes his head. "Honey, your mother and I have something we need to tell you."

I look at my mom, and she looks away. She's nervous.

Shit.

Dad continues, "We figure since you're graduating in two weeks, and you've been eighteen for a few months now . . . Well, I guess we both decided it was about time we tell you something very important."

I scan my brain for what this can be, then it hits me: *I'm adopted.*

I knew it. I was always different. I looked less Asian than I should, and I don't know where my nose comes from. No one in my family has this nose. Oh, God. Who are my birth parents? And what about Emily . . . Is she adopted, too?

"Mikayla?" Dad interrupts my raging thoughts.

I close my eyes, hoping that doing so may take away the sting of what he's about to tell me.

"Are you listening to me?"

I nod once, eyes still closed.

"Mikayla." He pauses for a long moment. "Boys have a penis . . ."

My eyes dart open. My parents are both stifling a laugh, and my mom's face is beet red with the effort. I glare at them with narrowed eyes, waiting for my pulse rate to decrease.

I want to junk-punch my own dad.

I know he's behind this. It's totally something he would do. My mom doesn't have it in her to think of something like this.

As I'm about to stand so I can turn and face them both, Emily comes running into the room with her life-size cardboard cutout of Justin Bieber. She's hiding behind it, cackling to herself. Then she breaks out in song, waving the cutout in front of her.

"And I was like penis, penis, penis, ohhhhh! Like penis, penis, penis, nooooo! Like penis, penis, penis, ohhhhh! I thought you'd always be mine, mine!"

I'm trying so hard to hold in my laughter, in case this is one of those situations that's funny for us but inappropriate for a nine-year-old girl. I look at my parents and wait for their reaction.

Mom giggles, and Dad breaks out in a weird dance, which I'm pretty sure is supposed to be something resembling the Dougie. He belts out, "You know you love me, I know you caaaare!"

I can't help but laugh. I start down the stairs to wait for Megan and James, shaking my head at their craziness. Of course they all follow, Justin Bieber cutout and all, and keep singing at the top of their lungs, Mom included.

"And I was like penis, penis, penis, ohhhhh! Like penis, penis, penis, nooooo! Like penis, penis!"

The front door swings open.

"What the fuhhhhhh—" Megan's words die in the air when she sees Emily—and the Biebs—behind me.

James scratches his head. "Are you guys singing about penises? To Justin Bieber?"

They snort with laughter. My family is insane, but I love them anyway.

—

After a good ten minutes of photos and my dad's retelling of the humiliating stunt they just pulled on me, we're on our way to Bistro's, an Italian restaurant in downtown Hickory. It's famous for its noisy atmosphere and big tables for large groups—perfect for pre-prom dinner.

When we get to the restaurant, we notice a few other tables with kids our age all dressed up. We don't recognize them; they must go to different schools. The air is thick with sexual tension and the smell of cheap perfume and hair products. It's everything prom should be.

We find our table and sit with Andrew and Sean, two of James's friends from his basketball team, and their girlfriends.

Megan decided to go stag. It wasn't like no one had asked her, because about a trillion different guys did. She said she wanted to keep her options open and not go with some guy because he was hot, only to find out he was a dick and have to put out at the end. (Her words.)

We make small talk until the waiter comes and takes our order. The restaurant is loud with conversation, like you would expect with a bunch of teenagers in the room. After we've all told the waiter what we want, James stands up. "Where's the toilet in this place? I need to take a leak. That champagne from the limo's gone straight through me."

He's charming, as always.

"I'll show you, since I need to use the ladies' room to readjust my underwear. It's riding up my ass," Megan states loudly.

They walk away toward the restrooms at the back of the restaurant.

I'm in the middle of talking to Andrew about the new gym being built at school when I feel something wet trickle down my back. I freeze for a second, then turn to find some dude in a tux looking at me wide-eyed, half a glass of beer in his hand. The other half, I'm sure, is down my back.

"Shit, babe. I'm sorry," the wide-eyed douche bag says.

Babe? Really? This guy has to be a joke.

"Jesus Christ, Logan. Turn down the asshole a little, would ya?" his friend behind him says. He has a British accent, or South African or Australian or something.

Logan turns around to face his friend so quickly that his hand holding the rest of his beer slams against accent boy's broad chest. Beer spills on the crisp white shirt under his open tux jacket. Logan stifles a laugh. Accent boy groans and pushes Logan aside, heading to the back of the restaurant toward the restrooms, I presume.

"Naw, don't be like that, Jakey," Logan jeers.

I stand up to go to the restroom to see if the dress, or this night, is worth salvaging, but douche bag Logan blocks my way. Eyeing me up and down, he walks a slow circle around me. He comes to a stop in front of me, a small smirk pulling at his lips.

"Well, hello there, little lady," he drawls.

I push him out of the way and head toward the restroom. I'm wearing a halter-style black dress that's open down to the small of my back, so I'm not wearing any underwear just in case it'd show. I'm hoping, fingers crossed, that the beer spilled just on my back and not on the dress. I can ask Megan to help me clean my back at least—more than I can say for accent boy.

As I turn down the hallway with the restrooms, I stop in my tracks. Megan is halfway out the door of the ladies' room. She's adjusting her dress, her hair in shambles and her lipstick smeared all around her lips. She's giggling and reaches her hands up to the face of some random guy who she probably just hooked up with.

Megan is every guy's walking wet dream. She's sex on legs: your typical leggy, blue-eyed blond. She loves sex and has lots of it. So it doesn't surprise me at all that we've been at Bistro's all of fifteen minutes, and she's been doing God knows what with some random dude in a public bathroom.

What does surprise me, though, as I get closer to her, is that her hands are not on just some random guy. They're on James. *My* boyfriend. She's cleaning the smeared lipstick from around his mouth. My eyes are drawn to his hands, which are at the front of his pants. He tucks himself back in and zips up his fly.

I feel the vomit creeping up my throat and gag. The noise must have been loud enough to distract them from each other. They both turn to face me at the same time in what almost feels like slow motion, their eyes huge and their mouths hanging open.

Like they're surprised *I'm* intruding on *their* intimate fucking moment.

TWO

JAKE

I'm in the bathroom, doing everything I can to save this beer-stained shirt that's clinging to my body. There's nothing I can do about it, though. It's dunzo.

I take off my tux jacket and start undoing the buttons on the shirt, hoping the tank I'm wearing underneath is okay. I'll have to run home and grab a new shirt. Luckily, Mom is always prepared for this kind of stuff and has a spare ready to go.

I can't believe Logan did that, and all to get that girl's attention. I mean, I get it—I noticed her the minute she walked through the door, smiling up at the kid whose hand she was holding. She walked in with another guy, so you'd think that was enough of a sign to call the game off. But not for Logan. The minute her boyfriend or whatever left her side, it was game on. I followed him for a laugh. I wasn't supposed to end up here. I roll my eyes at the mirror. I'm going to look like an ultra-douche walking out in suit pants and a beater. Fuck Logan.

I open the door and stop in my tracks. It's her again, but she's not the same girl who walked into Bistro's earlier. Her eyes are brimming with unshed tears and she's fuming. I've opened the door just enough so I can see her, but I haven't stepped into the hallway yet. She's staring daggers at something or someone.

I take a tentative step forward and see her glaring at a couple standing in front of the women's restroom. They look like they're frozen in time. The blond girl's hair is messed up, her dress is all twisted, and her hands are on the guy's face. I can't see him properly because his back is to me. I can, however, see that he's adjusting himself. It's obvious those two just screwed in the bathroom. At least *their* prom will be memorable.

I almost leave when I hear her strained voice. "How long?" she asks, her tone flat.

The guy turns to face her, and I realize who this asshole is. It's her boyfriend. At least, I assume he's her boyfriend. He's the dick she walked in with.

"How long?" she asks again, a little louder, but still with the same even tone.

"Baby . . ." her boyfriend says, reaching out for her.

"Two years," the blond says at the same time.

I look over at the cute brunette and wait for a reaction. I feel like I should leave, like what I'm witnessing is too intimate and personal. But my feet are glued to the floor. I have no idea why, but I can't look or walk away. I want to punch this guy for causing the pained look on this girl's face. No one deserves to be treated like that, especially her. I feel the need to protect her, but I don't even know her.

Two years—what the hell?

Her boyfriend steps forward, turning away from the blond. She glares at the back of his head. "Baby," he says. I ball my fists. "I love you, Mikayla."

What?

"What?" both girls yell.

The brunette and her boyfriend both turn to the blond.

"Shut up, Megan!" they shout in unison.

"Megan," the brunette says, taking a deep breath. "You're my best friend. What the fuck?" Tears start streaming down her face.

Megan looks at her, then at the asshole.

"I'm sorry, Mick." She shrugs. But you can tell she's not sorry, not even a little. She walks away, passing in front of me.

I still haven't said a word. I still haven't moved an inch.

Mikayla and her boyfriend are staring at each other. Neither of them knows I'm standing here like a creeper.

"Jesus, James," Mikayla whispers, her voice shaky now. "I've been with you for four fucking years, and half that time you've been screwing my best friend!"

He's silent as he wipes a tear from his face. Why the fuck is *he* crying?

"Why the fuck are *you* crying?" she says forcefully. He flinches. *Exactly, Mikayla.*

"For four years, I never so much as looked at another guy. I was loyal to you when you weren't even around, when you wouldn't have even known, because that's how much I loved you." She's in his face now, her words clear as day. She's beyond the broken girl she started as—now she just looks pissed. "Were there any others?"

"No! I swear it."

Silence. The only sound is their heavy breathing.

"Why her?"

"Come on, Micky. You don't want to hear this shit. Let's just go to prom and have a good time, okay?" He has an accent—Texan, I think.

"Why her?" she asks again.

He sighs, defeated. "Remember that away game a couple years back, when the team stayed overnight to support the cheerleaders at some tournament they were doing the next day?"

"The one I couldn't go to with you, because my dad was out of town and my mom and sister were sick?" she asks quietly, looking at the floor.

He nods. "Yeah, that's the one, Micky. It was so stupid. We just . . . There was alcohol, and she wanted me, and I didn't think. Well, I did, but not with my head."

"And all the times after? God, how many times were there?"

He flinches at the question. "I'm sorry, baby."

"Don't call me that!"

"I'm sorry, Micky," he sighs. "She just—I don't know. She always wanted me, and it was always so easy."

"What?" she asks quietly. Then fire burns in her eyes. "What?" she says, louder. "You're going to put this on *me*? At what stage did you think that I didn't want you? I gave it up to you whenever you wanted! I never said no to you, *ever*! I wasn't easy enough? Because we had to sneak around and wait for parents or brothers or sisters to not be around, or go to hotel rooms or our cars? Because she lived next door, and her mom was never home? That's why it was easy? What the fuck, James?"

She takes a deep breath and then her eyes go wide. "Oh my God . . . Did you use protection? I mean, she's been with a lot of guys—a *lot*. And that's only the ones I know about. I didn't even consider the ones she didn't . . ." She trails off. "James . . . ?"

"I always used a condom with her, always. I know I'm an ass-hole, but I knew she got around, and with you . . . Since you've always been on the pill, and we never needed to use protection, I didn't want to risk it. Babe, you have to—"

"You mean you didn't want to get caught?"

"Mikayla, I'm so sorry." He sighs. He at least has the decency to sound sincere. "Do you think you'll ever be able to forgive me? I mean, we had plans to go to college together. We planned our future togeth—"

11

"Oh my God!" she gasps, panic written all over her face. "Who was your first, James?"

He flinches. It's a small movement, but we both catch it.

"Our first time. At the hotel on my birthday. That wasn't your first time, was it?"

This guy just brought asshole to a whole new level.

"God, you faked it all, and the lies . . . I must be so fucking stupid!" she cries.

They're silent for what seems like the longest time. He must sense that nothing he says is going to make this any better.

A sob escapes her, and he moves forward to comfort her. I do everything I can to stay still. He holds her while she sobs in his arms. After a minute, she rears back from his embrace and pushes him away.

"Was I not good enough in bed? Is that what it was? Did I do it wrong?" She sounds so sad now. "If you didn't want to be with me, you could have just broken up with me, James. You didn't have to cheat on me, over and over again with my *best friend*. You could've just told me you didn't want to be with me anymore, and you could've had all the girls in the world. It didn't have to be like this." She looks up at him and whispers, "You didn't have to break my heart."

My chest tightens at her words. Tears are falling freely down both their faces.

She squares her shoulders and lifts her chin. "You need to go, James. I can't stand to even look at you right now."

"Mikayla, please," he begs.

"Please, James. Just go," she pleads.

He actually listens and walks away, passing in front of where I've been standing, unable to move.

I watch as she leans against the wall and, slowly, her body gives up. She slumps, sliding to the ground. Her body breaks into silent sobs, her arms shielding her head from the world.

She has no idea I'm still standing here. I need to do something. I need to comfort her, to make sure she's going to be okay. Or maybe I should just go out there and kick that guy's ass.

I step out of the bathroom and into the hallway.

Then I clear my throat.

She looks up, startled.

"Holy shit, accent boy! How much of that did you see?"

THREE

MIKAYLA

I can't believe accent boy just witnessed that whole thing. I'm so frickin' embarrassed by all of it, mainly because I was the dumb girl who got played for so long.

"So, that just happened, huh?"

He has this deep voice that doesn't belong to a teenage boy. It sounds like a rugged, middle-aged man's or something. He motions his head to the spot on the floor next to me. I nod once, not looking at him.

"So. Your boyfriend's an asshole, and your best friend's a selfish whore," he says, taking a seat next to me.

I can't help but laugh. "That pretty much covers it." I sniff.

"I'm Jake, by the way." He nudges my side with his elbow as he looks straight ahead. He's taken his dress shirt off. The beer obviously ruined it. I don't even know what my dress looks like—I never got the chance to check. I look down at the satin material.

"Mikayla," I say to the dress.

"Yeah, I figured that out."

We sit in silence for a few moments, then he clears his throat. It might be a nervous habit. I don't know. He clears it again, so I look to my left, at his profile. He senses my gaze and turns to look at me.

It's the first time I see him properly, and he's extremely hand-some in a masculine, not boyish, way—like he could grow five inches of facial hair overnight. He smiles at me then quickly looks away.

I was staring. Shit.

"So," he starts, "you're all dressed up and nowhere to go, huh?" Where is that accent from?

"Yeah, I guess so. Hey, um, where are you from?" I have to know.

He's confused for a second. "Oh, my accent? It's Australian, but I'm actually from here. It's a long story."

"Okay."

"So," he begins again. He rubs his hand over the back of his head. He has dark-brown hair with tiny curls at the base of his hair-line. His hair has a kink in it that could only be caused by his wear-ing a baseball cap anytime he's not sleeping or dressed up in formal wear. "You heading to senior prom?" he asks.

"Yeah," I sigh. "I mean, yes, I was. I don't think I can handle going anymore, though."

"To your prom, or any prom?"

I shrug. "I don't know yet. I haven't really processed everything, you know?"

"Okay . . . Well." He clears his throat again. "I mean, you can come to mine. I have a spare ticket, and it would be a shame to waste that amazing dress. You look beautiful, by the way." His gaze quickly darts to mine then back down.

James didn't even comment on the way I looked.

"I swear, I'm not a psycho," he continues, "and we have the limo for the whole night, so you can just leave when you want if you hate it, or me." He laughs. "God, you must think I'm crazy. And my mate, Logan, spilling his beer on you . . ." He shakes his head. "I'm sorry, by the way. He's kind of a dick." He won't stop rambling.

"Look, I just don't think you should let bad people dictate whether you have a good time. Come hang out with me and my friends. It'll at least take your mind off things for a little bit. I just think that maybe—"

"Okay," I cut in.

"Huh?"

"Okay," I say again. I look into his deep blue eyes and he smiles—a panty-dropping smile that most girls would swoon over. Too bad I'm not most girls.

He nods. "So . . . I'll just let the guys know what's happen—"

"Yo, Jake. What the hell, man? You've been in here for ages, I was about to—" Logan stops in his tracks when he sees us sitting together and the state of my face.

"Give us a minute," Jake says.

"Yeah, man, sure, of course." Logan starts backing away from us.

"I should probably go tell them what's up. I mean, they won't mind your coming along, but they'll probably want to know why. I can lie to them if you want, but I don't think they'd care either way. So whatever I tell them is up to you."

"It's okay." I smile at him. "You can tell them the truth. I'm just going to go freshen up, and then I'll be right out, okay?"

"Sure." But it comes out more like "shaw." It's the accent.

—

After ten minutes in the restroom of freshening up, I'm almost back to normal. I hope ten minutes is enough time for all his friends to ask whatever they need to. I don't want to ruin their night, but I don't want to downplay what happened here, either.

My phone's been blowing up with calls and messages from James. None from Megan—not one. There are two missed calls from my parents, and a text from Mom asking if I'm okay, because

James has called there a few times. I text back that everything's fine, and I'll see them at home later tonight and explain everything then. I write that I love them, because I really do, and nothing has made me realize it more than the shit that's just happened.

A few seconds later I get a text from Mom:

We love you, too, sweetheart. Have a good night. Emily is begging for ice cream. We'll bring you back a big batch of cookies'n'cream. It will be waiting for you in the freezer, wake me if I'm asleep and we can share some.

I'm actually really looking forward to that, I text back.

I walk from the back of the restaurant to the dining area. Jake and his friends are waiting for me in the foyer. They turn toward me and smile as I walk up, but I don't know them well enough to know if it's genuine.

Jake puts his hand on the small of my back to lead the way. I don't think he expected skin-on-skin contact. He tenses for a second next to me before asking, "Ready?"

I nod and smile up at him.

He smiles back. "Well, let's go then."

—

Once we're all seated in the limo, Logan goes outside to have a cigarette. We introduce ourselves while waiting for him. I can tell by their builds that all the boys are jocks. The guy opposite me looks familiar—maybe he plays basketball, and I've seen him play against our school. I did go to all of James's games.

"I'm Heidi," the blond girl sitting on his lap says, "and this is Dylan." Dylan does a quick nod then returns his gaze to her. Obviously a man of many words.

"Don't mind him, he's quiet." Heidi shrugs. "Likes to make me feel real special by not looking at other girls for more than a second. It's sweet, but it can be awkward if you don't know him."

"*Him* is sitting right here, Heids," Dylan says, rolling his eyes.

"It's nice to know there are actually guys like that around," I say flatly, looking out the window.

"Oh, shit!" Heidi gasps. "I'm such an idiot." She pounds her palm to her forehead. "I'm sorry, Mikayla. I really didn't mean anything by it."

"It's fine." I smile at her. "Honestly."

"I'm Cameron, or just Cam," the guy next to them says. I think Heidi is relieved to move on. "And that little lady," he adds, pointing to the girl on the other side of Jake on our bench seat, "is Lucy."

Lucy looks up from her e-reader with a timid smile on her face. "Hi, Mikayla. It's nice to meet you," she says quietly then resumes her reading.

I look over at Cameron, who shrugs. "She's on the last few chapters of some book she's been reading. She can't stay away from it. We're used to it by now. We always find her reading at the oddest times. Don't we, babe?" He says the last sentence a little louder to get her attention.

What? These two are dating?

"Uh-huh," Lucy says, not looking up from her book.

"I have the biggest dick you've ever seen, don't I, babe?" Cam is almost shouting at her, trying to distract her.

The car erupts in laughter, me included. Jake shakes his head next to me.

"Yeah, babe. I heard exactly what you said, and I'd deny it if it weren't true, but you're right. It's definitely the biggest I've ever seen," Lucy says with a small smirk, her eyes never leaving the book.

"Aw, I love you, babe. Best answer ever!" He gives her a shit-eating grin.

"But *babe*," Lucy says, eyes still on her book, "yours is the only one I've ever seen, so I have absolutely nothing at all to compare it to. It could be *tiny* and I wouldn't have a clue. Now, let me finish my book."

Everyone laughs again. Heidi leans over to give Lucy a high five, which she enthusiastically accepts.

I smile at Lucy. She's something else. "What are you reading?"

She looks up at me and blushes a little. "Um, it's called *The Sea of Tranquility*, and it's by—"

"Katja Millay, right? Josh Bennett is so swoon-worthy," I interrupt. Her smile is huge, like she's finally found someone she can talk to about this stuff. Inside, I'm kind of feeling the same way, since none of my friends read the kind of books I enjoy.

"I've definitely found my new book boyfriend." She mock swoons, holding her e-reader close to her heart. Cam just shakes his head at her.

"I bet you'll never look at wood the same," I say, faking dreaminess in my voice. The car is silent for a second, then everyone cracks up, including Lucy. What I said hits me.

"No!" I yell. "I meant . . . Because he likes to build things from wood." I'm animated now, gesturing to prove my point. All eyes go to my hands, and everyone starts laughing harder. I look down and almost die of embarrassment. Who would have thought that sanding a chair leg would look the same as jerking off?

I moan in defeat and embarrassment and try to hide my face on Jake's shoulder. He chuckles into my hair and shifts so he can put an arm around me. I've known this guy for less than an hour, and I'm already comfortable with him.

The laughter at my expense is still going strong when the door opens and Logan looks inside.

"What's so funny?" He looks around the group, but no one bothers to fill him in. "Fine, don't tell me."

He looks at the seating arrangement. Although it would make complete sense to sit opposite me, he squishes in next to me, forcing us all to move down until I'm almost sitting on Jake's lap. Lucy, still enthralled by her book, works out what's happening and moves to the other side to sit on Cam's lap. I smile gratefully at her. She reminds me of myself a little.

"Let me know when you get to the end," I tell her.

"Almost there," she says, lifting her finger to shush me. Her eyes go wide, and I know she's done. "No shit," she says.

"Shit." I nod. "It's my favorite book."

"We should totally be book best friends."

I laugh. "Yeah, sure."

"What are they talking about?" Logan looks between me and Lucy. No one says anything. "Hey, uh . . ." He nudges my leg with his.

"Her name's Mikayla, asshole," Jake says, slightly tightening his hold on my shoulders.

"Mikayla." Logan nods. "I owe you an apology about the beer thing . . . It was an asshole thing to do. I wasn't think—"

"Hey." I cut him off, waving my hands. "It's fine. Don't worry about it. Actually, I should probably be thanking you. If you hadn't spilled that drink on me, I would've never walked in on what I did. I'd probably be at my own prom right now, dancing with my so-called perfect boyfriend, clueless to the fact that he and my best friend were fucking for two years behind my back." I try to smile, but my anger overcomes me.

There's an awkward silence in the car. Jake slowly removes his arm from around me, probably because he thinks I'm crazy. Just as I'm about to apologize, Lucy pipes up.

"You should totally key the dickhead's car," she says. Everyone turns to her, then slowly to me.

I should laugh it off as a passing comment—a little joke between friends. But I can't help the smile that creeps across my face. "Well,

I do have his keys. And I know his truck's at his house and no one's home." I look at Jake and he grins, eyeing me sideways.

"Wait." Cam breaks the silence. "Are you saying you have his car keys, you know where his car is, and no one is around?"

I nod slowly, glancing at all of them.

"Uh-oh," Heidi sings.

"Operation Mayhem!" Dylan declares loudly, pulling Heidi off his lap and placing her at his side.

In two seconds flat, the boys somehow reposition the girls to one side of the limo so they can discuss whatever in private.

"What are they doing?" I ask Heidi, but Lucy answers. "Trust us, it's better you don't know. It's more fun this way."

FOUR

MIKAYLA

"You guys," I say, trying to catch up as we walk to the twenty-four-hour Walmart. "You're going to miss your senior prom."

"No one cares! As long as we're there at the end when they declare little miss Heidi prom queen, we're all good. But that's hours away," Logan says, tapping Heidi on the ass. She squeals and hides behind Dylan.

"Touch her again, and I'll break your arms, asshole." Dylan glares at Logan, who throws his hands up in surrender. Dylan's one of those guys who doesn't say much, so you listen when he does. Now that I see him at full height, I notice he's huge—bigger than the others. He seems loyal and protective, though, willing to give his all to his girl. I can see why Heidi loves him. I would, too. I thought I had that kind of guy.

"What are we doing here? I mean, what are we getting?" I ask them, walking into the store.

"Don't you worry your pretty little face." Logan runs his hand down my back, lower and lower, until he cups my ass.

"Get your hands off me, before I get Dylan to break your arms!" I say it like a joke, but I'm serious.

"I don't think it's Dylan I have to worry about," he mutters.

Jake gets between us and shoves him aside. "Leave her alone, asshole," he says to Logan. He holds his hand out to me. "Come with me."

I take his hand. "What about the others?" I really want to know what this Operation Mayhem is. I hope it doesn't break the law or cause permanent damage. I don't know these guys at all—they could be buying stuff to bomb his truck or his house. Oh my God, what if they're going to kill—

"Relax, Mikayla." Jake laughs. "We're not going to do anything crazy. It's just a bit of fun. Trust me, okay?"

He must have seen the internal meltdown I was having. I smile and nod. Because I do trust him.

"Now help me choose, please. I don't know anything about this stuff," he says, twirling his finger in the air.

"Huh?" I look around and see that we're in the men's formal wear section. "Oh, okay."

I glance at him. He's still wearing his suit pants and a plain white tank, which shows off his broad chest and muscular back. "What's wrong with what you're wearing?" I ask with a raised eyebrow.

"Ha-ha," he says flatly. "It would be fine if I wanted to look like Eminem circa 2001." We both laugh. "I'm thinking a black shirt and blue tie to go with your dress and flower." He starts sifting through the racks.

I look down at myself. My mind is so hazy that I had forgotten what I was wearing. He pulls out a black dress shirt and slips it on. He looks at himself in the mirror, then shrugs it off. He removes the tag and puts it in his pocket, then puts the shirt back on and starts buttoning up. I look away because watching him dress feels too intimate. Plus, I think he might be stealing, and I don't want to be an accomplice.

I head over to the accessories, where there are two-dollar ties galore. I find a blue one that matches the little dahlia pinned to my dress, just under my breasts.

He saunters over and smiles.

"Here, this one should do." I hold it out to him.

"Perfect." He grabs the tie from me and frowns. "My mom's going to be so disappointed." He laughs. "I have no idea how to knot a tie."

"I can totally help you with that." I grab the tie from his hands and begin to knot it the way Mom showed me. She said one day I'd meet a man who would appreciate my knowing how. Who knew she'd be so right? I start to twist it around his collar when I realize how close we are. I can feel his breath on my face. I'm surrounded by his cologne—it's subtle but strong enough to make my head swim. I close my eyes for a second to calm my nerves, but I can feel his eyes on me.

I take a small step back before opening my eyes and force a smile. "There, now you look more like Eminem circa 2005." He laughs as we head to the front of the store.

Everyone else is already waiting. Whatever they bought is hidden away in a few plastic bags, so I can't tell what it is. Jake starts walking through the checkout but stops abruptly in front of the cashier. I bump into him from behind, losing my balance. He turns quickly, steadying me by my elbows. He then pulls two tags out of his pocket and gives them to the cashier. She's a few years older than us but shamelessly eyes Jake up and down and winks at him.

"I need to pay for these," Jake says, adjusting his tie and looking past her. She doesn't speak, which seems to make him uncomfortable.

After the transaction, we make our way back to the group and walk out to the limo.

"Dude," Logan says. "That chick would've totally banged you in the storeroom."

"Not everyone's a pig like you, Logan," Heidi huffs as we settle back into the limo.

"I can't stand girls like that." Jake shakes his head. "I mean, what if Mikayla were my girl, and we're on a date?" He quickly looks at me then faces Heidi. "I'm not saying we are . . . But it's obvious we were *kind of* together. I mean, we walked up to the register together." He shrugs. "I don't know. It just seems disrespectful to Mikayla if, you know, she *were* my girl."

I blush and look at the floor. I can sense Heidi is staring at me, but I don't say anything.

"Aw, Jakey, always the gentleman," Logan coos.

"Whatever," Dylan huffs. "Let's cause some mayhem."

———

A bottle of food dye, a bag of sugar, dozens of bags of popcorn, hundreds of Post-Its, a roll of Saran wrap, and a death-metal CD later, we admire our masterpiece, laughing to ourselves. To the outside world, we're just a group of crazy kids playing an innocent prank on one of our friends. Even the limo driver chuckles to himself.

"How much do I owe you guys? This couldn't have been cheap. And I'm the reason we're here, right?"

Logan looks at Jake, who clears his throat. "It's nothing, Mikayla. We have a mayhem fund. We all chip in to do stupid shit like this. It just so happens that this time it's not someone we know. We love it, so don't even worry about it."

I glance at Logan, who smiles and nods enthusiastically. Jake bends forward to place his mouth near my ear. "All good, Mikayla?" he whispers.

I nod and smile up at him. Then I make the mistake of looking next door—at the silhouette of a girl watching us from the bedroom window where my now ex-boyfriend has probably had sex with my now ex–best friend hundreds of times. I feel a sob coming and cover my mouth, knowing tears will fall the second I blink. Jake notices and follows my eyes to the girl at the window.

Logan must see her, too, because he asks, "Is she going to be a problem?"

I shake my head. "That's Megan."

"Fuck," Jake mutters under his breath. A sob overtakes me, and he envelops me in his arms.

"Um, guys." It's Heidi. I don't look up. "They're announcing prom king and queen in twenty minutes."

FIVE

MIKAYLA

Megan and I are not as similar as you'd imagine best friends are. We're polar opposites in almost every way. She's the head cheerleader with the smokin' hot body, long, shiny blond hair, and sparkly blue eyes. She plays the field, and the boys are all for it. Megan knows what she has and uses it to her advantage. People tend to not take her seriously, because she acts the airhead role to perfection. But she is so much more than that, and I'm one of the lucky few to have seen that side of her.

I met her in fifth grade. She had just moved for her mom's job. I remember she sat behind me in class, chatting with everyone around us. All I could hear was her talking about her stationery. Girls love stationery. I was facing the front, trying to concentrate on the new art project we had just been given, but she continued to giggle, talking to whoever would listen about how she had two of everything. She called them "emergency" things—emergency ruler, emergency eraser, emergency sharpener, and on and on.

By that point, I had lost focus and turned to glare at her. She just looked at me and smiled a full, toothy grin. I huffed and turned back around, fishing through my pencil case. But I couldn't find it—I must have left it in the book I was reading during lunch.

I raised my hand. "Ms. Spencer?"

The teacher, sitting behind her desk, looked at me over the frames of her glasses.

"I don't have my ruler. Can I, um . . . May I please go to my locker to get it?"

Before she could answer, there was a light tap on my shoulder. I turned around to see a ruler inches from my face. I looked at Megan questioningly, and she smiled.

"For emergencies," she said, shrugging.

We became best friends.

—

One day, during the summer before freshman year, we were eating popsicles on Megan's roof just outside her bedroom window. We were working on our tans, because that's what high school girls did.

"Do you think people will make fun of us because we don't have boyfriends?" she asked out of nowhere.

I hadn't even thought about boys that way yet. I guess I was a late developer. I shrugged.

"I'm going to have a boyfriend within a month," she declared, more to herself than anyone else. She nodded as if agreeing to it.

"Okay, Meg, just don't go dragging me into any of it. I'm happy with the way things are," I said, rolling my eyes.

She snickered. "As if I'd even consider it. Do you think I don't know you at all?" She faked hurt in her voice and held her hand to her heart.

"I just don't want to be one of those girls who's in a serious relationship through most of high school. It's so not my thing. Then when we graduate, I don't want to do that whole 'Where are you going to college? Should we go to college together? Whose hopes and dreams are more important?' thing. Blah yadda blah."

She looked at me for a second then shook her head. "Well, miss fifteen-going-on-fifty . . . I want to fall in love *lots* and I want to break hearts *lots*. I want to have so many awkward first dates and first kisses with lots and *lots* of boys. I want to hold hands down the hall with some amazingly gorgeous guy and make girls jealous because that guy only has eyes for me. I want to chase and be chased. I want to really *live* in high school. I want to *love* in high school. And I want to have sex. Oh my God, like, *so much sex!*"

I stared at her, my mouth open in shock. She looked at me and broke into a fit of laughter. It was a joyous sound that, to this day, still makes me crack up whenever I hear it. We sat on that roof and giggled like the innocent girls we were for what seemed like hours. Our laughter broke off when we heard a beeping noise. The sound was coming from the house next door. A U-Haul truck was reversing into the driveway.

"Oh, God," Megan sighed. "The house has finally sold. I hope they're not sucky neighbors. I can't think of anything worse! Like old people hoarding random shit, so they have to call the fire department to clear the house only to find . . ." She looked at the sky, thinking. ". . . a five-billion-pound woman stuck under a pile of empty snack-sized chocolate-pudding containers. Then a crane has to lift her body out of the house like in *Gilbert Grape*, and they take her to a hospital to pump all the fat out of her body. Then three years later some random kid emerges from the house, knocks on our door, and asks, 'Have you seen my baseball?'"

I looked at her for a second then burst out laughing—uncontrollable laughter that had the sides of my body aching. I heard her laughing with me, then: "Holy shit, Mick . . . Who the hell *is* that?"

I stopped laughing and followed her gaze.

It was a boy—a boy better than any boy I'd ever seen. He could have been our age, but he had a bigger build—not an "I work out, I'm a jock" build, but an "I lift heavy stuff" one. Big like a farm boy? I didn't know. I'd never really thought about boys and bigness before.

"Let's go introduce ourselves," Megan said, already climbing through the window back into her room.

I sat frozen, staring at him as he slowly made his way to the front door. He took in his surroundings as though he hadn't yet seen the house. Maybe he hadn't. He had dark-blond hair hidden under a baseball cap and wore dark jeans and a plain gray T-shirt. I was wondering what color his eyes were when he looked up and caught me mid-stare.

I was sure a blush had crept up my face, and I was even more sure that he could see it. A slow smile tugged at the corners of his mouth, and he raised his right hand in a small wave. I forced a smile, which probably made me look more like I was constipated than actually smiling. I started to lift my hand to wave back . . .

"Mikayla! Come on!" Meg screamed at me like a banshee from inside.

I stood up suddenly and hurled myself through the window, tripping on the windowsill and falling, unladylike, flat on my ass.

"What is *wrong* with you?" She looked at me like I'd grown a second head.

"Big boy farm."

What? Please kill me now.

By the time I'd calmed my rapidly beating heart and convinced Megan that I wasn't completely insane, I found myself stumbling down her driveway to the driveway next door. A woman who looked in her late thirties greeted us. She wore sweats and was unloading boxes from a cherry-red truck. She saw us and instantly smiled.

"Hi! You young ladies must be our neighbors?" she said, wiping sweat from her brow.

"I am. My name's Megan." Megan reached out to shake the woman's hand. "This is my best friend, Mikayla." She nudged me.

"Hi, I'm Mikayla," I repeated, shaking her hand. I glanced down at my feet. I didn't want to look at her since she was more than likely the mother of the boy I'd just been checking out.

"Well, aren't you girls just the prettiest picture," she drawled in a thick Texan accent. "I'm Sam." She faced the house and called out, "Henry! Boys!"

I was still looking at the concrete of the driveway when I heard the front screen door open and close. "Yeah, Ma?" said a male voice.

I jerked my head up and saw him—really *saw* him. His eyes were brown like the color of maple syrup. He seemed to recognize me and stood in front of me, smiling.

"Honey, this is Megan. She's our neighbor."

He took his cap off and shook Megan's hand, never taking his eyes off me.

"And this is her best friend, Mikayla."

We shook hands and, I swear, sparks flew. My hand tingling, I felt rooted to the spot, something I had never experienced before.

"Girls, this is my son James. My husband Henry and our younger one are around here somewhere. I'm sure you'll see him soon."

"Nice to meet you." James finally let go of my hand, and I wept internally.

Megan was looking at me like a third head just oozed from the second one. Luckily, she saved the day by actually talking to this James guy. I was still trying to get over the physical shock that had just sparked my body to life. They talked about school, sports, why they moved here, things to do in our small town, and everything else small talk might consist of. I learned that he was a freshman, too, and would be going to our school. Great. I'll be struck dumb and mute for the next four years.

I heard my name, but I didn't catch anything else. Megan nudged my side, and I looked up at her. Her eyebrows were raised, and her head jerked toward James. I slowly looked at him. "Huh?" I was so eloquent.

He cleared his throat. "It was nice meeting you, Mikayla. I have to get back to unpacking. Hopefully I'll see you around school or something?" He said it more like a question than a statement.

Before I could answer, a kid no more than eight years old came barreling toward us. He ran so fast, I didn't think he could stop in time. Both Meg and I put our hands out to stop his crashing into us, but he stopped mere inches away. He glared at Megan then at me.

James put his hand on the boy's shoulder. "And this is my brother, Bradley."

Bradley smiled. "Hey, have you seen my baseball?"

Megan and I couldn't help it. We laughed.

Two weeks later, James and I were dating.

—

"You okay there, Miss Mikayla?" Heidi asks from across the limo.

I must've zoned out. "Yeah," I sigh. "I just can't believe I didn't see it coming." I pick imaginary lint off my dress.

"No one suspects the people they love of douchebaggery." Heidi looks at me sympathetically.

"Or slutbaggery," Lucy adds.

Six

Jake

We get to prom within seconds of the announcement. Heidi, the new Prom Queen, changes from the girl we know to the girl everyone expects her to be. Prancing onstage, she smiles and gives a short speech. The Prom King is Doug, the quarterback, of course.

They pose for photos, but it's awkward as hell because Doug knows Dylan's watching, and you don't fuck with Dylan. There's only one thing Dylan loves more than basketball, and that's his girl. Physically, they'd be a decent match, but to Dylan there's a huge difference between sports and Heidi. Doug would probably not survive that fight. We'd give Dylan shit if he weren't so serious about her. He's not the hearts-and-flowers kind of guy—he's the heart-and-soul kind, and fuck if every girl would rather have that than the flowers.

—

We're all watching the stage when I see Casey sauntering toward me. Casey is my crazy ex. I panic and step closer to Mikayla. It's a dick move, but it's instinct. Mikayla looks up at me, eyebrows drawn in. I guess she must sense my panic, because she follows my eyes to Casey. I think she understands. She wraps her tiny little arms around my waist, her side pressing into mine. I put my arm around her shoulders, and she rests her head in the crook of my arm.

"Hey, Jake," Casey says, inches away from us. "Who's your little friend? I haven't seen this one around before."

I flinch at her words and feel Mikayla tense next to me for a second. "Casey, this is Mikayla."

Mikayla laughs. "Baby, you don't have to be so formal." She reaches a hand out to Casey. "Jake calls me Kayla. Do you go to school here, Lacey?"

"It's Casey."

"Oh." Mikayla nods, smiling at her. Then she looks at me with her big brown Bambi eyes and runs her hands up and down my chest. "I'm thirsty, babe. Let's get a drink then head to the hotel," she says, loud enough for Casey to hear. On tiptoe, she whispers in my ear, "I'm not wearing any underwear."

I don't know if Casey could hear that, but I know she can see my eyes widen in surprise. What she can't see is my dick twitch at the thought. I'm such a guy. I look down at Mikayla, who smiles innocently up at me.

"Well, have a good night," Casey interrupts, backing away.

"Was that Casey? What did she do to you this time?" Heidi approaches us from the stage, watching Casey return to the dance floor. She points her finger at me then Mikayla. "And what's going on here?"

We realize we're still locked in each other's arms and abruptly let go. I'm a bit more hesitant than she is, though, because I can't help trying to look down the back of her dress to see if she really isn't wearing any underwear.

I'm an asshole.

"Let's go. I'm bored," Cam says as Logan walks up to the group, his hair disheveled and his tux all out of sorts.

"I'm ready," Logan says as we stare at him. "What? I just gave some band geek a night she'll never forget."

———

We're in the limo driving through some heavy woods. I can tell Mikayla is getting worried because her eyes dart between the window and her phone.

I nudge her. "Don't worry. I told you, I'm not a psycho. I'm not going to kill you. We can drop these guys off, and you can take the limo home if you want."

"It's okay." She smiles. "I'd rather be here than anywhere else."

MIKAYLA

The limo stops at a clearing in the middle of nowhere, and we all file out. I see an old truck that surely doesn't run anymore and a bonfire pit. Logan and Dylan light a fire, while Cam and Jake jump into the bed of the truck and pull down three chairs and a cooler full of beer. They pass the bottles around after the girls set up the chairs around the fire.

Cam and Lucy sit on the bed of the truck. Dylan's in one chair with Heidi on his lap, and Logan's in the other. Jake is holding the back of the third and last chair. "Here," he says to me. "Take a seat. I'll stand."

"Sorry." Heidi holds up her beer. "We weren't expecting company. Not that you haven't been a great surprise, though."

I face Jake. "No, it's fine. I'll stand. It's your chair, your bonfire, your—"

"I got a place for you right here, sweetheart," Logan says from behind me, patting his lap.

I scrunch my nose at him. Lucy notices and laughs. Don't get me wrong—Logan is a good-looking guy. If I were any other girl, I'd be swooning over him. But the fact that he spilled beer on me, screwed some innocent girl at her prom and left, and generally has been acting like an ass . . . Well, all that kind of downgrades his swoon-worthiness.

Before I can react, Jake wraps his arm around my waist and sits me down on his lap. I lean against his chest, my legs to one side. "I think she'd rather not," he says to Logan. His accent makes it sound like "ruh-thuh nawt."

I have to admit that accents turn me on. James has a sexy accent—a nice, not-too-dirty Texan drawl. I used to love how he dipped his cap forward a little and said, "Yes, ma'am," when I asked him to do something. He knew it turned me on, so he did it as often as possible. Fuck James. I really do love him.

Jake is wiping away tears I didn't realize were falling. He places his hands on either side of my face, looking into my eyes. He must see so much sadness, hurt, anger, and regret, but all I see in his are comfort and understanding. He brings my head to his lips and gives me one short, sweet kiss on my temple. It's all I need to keep going and believe that everything will be okay.

Everyone around us continues to chatter, and I realize I've totally spaced out.

"I can't wait to hit the bars around UNC," Cam says.

"Huh?" I look up. "Who's going to UNC?"

Cam laughs. "We all are. Why? Are *you*?"

"Yeah, I am," I say, wide-eyed. "What? *All* of you are?"

Cam eyes Jake for a second then looks at me. "Yeah, your boy Jake got a full–ride athletic scholarship." He smiles like a proud dad. "He'll probably be starting pitcher as a freshman."

I whip my head in Jake's direction and see him nodding shyly. "No shit?"

"Shit," he deadpans.

"And what about the rest of you?" I eye Lucy in particular, because I think we're probably going to study the same things.

"I got a partial academic scholarship and am planning to major in either creative writing or journalism. I haven't decided yet." She shrugs.

"No effing way!" I cry, my voice laced with disbelief. "Me too! Like, exactly—partial scholarship and all."

"No shit?" she says.

"Shit," I return.

"Jake and I are the only ones lucky enough to get scholarships. Cam and Dylan are hoping to share a dorm, and Heidi and Logan will be majoring in the Greek system." She laughs, and the rest join her. I see her glance at Jake and feel his body move under me.

"What about you?" I ask him.

He shrugs. "I haven't thought that far ahead yet."

———

We continue to drink and talk the rest of the night. I'm feeling slightly buzzed—okay, maybe a little more than slightly. I'm smiling and having a good time, and the ache in my heart from earlier tonight is a fraction less painful.

Lucy shuffles through her bag to find her e-reader.

"Seriously, Luce?" Heidi says.

"No, let her read," Cam says with an evil smirk. His eyes look heavy—he's definitely drunk.

"Shut up," Lucy mumbles under her breath.

"What's going on?" Logan looks up from his phone.

Cam starts laughing. "Oh, I love it when she reads." He turns to Lucy, whose face is turning a bright shade of red. "She reads these smutty books—like, full-on dirty sex and BDSM shit."

"Oh my God, Cameron. Shut the hell up!" She reaches out to cover his mouth, but he's too quick. He jumps off the truck and starts walking around.

"Sometimes when we're in bed, she'll be reading and make these little moaning sounds," he continues, trying not to laugh. We're all cackling with him.

Lucy jumps off the truck, too. Removing her heels, she stalks him like prey. "I swear to God, Cameron *Aladdin* Gordon! You better shut your mouth or I won't put out for one year!"

"Aladdin?" we all yell and erupt into fits of laughter.

For some reason, Cam decides to keep talking. "She reads these books, right . . ." He walks backwards around us as Lucy advances. She occasionally tries to cover his mouth, but he slaps her hands away. She's fuming, but I can see she's also trying not to smile. She doesn't know whether to laugh or cry.

"I'm not joking, guys! They're pornographic, all about silky shafts and veined dicks," he continues. Logan is on the ground, holding his side from the pain of laughing too hard. "Sometimes she suddenly puts her book down and looks at me like she wants to eat me—*literally* eat me!" he yells, laughing harder and swatting her hands away. "I mean, I don't mind it at all. It's hot as fuck. She wants to try everything she reads in these books—*everything*. So I don't give a shit when or how much she reads, because I get the rewards."

I bury my face in Jake's neck to stop a hyena laugh from bubbling up. Logan's still rolling around on the ground, and Heidi is wiping tears from her eyes. Even Dylan has his head thrown back, his body convulsing with silent laughter. Jake's deep, rumbling chuckles are so close to my ear that I can feel his breath.

Cam runs away from her faster. "The other week she even let me do her in the a—"

Lucy squeals. We burst out laughing even harder. Her face is bright red now, and she's given up trying to catch him. She stands defeated, and when Cam strolls over to her she slaps him *hard* across the face. We all quiet down and, still giggling, stare at them, waiting . . . Then Cam says, "Yeah, baby! You know I like it rough!" and throws her over his shoulder. They head into the bushes, Lucy laughing and pounding his back.

—

They return thirty minutes later, changed out of their prom clothes. It's obvious what just happened. Where did they go, anyway? I look in the direction where they came from and see lights on in a little wooden cabin.

"Where the hell *are* we?" I ask. The group chuckles.

"This is my family's property," Lucy says, sitting back down on the truck bed. "We live on a billion acres or something. My dad built that cabin for me to use whenever I want to escape. My mom passed away a few years ago, and I have six younger brothers, so it's just me. They can't hear anything from the main house. Cam and I practically live there."

"Your dad doesn't mind that you're out here by yourself or with Cam?" I ask, cocking an eyebrow.

"My dad acts naive and likes to think that Cam leaves every night. I'm his only daughter, so as far as he's concerned all I do is study and read books. He probably doesn't want to think too much about it. It's not like I'm a crackhead or goth or covered in tattoos and piercings." She shrugs. "Would you worry if I were your daughter?"

"Probably not," I say. "But if I knew you were a lady in the street and a freak in the bed, I'd have my doubts."

Everyone cracks up. Logan goes to an iPod dock that's sitting in the truck and plays "Nasty Girl." When Ludacris says the "A lady in the street and a freak in the bed!" line during his rap, we all yell it. Logan knows the entire rap word for word. He then plays "Yeah" by Usher. We stand up and dance like fools, thinking we actually have moves like Usher. We try to pop and lock but look like we're having epileptic fits. Even Dylan gets in on it.

As the song fades to an end, Heidi raises her beer. We're standing in a circle. "To good friends and new ones," she says, winking at me. We take a sip.

"To finding the perfect girl of your dreams and having your entire future to spend with her," Dylan says, hugging Heidi around the waist and kissing her on the cheek. The girls swoon, and the guys make gagging noises. We drink.

"To easy college chicks!" Logan is practically panting. And we drink.

"To whoever wrote *Fifty Shades of Grey*." Cam clasps his hands and looks skyward like he's thanking the Lord. We laugh . . . and drink.

Lucy playfully smacks him on the chest, probably harder than he expected because he actually flinches in pain. "To Josh Bennett," she says, clinking her beer against mine. Cam rolls his eyes. We're the only ones who drink.

Everyone looks at Jake, who is standing next to me. "To baseball," he says quietly. His friends moan.

"You're a pretty shit kid, you know that, Jacob?" Logan says. It's the first time anyone has called him that. Jake shrugs, and everyone takes a reluctant gulp of beer. Logan eyes me. "What about you, Mikayla?"

I think for a bit then smile. "To not letting bad people dictate whether you have a good time."

It's quiet for a moment, then Cam yells, "Hollaaaaa!" Logan searches his iPod. I know what song it is from the first note. It's "Baby" by Justin Bieber. I shake my head in amusement.

The boys start to serenade us girls like they're from some boy band. They surround us, and Logan has the Ludacris rap down *again*. We're in fits of giggles, tears streaming down our faces. I can't wait to tell Emily and my parents about tonight. They'll love it—minus the cheating boyfriend and backstabbing friend.

Everyone plans on staying the night at Lucy's cabin—everyone but Jake. He apparently gets up at five every morning to go for a run, work out, and do whatever else he does that early in the day. So after exchanging numbers with all his friends and saying "See you soon" instead of "Good-bye," I get into the limo with Jake to head home.

Seven

Jake

It's just the two of us in the limo, heading back to her house. We're both buzzed. Well, I *think* she's buzzed—I know I definitely am. Her sitting on my lap the whole night didn't help. I needed something to calm me down. It was a bad idea, but it was either my lap or Logan's. Logan would've probably gotten her wasted and done God knows what with her.

I sit on one bench seat, and she sits on the other. It's the farthest we've been apart since the restaurant.

"Jake, get the limo to drive you home first. I'll be okay. It's almost forty minutes to my house, then you have to go back past here to yours . . . It's stupid."

I tilt my head back against the seat and close my eyes, trying to steady the spinning. I open one eye and look at her. She's lying down, her whole body sprawled across the bench seat.

"I'd rather make sure you get home safely," I say. She smiles but doesn't respond.

A few minutes of quiet pass. I'm replaying the night in my head. I wonder if she is, too. I bet our versions would be completely different, though.

The limo driver swears and slams on the brakes. Mikayla falls to the floorboard with a thud. "Sorry." The driver waves his hand in the air. "Goddamn rabbits!"

I kneel next to her. She's giggling to herself—she may not hurt now, but she sure will be hurting tomorrow. "Hey, Mikayla. Are you okay? Are you hurt?" I lightly shake her.

She tries to sit up but struggles, more than likely from the alcohol. She wraps her arms around my neck and I bend to lift her back up. "Call me Kayla," she says into my chest.

"Okay . . . But your friends call you Micky, right?"

She looks up at me with those Bambi eyes. "Yeah, Jake," she sighs. "They do. But you"—she shoves a finger into my chest—"can call me Kayla . . . all right?"

I nod, this stupid, goofy grin plastered on my face. As I place her down on the seat, her grip tightens around my neck. "Just hold me, Jake. Please?"

She doesn't need to ask. I make myself comfortable and help her position herself sideways, leaning against me. She puts her arms around my shoulders and burrows her face in the crook of my neck.

"Thank you for tonight. God, if you hadn't been there, I don't know what I would have done. And your friends accepted me and didn't ask any questions . . ." She takes a breath and sniffles. I can feel the wetness from her tears on my skin. "Thank you . . . so much . . ."

She kisses my neck. I freeze, but she keeps going with soft, gentle kisses along my jaw, looking for my mouth. I shouldn't let her do this—she's a mess, emotionally and physically. I turn to face her and tell her to stop, but my mouth accidentally brushes against hers. Her lips are soft on mine as she kisses me once . . . twice . . . The third time is a little longer and more intimate. My eyes drift closed. Her tongue tastes my lips so softly that I would have missed it if I wasn't focusing so hard to remember this forever.

"Mmm," she murmurs, pulling away with a smile and resuming her position.

Shit.

Now I'm hard and she's sitting on me.

——

She's fallen asleep on my lap. I cradle her in my arms. She's snoring gently, which is pretty much the cutest thing I've ever heard.

The driver lowers the glass partition. "We're on her street, but I can't go any farther. What's the house number?"

"What do you mean you can't?" I shake her. "Kayla, which one's your house?"

She wakes up drowsily and takes a second to get her bearings, looking around the limo.

"Look outside," the driver says. "I don't know what's happening. The street is blocked."

I press the button to lower the window. There are police cars, fire trucks, and ambulances everywhere. I can't see much past the crowd in the street. Kayla's eyes widen.

"What the fuck?" she mutters, fumbling to open the door. She's out of the car so fast, I don't have time to comprehend what's happening. I jump out and follow her. She's trying to push through all the people in front of the house, but her tiny frame doesn't make it far before she turns to me. There are tears in her eyes and panic all over her face.

"This is my house, Jake. What's going on?"

I grab her hand and start pushing people aside. I'm not nice about it, so some people are pissed. We make it to the front of the crowd. The house has been cordoned off with police tape, and cops are swarming all over the place. I smell smoke—there must have been fire. Kayla looks at me like she's four years old and can't understand what's happening. I pull up the police tape and duck under it.

"Hey, you kids can't go past that line," an overweight cop with a clipboard yells, walking toward us.

"I live here! Please tell me what's going on. Where are my mom and dad and sister?" I hold her as she starts to sob. She looks up at the cop, her voice breaking. "Please tell me what's happening . . . I need to see them."

The cop looks at her, sadness and pity in his eyes. "Sweetheart, just give us a minute, okay? We need to do our jobs." He squeezes her shoulder. "Mendoza!" he calls. A younger cop talking to people in the crowd and taking notes comes over to us. "This is Miss . . . ?"

"Jones," Kayla says.

"Mendoza, this is Ms. Jones. Can you please escort her to the ambulance until we finish up here?"

Mendoza's eyes widen in surprise then understanding.

"Sure, boss." He nods. "Come with me."

Kayla digs her heels into the ground and grips my left arm tightly. "With all due respect, *sir*," she says to Mendoza, "just tell me what the *fuck* is happening!"

"Micky!" a guy's voice booms behind us. We both turn to see James running toward us. Kayla hides behind me, and I step protectively in front of her.

"Get the fuck away from me, James. I don't want to deal with your shit right now!" she yells.

"Micky . . ." he sighs. "I just want to make sure you're okay." He tries to reach behind me to get to her, but I block him. "Who the fuck are *you*?" he spits, squaring his shoulders.

"James, I swear to God, just go! I don't want you here!"

"Micky . . ." He tries to reach for her again.

"I don't think she wants you here, asshole," I say between gritted teeth, my hands balling into fists.

"Fuck you!" he shouts and lunges for her again.

So I punch him.

Right in the face.

Like I should have the first time I saw him.

He falls to the ground.

Cops start coming over, but a guy who must be his friend peels him off the ground and helps him limp away. "Asshole," I mumble under my breath.

Then I hear her gasp, and she seizes my arm again. I turn to face her. All the blood has drained from her face. Her body gives out and I struggle to help her fall to the ground gently. I envelop her small frame. Then she wails, a scream so deafening that the crowd instantly falls silent.

I look toward the house and see them.

Three gurneys. Three body bags. And one so small it can only be a child's.

EIGHT

MIKAYLA

Somehow I end up in the back of an ambulance. I hear voices and smell Jake all around me. I sit up, a little dazed, and realize I'm wearing his tuxedo jacket. I sniff it.

Then I remember.

My entire family is dead.

I close my eyes and pray this is a dream—a nightmare. But when I open my eyes, I'm exactly where I was. I feel my heart pounding hard against my chest. I can't breathe. My throat tightens and my vision blurs. I need to find a way to make this better. I need James. I need Megan.

Then I remember more.

How can *everything* be taken from me instantly? Anger consumes me, and my body trembles with the need to release something from within.

I want to die.

I want to be with them.

There's nothing left.

No one.

Nothing can hurt more than this.

Nothing.

My face burns, and my voice is hoarse from crying. I feel strong arms wrap around my shoulders, rocking me like I'm a child. Jake sits next to me, smoothing my hair away from my face and shushing to comfort me.

"It's going to be okay, Kayla. I promise." He kisses my temple.

I open my eyes and look into his midnight-blue ones, red and raw from his own tears.

"Jake . . ." My voice breaks, and I begin to sob again in his arms.

We stay like that for what feels like hours. My mind is completely void of any thoughts. I'm a shell of a person.

"Ms. Jones?" Mendoza tries to get my attention.

I bury my face deeper.

"Have you got somewhere to stay tonight?" he asks cautiously. "The house is going to be a crime scene for a while. You'll need to stay somewhere until we clear out all the evidence."

I *still* have no idea what happened to them. "What happened?" I whisper, looking at Jake.

"It's okay. We'll talk later," he reassures me. To Mendoza, he says, "She can stay with me."

"And what's your relation to Ms. Jones?" Mendoza sounds suspicious.

"I'm her boyfriend."

"I don't know if that's appropriate. Has she got any friends she can stay with?"

A sob escapes me, and I grip Jake more tightly.

"Seriously, dude?" He sounds pissed. "We're both adults! And do you really think I'd *be* here right now if I didn't care about her? What the fuck?" Jake's accent is so thick right now, I barely understand him.

"Jake?" A woman hesitates at the open ambulance doors.

"Mom?"

"She's your mother?" Mendoza asks.

"No shit, Sherlock!" Jake growls.

"Jacob!" his mom reprimands him.

"Ma'am," the cop begins, "your son says that he's Ms. Jones's boyfriend. He says she can stay with him tonight. I just want to confirm that this is a suitable arrangement."

Jake's mom doesn't miss a beat. "Officer, my son is an adult. I am here for moral support, not to write out permission slips. It's obvious my son cares for Ms. Jones, or they would not be in the position they are in." I'm still sitting next to him, cradled in his arms. "You might consider being a bit more sensitive in a situation like this."

"Yes, ma'am, just trying to do my job," Mendoza replies. I hear his footsteps as he walks away.

"Jake, honey, let's go home."

Jake pulls away from me so he can see my face. He has to hold my head up, because I can't seem to function at all. "Kayla?" I blink. "I'm going to carry you to our car, and you're going to stay at my house tonight, okay?"

I nod.

"Okay," he says, pulling the hair away from my eyes and planting a kiss on my forehead. Then he lifts me and carries me to a minivan. He sits in the back with me and resumes his hold. His mom drives to their house in complete silence.

I must have fallen asleep because the next thing I know I'm being carried upstairs and tucked into bed.

"Jake," I whisper. "Where are you going?"

"I'm going to sleep on the sofa downstairs." He hands me some clothes to sleep in. I'm still in my prom dress. "No one will bother you here. Just try to get some rest, okay?"

I start to cry. He sits down next to me instantly, holding and soothing me.

"Please, Jake. Can you stay, please? I don't want to be alone."

"Sure . . ." It sounds like "shaw"—his accent again.

"Get dressed, and I'll be back in a few minutes." He kisses my temple and leaves the room.

I get out of bed and undress. I put on the clothes he handed me: a plain white T-shirt and boxers. I have no underwear, no bra. I have none of my own clothes. I don't even think I can go to my house to get them. Oh God, what happened?

When I get back into bed, I can hear hushed conversation just outside the door.

"Get some rest, sweetheart—both of you. Well . . . try, anyway."

"Thanks, Mom, for everything. I mean it."

"Honey, you don't need to thank me. You did such a good thing today. We're very proud of you."

"I didn't do anything, Mom."

"Try to get some sleep, son," a deep male voice says. It must be his dad. "You have a meeting with your agent here at nine in the morning. Don't forget."

"We can't cancel?" Jake asks.

"Son, he's traveling from LA. Just tell him you're not interested right now and send him on his way."

"Good night, guys," Jake says, opening the door. He closes it behind him then leans against it. He's holding an ice pack on his hand, injured after punching James. He takes a deep breath and exhales, puffing his cheeks out. He looks at me—for a few seconds, minutes, hours . . . Who knows.

"God, Kayla. I'm so sorry." His voice breaks.

I stare at him.

He puts the ice pack down on the dresser and starts to strip out of his clothes. I look away. He then slides into bed with me, dressed in his tank and boxers. We face each other.

He suddenly sits up and rips his tank off. "Smells like beer," he says and gets back under the covers. We pull the blankets up to our chins.

"What happened to them, Jake?"

He looks at me, and tears fill his eyes. He pulls me in and wraps his arms around me, resting his chin on top of my head. He clears his throat.

"The police think your family walked in on a burglar, and the asshole shot them, Kayla."

I tense.

"He got away, but he tried to burn the house down first—to get rid of the evidence, I guess."

I lie silently, tears streaming down my face. I wipe them on his chest.

"The place is covered in fingerprints, so they should be able to catch the asshole soon. They got a lot of witnesses, too. The police are calling it a random act of violence." He runs his fingers through my hair and kisses my forehead again. "I know it doesn't bring them back, Kayla, but I'm really sorry about all of it—about James and your best friend, and now your family. I can't even begin to imagine what you're feeling. Just know that my family and I, and my friends—*our* friends—are here for you. I know that I just met you tonight, but I truly do care about you, Kayla. If there's anything you need or want, just tell me, okay? Promise me you'll do that?"

I nod, the lump in my throat preventing me from speaking. I fall asleep in Jake's arms, sheltered from all the evil in the world.

NINE

MIKAYLA

The next morning I wake up needing to use the bathroom. The bed is empty. My head is pounding from the previous night's crying, and I try not to think about any of it too soon. I look around the room and notice two doors on the right. I pray that one of them is a bathroom.

I get up and creep over to one of the doors. The first one I open is the one I need. I then crawl back into bed.

I hear men's voices downstairs. I look for my phone on the nightstand and see a glass of water and two aspirins. A note is leaning against the glass: "Had to take care of some business, be back as soon as it's done. Take the aspirin for your headache." It's signed Jake.

I do as the note says then look at my phone: 178 missed calls from James and several unknown numbers and thirty-two new text messages. I check if there are any texts that aren't from James. There's nothing from Megan—not a single call or text. Then I read my mom's text from last night:

We love you too, sweetheart. Have a good night. Emily is begging for ice cream. We'll bring you back a big batch of cookies'n'cream. It will be waiting for you in the freezer, wake me if I'm asleep and we can share some.

They must've come back from getting ice cream and walked in on the burglary. I close my eyes and wish it would all go away.

I lie in bed for a long time before I realize I should be doing something—anything—else. I start to panic. I'll have to deal with lawyers, insurance, and funeral planning. I'm legally an adult, so I won't have any help.

I'm going to have to bury my entire family.

I suddenly feel claustrophobic. The walls closing in, I rush to the door and pull it open. I stop in my tracks. Jake's mom is bending down to put a tray of food and a change of clothes in front of the door.

She gasps when she sees me, startled. "Good morning, Mikayla," she says, smiling awkwardly. "I'm not sure what your size is, but I think you'll fit in my sweats."

She hands me the clothes and picks up the tray. She walks into Jake's room and sets it down on his dresser. Wandering over to his desk chair, she fingers the dress from last night. It's laying across the back of the chair. She won't look at me. I sit on the edge of the bed with the clothes on my lap and wait.

"This must be incredibly hard for you," she finally says, trying to hold back tears. She comes to stand in front of me, leaning against the dresser, and clears her throat. I notice she doesn't have an accent. "Sweetheart, I need you to understand that I'm not asking you this because . . . Well, because we don't want you to stay here. You can stay as long as you need to—we've already told Jake that. I'm asking because it's an important step in the process, I guess. Is there anyone you should call—aunts, uncles, cousins, grandparents? Anyone?"

My parents had a lot of friends and acquaintances, but we were a small family. People cared about them, but there isn't anyone in particular who would care *for* me—except maybe my aunt Lisa. She wasn't really my aunt. Both my parents were only children, and my grandparents are dead.

"Just my aunt Lisa. She's my mom's best friend from college. Otherwise it's just me."

"Oh, sweetheart," she coos, sitting down next to me and taking my hand.

"Um, where's Jake?" I look at the floor, feeling uncomfortable and awkward.

"He's downstairs meeting with his agent. He won't be too much longer."

"Agent?"

"Yeah, he plays baseball. He didn't tell you?" She looks at me curiously. "Sounds like Jake." She shakes her head. "Yeah, baseball. He's kind of a big deal."

I don't say anything.

"How long have you and Jake been dating?"

"Oh, we're not." I look at her, and she cocks an eyebrow at me. "It's a long story."

"Okay, sweetheart." She pats my hand. "I'll leave so you can change and make that phone call." She gets up and goes to the door. Before closing it behind her, she says, "And please, call me Mandy."

———

"Aunt Lisa?" I say the second the phone connects.

"Oh, honey. Tracey rang me last night. I'm at the airport catching a flight out to you right now." She sounds like she's been crying, too. "Just sit tight, Kayla. I'll be there soon. I'll take care of everything, okay? I promise."

"Okay," I say quietly into the phone, looking up at the ceiling wide-eyed to stop the tears from falling.

I hear a soft knock, and Jake pokes his head into the room. I motion for him to come in. He sits down on the edge of his bed and waits until I'm done.

"I'll call you as soon as we land, and I'll try to be there as fast as possible, okay?"

"Yeah."

"Do I go to James's house or Megan's?"

I can see Jake watching me.

"Um, neither. I'll give you the address when you call."

"Okay, honey."

"Aunt Lisa?"

"Yeah, hun?"

I turn so my back is to Jake. I don't want him to see my humiliation. "Do you think you could go to the store on your way here? I kind of have no underwear."

"What?"

"We, um, had prom last night. I wore only my dress—like, *only* the dress." I'm beet red. "I need bras and panties, please." I basically whisper the last sentence.

"Uh, no problem. Same size as the ones I sent you for Christmas?"

"Mm-hm."

"Okay, hun," Aunt Lisa says, maybe a bit too brightly. "And Kayla?"

"Yeah?"

"I'm so sorry."

"Me too."

We hang up, and I sit next to Jake. I'm still wearing his clothes. I self-consciously cross my arms over my breasts, so he can't see my nipples through his thin white T-shirt—though he probably already has.

He clears his throat. "So, your aunt's coming?"

"She's not my real aunt—just my mom's best friend. She already found out from their friend Tracey. They were all best friends in college. Aunt Lisa's already on her way here."

He nods.

"So . . ." I say, trying to find my voice. "Your mom tells me you're kind of a big deal in baseball."

He blushes and looks away. "My mom has a big mouth."

Silence.

"Thank you, Jake."

"You're welcome, Kayla."

Ten

Jake

Kayla's aunt Lisa is on her way here, and I guess they'll need to discuss funerals and things. I'm just glad she'll have someone around who she's known for more than two days. I hear her phone going off constantly, but she ignores it every time. I bet it's James.

I had to practically kick Ryan, my agent, out of the house this morning. He wouldn't take no for an answer. Then he saw the swelling and bruises forming on the knuckles of my pitching hand and lost his shit. My dad hadn't noticed the injury till then, either, so he wasn't very happy about it, too. I told them what happened, and Ryan told me not to let "bitches" (his words) ruin my dream. That's when I told him to fuck off—in a nice way. I then came upstairs to check on Kayla. I could think about only her the whole time I was with Ryan.

I didn't expect to walk in on her conversation with her aunt. And I couldn't help but notice that her nipples were poking through my T-shirt. I know, I'm a dick. The girl's so fragile right now, having just lost everyone, and I'm the creepy perv staring at her tits. I'd punch *myself* in the face if my hand weren't so fucking sore.

—

The doorbell rings, and I answer it to find a tiny woman with a pixie cut on our doorstep. She looks about my mom's age. She smiles warily at me.

"I assume you're Jake?"

"You must be Lisa. Come in." I lead her into the family room and gesture at the sofa. "Have a seat. I'll get Kayla—she's upstairs."

"Thanks, hun. Oh, and give her this." She hands me a bag—probably of bras and panties.

I run into my mom on the staircase and tell her that Lisa is downstairs waiting. She leaves to introduce herself. I knock on my bedroom door and open it slightly, peeking in. Kayla's lying in the middle of my bed in the fetal position, quietly crying. My heart breaks.

I clear my throat, and she looks at me. She sits up and wipes frantically at her tears. I sit down next to her. She showered and is wearing my mom's sweats, which are a little small for her. They hug her curves, but this time I don't look for too long. I cradle her face in my hands and wipe the tears away with my thumbs. I don't know if she means to, but she leans into my hand a little, and it takes everything in me not to kiss her.

"Your aunt Lisa's here," I tell her. "And she wanted me to give you this." I hand her the bag. She blushes.

"Thank you . . . I'll just go to the bathroom and, uh, dress. Wait here, okay?"

I nod, because being in the next room while she tries on underwear is going to be *fine*.

She's out within minutes, a shy smile creeping across her face. She sits back down next to me. "I know that I've already said this, but I don't think I can say it enough, Jake. Thank you for being here and helping . . . I need to thank your mom, too—and your dad. I haven't even met him yet! God, I'm so rude. I just—"

"Kayla, stop. It's fine. We honestly don't mind. And you'll meet my dad soon. He should be home with Julie any minute now."

"Julie?"

"My little sister. She's eight." Sadness shadows her face, and I know she must be thinking about her sister. "How old is—I mean, was—Emily?"

"She was nine." She stops breathing for a second and closes her eyes. When she opens them, they look resolute, like she realized she must accept this horrible fate. She grabs my hand. "Can you come with me, please?"

I lead her downstairs into the family room. Mom's there, too, with a tea set on the coffee table. Lisa stands up when we walk in, and she and Kayla hug for a long time. I sit on the love seat opposite them, and assume Kayla will be next to Lisa on the sofa. But she surprises me by sitting next to me and taking my hand. She presses close to me, almost climbing into my lap.

She's afraid.

I adjust our positions so I can loop one arm around her waist and hold her hand with my free hand. She burrows even closer. I'm not blind to the confused stares we're getting from the grown-ups, but I don't care. If she needs me, I'll be there for her.

I suddenly realize that this might be the last time I see her. I don't know what her plans are or where she'll live after this. Is she still going to go to UNC? She may not even want to see me again. I've been a part of the worst night of her life. I didn't even *think* of that. My stomach drops.

Lisa clears her throat, glancing between the two of us. "I'm sorry." Her eyebrows are drawn together in confusion. "I know there are more pressing things we need to discuss, but what's going on here?" She looks at Kayla. "Kayla, your mom sent me a picture of you last night. You were cozied up next to James, and Megan was there, too. She said you had just left for prom. Am I missing something?"

I look at Mom, but she's just as confused. She leans forward in the recliner, waiting for an answer. She won't get one from me.

Kayla's voice is so quiet, I can barely hear her words. "I walked in on James last night."

Lisa gasps, knowing where this is heading.

"With Megan."

Lisa's face falls.

Kayla continues, "They were seeing each other behind my back for two years."

It's Mom's turn to gasp. I hold Kayla more tightly.

"That's when I met Jake. He was there . . . He helped me. He—"

"Wait," Lisa interrupts. "You guys have known each other for only *one night*?"

Kayla's quiet for a long moment before she answers. "I don't think that really matters, Aunt Lisa. I've known James for four years."

Lisa nods slowly, trying to understand.

"I know it's strange, and I know it might just be circumstantial. We shared an experience that somehow makes us closer . . . But Aunt Lisa." Kayla looks up from her lap. "Jake makes things hurt a little less. He's *home* for me now. If being around him takes the pain away just a tiny bit, then it doesn't matter how or why he's here with me. I just . . . Oh, you can't understand . . ."

Lisa settles back on the sofa, lost in thought. My mom smiles at Kayla, and I kiss her on the temple and lean us back.

Just then the front door bursts open, and Julie comes running down the hallway. Her shoes squeak as she makes an effort to stop abruptly, then she slowly walks into the room. My dad comes up behind her and places his hand on her shoulder. She looks at everyone in the room one by one. When her eyes land on Kayla, she does a double take. She notices how close we are.

"Oooo," she says, stepping closer to us. She studies Kayla's face. "You're pretty!" Looking at me, she adds, "Better than the last one, *Jacarb*." She says my name like she did when she was a baby. She does it when she wants to be a brat, because she knows it pisses me off. Now is not the right time. I'm about to tell her to get lost when she leans in even closer to Kayla.

"Hey, I know you! You're Emily's sister, right? Man, she looks so much like you. She's going to be just as pretty when she grows up. We have dance together. She wasn't there today, though . . . Is she sick?"

"Okay, kiddo, time to get some homework done. I'll let you do it in my office on the big spinny chair," my dad says and mouths "Sorry" to Kayla.

"Oh, no . . ." My mom covers her mouth with her hand. "Emily Jones? Your parents are Kevin and Denise?" Recognition dawns on her face.

Kayla nods. Her eyes are wide with unshed tears.

"Oh, sweetheart!" Mom cries. Lisa looks between my mom and Kayla. It's not enough that Kayla lost her entire family, or that Lisa lost her best friend, but now Mom's lost people she cares about, too—she just didn't know it yet.

"Well." Lisa looks between my mom and Kayla. "I thought you'd be staying with James or Megan, but now I see that's not an option." She glances at me then down to our entwined hands. "We can figure something out. I'm sure Tracey won't mind having an extra guest till we sort out what's happening with the house." She tries to smile.

"She can stay here!" I blurt out.

Kayla turns to face me.

"Right, Mom?" I plead with my eyes.

"Yes, sweetheart, of course she can stay here until things settle down a bit and she finds a new place to live." She smiles reassuringly at me.

"I can't stay here—" Kayla begins to say.

"What?" I look at her.

"You can, and you will," my mom says firmly in a tone that means the subject is closed.

——

Lisa stayed for dinner, and Julie is spending the night at a friend's house. Dad apologized to Kayla again and assured her that he explained the situation to Julie. It might be a little hard for an eight-year-old to comprehend, he said, but he did the best he could. I know Kayla appreciated it—and they finally had a chance to meet.

Lisa and Mom made plans to catch up the next day. I think Lisa is glad someone is here to help both her and Kayla, and I know Mom doesn't mind, especially now that she realized she knew Kayla's parents.

Lucy and Heidi arrive after dinner. I rang them earlier and told them about Kayla's clothing situation—she doesn't have any, aside from underwear. While they wait in the family room, I run upstairs to get Kayla, who's been holed up in my room since dinner. She didn't eat. I don't know how she'll feel about my telling them everything and their being here. I knock on the door and wait for a response.

She opens the door a crack and peeks out. I can tell she's been crying by the puffiness of her eyes.

"Hey," I say.

She fails her attempt at a smile.

"Um, I really don't want you to get mad, but . . ." I rub the back of my head—a nervous habit. "Lucy and Heidi are downstairs . . ."

"Jake, I can't—"

"It's my fault. I called them earlier. I just . . . You need clothes and probably other girl things, and I didn't know what else to do . . ."

Her eyes were cast downwards, but when she heard my explanation, she looked up at me and a small smile broke through. She opens the door wider and steps into the hallway. She takes my hand as we climb down the stairs. We pause in the doorway of the family room, and Lucy and Heidi both turn to face us. They look at our hands then smile at us.

Lucy speaks first. "We're really sorry about what happened, Mikayla. If you need anything at all, just let us know, okay?" She's standing in front of Kayla, looking straight into her eyes.

Kayla nods.

Heidi stands next to Lucy. "We brought some stuff over that you might need, since Jake mentioned you can't go to your house. So we bought the essential stuff. I know it's not much, Mikayla—"

"It's more than enough," Kayla interrupts. "And my friends call me Micky."

I let go of her hand and bring her head to my lips, kissing her on her temple. She doesn't seem to mind, so I'll keep doing it until she tells me to stop.

"I'll get some drinks," I tell them.

Eleven

Mikayla

"Jake didn't really know what you'd want. He was actually pretty adorable when he rang—all shy and awkward about it." Heidi pauses. "Micky . . ." She waits until I'm looking at her. "Jake's good people, you know. I'm glad you ended up with him last night."

I nod slowly. "I know. Me too."

"Anyway," Heidi continues, perking up, "I bought some toiletries: body wash, shavers, toothbrush, lotions, feminine hygiene products. I don't know what you like, so I got whatever I could think of. We brought some clothes, too. We don't know how long you'll be staying here, so we weren't sure what to pack. Hopefully we're about the same size."

"You guys . . . Whatever you've got will be perfect, I'm sure." I genuinely smile, because these girls barely know me and they're doing whatever they can to help.

I still haven't heard from Megan—not a word.

Lucy pipes up. "Heidi and I obviously don't dress the same, so at least you'll have some variety." She smiles. "I also brought my spare e-reader. I don't know . . ." She looks at the ground, her voice getting softer. "I don't know if you'll want to read, or if you can even concentrate on reading, but it's here just in case."

"Thanks, my book best friend," I tell her. She beams.

We fall silent. I can't even imagine how awkward trying to console a girl they barely know must be for them. "So," I speak up. "Justin Bieber's your jam, Heidi?"

They both laugh, and the awkwardness leaves the room for the moment.

"It's kind of an inside joke," Heidi says, giggling.

"Not really." Lucy smirks at Heidi. "Heids here had a wee little obsession with the Biebs when he first blew up. She went a little too stalkerish when he was in town once, and his security detained her. Her parents had to pick her up and everything."

"No way!" I say, eyes big in disbelief.

"Yes way," Jake interrupts, walking in with drinks. He places the tray on the coffee table between us and comes to sit next to me.

"The next day at school, everyone knew about it. People called her 'wannabieber.' She didn't care, though—she wore it proud, like a badge. Dylan's eye still twitches whenever he hears Justin Bieber."

Our laughter fills the room. Talking about Justin Bieber reminds me of Emily, so I tell them about her version of "Baby" and how my dad tried to dance the Dougie, and how they followed me around, belting "Penis, penis, penis, ohhhhh!"

When the laughter fades, sadness washes over me. "I can't believe it was just last night," I say to no one in particular. "It feels like so long ago. Today has gone on forever." I look at Jake. "Is this, like, the longest day in history? What is *with* today?"

He puts his arm around my shoulders and kisses the side of my head. I love it when he does that.

"We'll let ourselves out," Lucy says, halfway out the door with Heidi.

"Let's get you to bed." Jake helps me up.

—

I've been lying in bed for two hours and can't seem to settle down. I'm exhausted but restless. I want to go home and I don't. I don't have words for this. I guess I won't know how I feel until I'm faced with the opportunity to go back.

An hour later I'm still wide awake. I need to get out of this bed and out of this room. I head downstairs. I can hear the murmur of the TV but stop in my tracks at the bottom of the stairs when I hear my name. The conversation is coming from the kitchen.

"Does Mikayla have nowhere else to stay?" Jake's dad, Nathan, is asking.

I freeze and my stomach drops to the floor.

"Dad, seriously?"

A moment of silence.

"I'm sorry, son. That came out all wrong." Nathan's voice is now softer and more sympathetic. He doesn't have an accent, either—come to think of it, neither does Julie.

"Look," Nathan continues, "it's not that we don't want her here. You have to know that. But you also need to understand that we're worried about *you*—"

"Dad—"

"Hang on, Jake. Let me finish. What you guys experienced is a lot to take in, even if you'd known each other for *years*. Your mom told me that you guys met just last night. We're not blind, Jake. We see the way you are together. I know there's something there. But we worry—and not just about her, Jake. This is a lot to process for someone your age—for anyone. I guess what I'm trying to say is that your mother and I are afraid she'll come to depend too much on you, and you'll get too involved. She really has *no one* else?"

"No, she really doesn't. I don't know what you want me to say, Dad."

"I don't want you to say anything. I said what I needed to say." Nathan sighs. "Now that that's out of the way, we also want you to know that we're proud of you, Jake. You've changed and grown up a lot in the last year or so. You've become a good man, and we love you. Just remember that you've worked hard to get to where you are—all of us have. Your mom and I . . . Well, we trust you to make the right decisions—not just with this girl, but with everything."

"Thanks, Dad." Jake's voice breaks.

I hear footsteps heading toward me and panic. I can't run back upstairs—they'll know I listened in on their conversation. *Idiot!*

"Kayla?" Jake says.

I turn around to face them. They have to know I just heard everything they said.

"Good night, Mikayla." Nathan gives my shoulder a little pat and brushes past me to the staircase.

I struggle to find my voice. "Good night . . . sir." I cringe.

"Can't sleep?" Jake asks.

I shake my head.

He's wearing only sweatpants and nothing else. His broad chest and shoulders are on full display. His abs are ripped down to the V that leads to his . . . I'm staring.

"Do you want to watch some TV with me?" He holds out his hand. "Nothing like infomercials to make me want to crash." I take his hand, and he leads me to the sofa, which is now his bed. We sit down, and he turns to me. "You heard that, huh?"

"Yeah . . . I'm sorry. I'll make some calls first thing in the morning and find somewhere else to stay as soon as possible . . ."

"Kayla, that's not at all—"

"Let's just not talk about it tonight, okay?" I suddenly feel exhausted.

He nods and looks away.

"Today was Mom's birthday," I say quietly.

"Christ, Kayla." He rubs his jaw. Silence fills the space between us.

"And Megan hasn't tried to contact me once," I add.

He pulls me in and places my head on his chest. The heat from his bare skin is overpowering. "I hate to state the obvious here, but Megan's kind of a shitty person."

I let out a tiny laugh. He strokes my hair from roots to tip, which is making me drowsy. "You know who isn't a shitty person?" I say through a yawn. "You, Jake Andrews, are not a shitty person—not even a little bit."

"Thanks." He chuckles.

My eyelids are getting heavy. "Mmm," I murmur. "My mom used to do this when I was little and couldn't sleep. It always helped."

"Go to sleep, baby . . ."

His words are the last thing I hear before he kisses the side of my head, and I give in to exhaustion.

Twelve

Mikayla

I'm woken up by the sound of a woman clearing her throat.

My eyes snap open to see Mandy standing in front of the sofa, hands on her hips. She's looking at something next to me. I take a few seconds to work out what the hell is happening.

I hear a moan and feel movement next to me. I sit up quickly—too quickly. The room begins to spin.

"Shit," Jake says. "We must've fallen asleep."

I feel something wet on the side of my face. I reach my hand up to touch it. *Drool.* I drooled—*on him.* My eyes go to his lap to see if there's evidence. I instantly regret it.

He's got morning wood.

I immediately look away but not before a tiny squeal escapes me.

"Shit," he mumbles, standing up to hide or at least adjust himself. He must know I've seen it. My eyes dart to his lap. I try to avoid *that* area but I can't. I squeal again like I'm a twelve-year-old virgin.

Jake grabs a cushion from the sofa and covers himself. His mom giggles. "Aw, Jake, don't be embarrassed. It's a nat—"

"*Mom!*" he yells, interrupting her. "Stop! Please. Just get out!" His hand not holding the cushion points to the door. She's all out laughing as she exits.

It's just the two of us in what suddenly feels like a tiny room.

"This isn't awkward at all," he sighs, shaking his head. Then we both start laughing. For a second, I almost forget about the pain.

Almost.

JAKE

So, she's pretty much seen my junk in all its glory. At least it was covered up. It could be worse—I don't know how, but I'm sure it could be.

Lisa will be here soon. Kayla says she's coming because she wants to take care of some stuff before everyone has to go back to work tomorrow. Personally, I think a part of it has to do with the stranger's bed her best friend's daughter is sleeping in. She's probably coming just to check on her.

After breakfast, I go looking for Kayla. I find her sitting on the sofa in the family room. She's looking down at her phone, her eyebrows bunched together in confusion.

"What's up?" I sit next to her and nudge her leg.

"Huh?" She's distracted.

I watch her as she stares at her phone.

"Have you heard from Megan?"

"Huh? Oh . . . No."

I remove her phone from her hand so I can have her full attention. She looks at me. "What's going on, Kayla?"

"I'm just trying to work up some courage." She looks resolved.

"What do you mean? Courage for what?"

She's quiet for a beat. "Sam, James's mom, has been calling me. I haven't spoken to her yet. She's sent a few texts, too." She looks away. "She's asked that I stay with them. I don't think she knows about James and Megan, but she knows something's up with me and James." She pauses. I wait for the rest.

She looks back at me now, tears in her eyes, "I think I should stay with them, Jake, until everything gets sorted out." I try to interrupt but she stops me. "I was with him for four years. I'm like a daughter to them. I just think that maybe . . . maybe they might need me there."

The lump in my throat makes it hard to speak, so I have to clear it a few times before anything comes out. "Kayla, if that's what you want, then I can't stop you. But it's not what my family wants, and it's definitely not what *I* want."

She sighs. "I think I need to, Jake."

"But what about James?" I can't help but spit out his name.

"What about him?"

"Are you guys going to get back together? I mean, do you still love him?"

"I—"

The doorbell cuts her off. Lisa's here.

—

Lisa spends the day with Mom and Kayla, making phone calls and arranging appointments for next week. I can see Kayla's preoccupied, because she's just nodding and agreeing with everything. I don't think she actually has a clue about what's happening.

Logan comes by to check on Kayla, but she's not really in the mood for hanging out, so he leaves soon after. Logan might be an ass most of the time, but the guy's got heart. There's a reason he's one of my best friends.

I don't know where Kayla's decided she's going to stay. I hope to God she doesn't go to James's house—not just because he's an asshole, but because . . . It's selfish, I know, but I honestly don't want to be without her.

Lisa stays for dinner again. The funeral director is coming tomorrow morning to make arrangements, then the cops will come by with an update after that. There's an appointment the following day with the family lawyer. I think Lisa's hoping the funeral will be the day after that. Turns out she's getting married in a couple of weeks (the weekend after graduation). It's her second marriage, Kayla told me, and apparently this new guy is way nicer than her first husband. Kayla was planning on going, but because of everything that's happened she told me she wasn't sure she'd go. Anyway, Lisa has to head home the day after the funeral.

We're sitting at the dining table, eating dessert. Julie is still at her friend's house. Kayla hasn't touched her plate.

"I know this is far from important right now," Lisa says, putting down her fork. "But Kayla's mom was going to be my maid of honor." She looks across the table at Kayla. "I was hoping that maybe you could take her place. I think it's fitting—I love you just as much as I loved her."

Kayla looks at me and bites her lip. She twists the napkin in her lap and nods. "Of course, Aunt Lisa," she says quietly. She clears her throat and speaks louder. "I'd love to."

Lisa smiles. "Oh, thank you, hun. It means so much to me that you're still able to go." She invites my parents, but they politely decline—Julie has a dance recital that weekend. "Well." Lisa purses her lips. "I don't want you traveling alone . . . I guess you'll have to travel with Jake, then."

What? What an awesome frickin' lady! Of course I have no choice but to go with her.

Kayla insists on cleaning up after dinner. We then head to the back patio. It was a nice summer day, but it's cooled down in the evening. We sit on the swing together with a light blanket over our shoulders. I put my arm around her and she leans into me. Our legs entangled, we swing in silence.

"Are you adopted, Jake?"

I laugh, because it's not the first time I've heard the question.

"Don't laugh! It's the only conclusion I can come to. You're the only one in the family who has that sexy—I mean . . ." She blushes. "You're the only one who has an accent."

"You think it's sexy?" I try to hide my smirk.

"Shut up." She sits up a bit and swats my chest. "I know I'm not the first girl to think *or* say that. I'm sure that Casey girl has mentioned it." She looks at me, waiting for a reaction.

I flinch at the mention of her name.

"What's the deal with her, anyway?"

"Nothing."

"Bullshit."

"So, back to my being adopted . . ." I try to change the subject. "I was actually born here. My parents grew up here, and so did I— until I was five, anyway. We lived, like, two streets down from this house. My dad got offered a job he couldn't refuse in Australia, so we packed up and moved there."

"What does your dad do?"

"He's a lawyer. What he does is actually amazing. He specializes in child and family law. He works with disadvantaged kids, and kids who are beaten or neglected. He's their voice when they don't have one, you know?" I look at her. "You're probably thinking he's a big softie, right? It doesn't seem like he could be, but he's intimidating in the courtroom. When he speaks, people listen.

"He takes on a lot of pro bono jobs, so there's really no money in it for him—not here, anyway. I was too young to really grasp it back then, but he did the same kind of work in Australia. But there he was in charge of all these junior lawyers who were just starting out and were interested in doing the same thing. The company he worked for was funded by private and government donations. The junior lawyers were mainly volunteers, and Dad apparently got paid quite well to oversee them."

"That's awesome, Jake. He sounds like a good guy."

"He is," I agree.

"And you got into baseball growing up in *Australia*?"

Jake laughs. "My dad was always a baseball fan, so when we moved to Australia, he found a baseball team for me to join. You're right, baseball isn't really a big thing there. They have rugby, cricket, and something called AFL, or Australian Rules football. It's kind of like American football, but it's really rough—you don't wear any padding. I got into it for a bit, too. After a few years, though, my dad and coaches noticed that I was starting to get pretty good at baseball. They didn't want me to get injured playing AFL, so I had to choose one or the other. I chose baseball.

"When I was about fourteen, Dad thought that I might be good enough to get into a decent college in the US. But it was hard to know how I compared to others from here, so he sent me back for six months to live with my aunt and uncle up the road. I met with a bunch of specialized coaches and talent scouts and stuff.

"When Dad learned that I might be good enough to go pro one day, we packed up everything and moved back here. I guess I adopted an Australian accent and it's stuck. Julie was actually born there, but she was four when we moved back, so she doesn't have an accent. You think mine's thick, but it's half-assed compared to the real thing. You should hear some of my mates when they call on Skype! Even I have a hard time understanding them."

Kayla's been listening so intently, I can practically hear the wheels turning. "What about your dad's job?" she asks.

"He does the same work here, but for not as much money." I shrug. "They kind of gave up everything so I could make it pro. It's hard not to appreciate that."

"Why didn't you go pro straight out of high school? Aren't they disappointed?"

"Not at all. I could have gone pro if I'd wanted—I got offers, but my parents always left it up to me. I want to get a college education. I mean, who knows what the majors have in store for me? I could play two games then injure my arm, and it would be over. I have to be smart about it, you know?"

"Wow, Jake." She looks at me wide-eyed. "Your mom wasn't kidding—you really are kind of a big deal."

"Shut up." I laugh.

After a few minutes, the patio door slides open and Julie comes out. She looks at Kayla and smiles shyly.

"What's up, JuJu? Did you have a good time at Cindy's?" I raise my hand for a high five.

She returns it. "Yeah, I did." She turns to Kayla. "Hey, Mikayla," she says. "I'm really sorry about Emily and your parents and about what I said. I didn't know—"

"Oh, sweetie." Kayla slides out of my arms to kneel in front of her. "Don't worry about it, okay? It's fine," she reassures her.

Julie nods her head slowly then hands Kayla a little wooden box.

"What's this?" Kayla asks. She opens it.

"When I got to Cindy's house, I told her about Emily and Mr. and Mrs. Jones. We rang the other girls from dance class and together we decided to make these cards for you. Cindy's mom drove us and we collected them from everyone. I chose the box. I know it's not much, but we all wrote stuff we liked about Emily and what we remember about her. She always made us laugh. We just thought you might like it, that's all."

Kayla holds the cards in her hands, tears, seemingly endless, flowing from her eyes. She places the box carefully on the ground and gives Julie a gigantic hug. Kayla starts to sob, which makes Julie begin to cry, too. Kayla pulls back and, holding Julie's face in her hands, wipes away her tears with her thumbs. She looks from Julie to me, then back to Julie.

"You have just given me the greatest gift in the history of the world," she tells Julie through her tears. "Emily was so lucky to know you, and so am I."

"Can we be friends?" Julie asks hopefully. "You're staying here for a while, right? Can we hang out and do girl stuff? I always wanted a big sister!"

Kayla looks at me and I know my smile is huge—I can't help it. She turns back to Julie. "Of course, sweetheart."

Thirteen

Mikayla

It was the first night I spent in Jake's bed alone. I slept a couple of hours, which I guess is better than nothing. I can already hear Lisa talking downstairs, which means the funeral director will be here soon.

I take a shower, mentally thanking Heidi and Lucy for bringing me what I need. I'm not used to bringing clothes with me into the bathroom, because I had my own bathroom at home, too. So when I walk out in nothing but a towel and see Jake standing in front of the dresser, I almost shit myself. I must squeal or something, because he turns around and drops whatever he's holding.

"Whoa," he breathes out. I know he's trying not to stare, but he's got that deer-in-headlights look, his eyes glued to my chest. I *think* I squeal again, because whatever noise I make forces him to snap out of his trance. He turns his back to me and heads for the door, mumbling "Sorry" as he walks out.

Once I'm fully dressed, I step out of his room and practically walk into him. He's leaning against the wall.

"I'm sorry about that . . . I knocked but there was no answer, so I assumed you were downstairs. I just need to get my stuff for training." Only now do I notice that he's in full baseball gear, from cap to cleats. It's hot as hell.

Wait . . .

"It's Monday. Don't you have school?" I know I do, but I've been excused. We're seniors, so it's not a big deal. But I hope he's not skipping because of me.

"I have permission." He rolls his eyes. "Besides, it's senior year. We graduate in two weeks, so who cares, right?"

"I guess." I shrug.

"I actually have a specialist pitching coach from UNC meeting me at the field. We're going to go over some things to prepare me for the season. They normally don't come out to individual players like this."

"That's awesome, Jake." I smile proudly at him.

"Yeah." He takes off his cap, runs his hand up and down the back of his head, then puts it back on. It's a nervous habit of his, I've noticed. "It's just that I might not be here when the funeral director comes."

"Oh." *Oh.*

He must sense my panic because he grabs both my hands and bends his head to look into my eyes. "I can cancel, Kayla. It's not a big deal. I'll just call—"

"I'll be fine, Jake." I smile, hoping it's genuine. "Go—you have to. You *are* a big deal and all." I try to laugh.

"Shut up and quit being cute," he says, flipping his cap backwards. He hugs me tight and kisses my temple, then makes his way into his room to get his gear bag out of the closet. He double-checks that everything is in there, then we walk downstairs hand in hand. I say good-bye to him at the door, and he reassures me that he's going to try to get back as soon as possible.

—

A couple of hours later, the funeral director is sitting opposite me in the family room. He's brought a bunch of brochures with him, and they're sprawled all over the coffee table. I space out through most of it, but I know that I have some decisions to make.

"Will the gathering afterward be held at our establishment or elsewhere?" he asks. His name is Wes—or Les maybe? I'm not sure.

"It will be held here," Mandy answers. I look at her, and she just smiles and nods, leaving me speechless.

"Okay," Wes/Les confirms. "Have you got a budget in mind?" he asks me.

Me.

I shake my head.

"Have you got numbers on how many guests?"

Guests? He makes it sound like it's a fucking party. I shake my head again, staring past him.

He sighs. "Oh, honey. Let's have a look at the caskets then, shall we? Let's start with what we call the junior range, for the child . . ."

He hands me a brochure and I tense. I cannot breathe. The blood drains from my entire body, and my vision blurs. In the distance, I hear a door open and close. I'm still staring into space when I see Jake. He's crouching in front of me, cap on backwards, and his hands are cupping my face to get my attention. I focus on him and his concerned look.

"Hey," he whispers.

"Hi," I whisper back.

"Would you please give us a minute?" Aunt Lisa asks Wes/Les.

"No problem, I'll be just outside." He closes the family-room door behind him.

"Are you okay, hun?" Aunt Lisa asks. I nod, never taking my eyes off Jake. "Honey, if you don't mind, why don't you let Mandy and me take care of this part?"

"That's a great idea," Mandy agrees. "Why doesn't Jake take you out for a bit?"

I nod again, and a second later Jake is leading me out the door. As soon as the family-room door closes behind Wes/Les, I hear Mandy screech, "How dare you!"

Jake leads me outside to his truck. He helps me into the passenger seat and puts my seat belt on like I'm a child. We've only said those two words to each other since he came back.

"Wait here, okay? I'm just going to run in quickly and change." He's still in his baseball gear. He returns what feels like a minute later wearing the same cap, dark jeans, and a light-gray Henley shirt with the sleeves pushed up.

"Feel like hitting something?" he asks, settling into the driver's seat.

"You know a way to a girl's heart," I joke, still feeling dazed.

He reverses out of the driveway, changes gears, then holds my hand the rest of the way.

We end up at the batting cages.

Of course we do.

—

Jake's standing at the pitching machine, adjusting some dials while I stand in the cage, bat in hand. He comes over to me and adjusts my hands on the bat. He tells me when the right time to swing is. I take in everything he says.

He goes back to the pitching machine and presses a couple of buttons. The balls start shooting out. I hit the first six out of the park.

His eyes bug out of his head. "Okay, smart-ass!" he yells, but it comes out "smuht-uhs." Australians don't use *r*'s, apparently.

He plays with some more buttons. The next few pitches come out faster, but I still manage to hit every one. He's chuckling and shaking his head in disbelief. He turns it up faster.

This next lot gets me. I'm probably fifty-fifty hits to misses. After no less than thirty swings, I shout, "Okay, I'm done!"

He turns the machine off and strolls over to me. "Want to tell me what that was about?" he asks, chuckling in amusement.

I ignore his question and hand him the bat and helmet. "Thanks, Jake. I really needed that." And I did—I *really* did.

"Seriously, though—where did you learn to hit like that? I would never have expected that."

Just as I'm about to answer, someone yells out his name. We turn to see about five guys walking over to us. When they reach us, they do that weird bro code handshake/fist bump/shoulder slap/ half hug greeting then shoot the shit for a few minutes. I see one of them staring at me, eyes roaming up and down my body. He creeps me out.

"Who's your friend here?" Creeper says loudly, interrupting their conversation.

Jake throws a possessive arm around my shoulders, and I lean into him. "Guys, this is Mikayla. Mikayla, these are—"

"She your girl?" Creeper asks, interrupting him again. His eyes are trained on my tits. *Ugh.*

"For now," a girl says from behind them. She makes her way to the front of the group.

Casey.

Where the fuck did she come from?

Jake tenses. Luckily for us, my phone sounds with a text. Aunt Lisa is letting us know that the detectives are on their way. I show him the text, and he excuses us. We walk back to his truck, his hand on the small of my back.

We ride back in silence, but halfway there I look over at him. His cap is pulled down low on his forehead, almost past his eyebrows. He senses my looking at him and glances at me. He smiles that panty-dropping smile then turns back to face the road, smile still in place.

"So . . . Casey, huh?"

His expression falls instantly, and we don't talk for the rest of the ride.

JAKE

When we pull up to the house, an unfamiliar black sedan is already there. We make our way into the living room to find them seated, waiting. Dad's here, too.

The detectives stand up to shake Kayla's hand. Kayla sits in the recliner, and I sit on its arm. She takes my hand in hers and tries to get comfortable. They wait for her to be settled before they sit back down.

"Ms. Jones, I'm Detective Richards. This is just a courtesy visit—" the first detective starts to say.

"Micky. Call me Micky, please."

"Micky." The detective nods at her.

The second detective speaks up. "And I'm Detective Frances. We just wanted to update you on the case. There's not much to report. We're doing everything we can, but we still haven't found the person who did this."

"Okay," Kayla says quietly.

"We continue to be under the impression that it was random. There is no evidence to indicate otherwise, unless you have further information that might change that."

Kayla shakes her head.

Detective Richards jumps in. "It looks like the perpetrator was there for a simple burglary. We suspect that your family walked into the middle of it." His voice thickens. "We also believe that they tried to burn the evidence. They started a fire in the garage, which got to all three cars and to most of the kitchen. Unfortunately, by the time the fire department arrived, the fire had consumed the entire front of the house. We've swept the place clean of any evidence we might need, so you can return to collect any personal belongings that may remain. But the fire department has deemed the house structurally unsound, and it will need to be torn down. We're very sorry, Micky."

Kayla's eyes brim with unshed tears, and Lisa moves to the other side of the recliner to comfort her.

The detectives share a look, then Detective Frances eyes Kayla. "Ms. Jo—uh, Micky." He corrects himself. "There's one other thing. We don't want to go into too much detail about the crime, but we thought you should know that the victims . . ." He takes a deep breath.

Kayla grips my hand so tightly that the blood drains from it. She leans forward in the chair, waiting.

"The victims all had a single gunshot wound to the head. They died instantly. They weren't in any pain, Micky."

Kayla's entire body convulses, and she falls to the floor. I scoop her up and sit down in the recliner, rocking her in my arms. I sweep the hair off her face as she cries into my chest.

The detectives stand up. "We'll see ourselves out," Detective Richards says. "Thank you for your time. We'll leave you to grieve with your loved ones, Micky." Dad shakes their hands.

Loved ones.

I think I do. *Love her*, I mean.

I think I'm *in love* with this beautifully broken girl.

I carry her upstairs to my bed, and that's how I spend the night—with her crying in my arms.

Fourteen

Jake

I miss my morning workout *again*. Kayla finally fell asleep around five. I didn't.

I carefully extricate myself and get out of bed. She needs to sleep. She has a meeting with their lawyer today at his office—I guess it'll be about her parents' wills and the house. I'm not sure. Dad will be there. I won't. I have to be at school for the morning at least. Some of the trainers and players from UNC are meeting me at the field for pre-orientation—whatever that means. I'd much rather be here with Kayla.

When I get out of the shower, she's sitting up in bed. Her eyes and nose are puffy and red from crying all night, and her hair is matted with one part sticking out to the side. She looks at me shyly. She's pretty much the cutest thing I've ever seen. Don't get me wrong—I've seen plenty of girls the morning after, but none like her. She's just *different* than anyone else. We haven't even slept together . . . yet she somehow means *more* to me already. Eventually, I'll want to kiss her again. Hell, who wouldn't? I just don't want to now—not with all this.

"Morning," I say and sit down next to her on the bed. I give her a quick kiss on the temple. She kisses me softly on the cheek. It's the first time she's kissed me since the limo ride.

"Good morning." She tries to smile.

"I *really* have to be at school this morning. If I could get out of it, I totally would—just so you know."

"It's okay, Jake."

"My dad's going to be there with you. If you have any questions or don't understand something, just ask him, okay? Seriously—I know he can be intimidating, but he's—"

"Jake, thank you. I'll be fine. I really appreciate your dad's taking time out of his workday for me. All you guys—you're amazing, you know that?"

"I know my family's amazing. But me? I'm kind of a *big deal*," I joke, trying to lighten the mood.

She swats my shoulder playfully then falls back onto the pillows with a huff, covering her eyes with one arm. "Get out of here, Jake, before I make you crawl back under these covers and snuggle with me." Her free arm points to the door.

I make a strangled noise, because I'm certain there's absolutely nothing else in the world I'd rather be doing.

—

By the time I get to school, the hallways are packed. Coach says they'll just excuse me from class whenever the UNC guys get here. Hopefully, they aren't far off, because I need to get back home to Kayla.

"Hey, asshole!" Logan yells as he walks over to me.

"Mr. Matthews," a teacher I don't know reprimands him. "This is a place of learning, not the basketball court."

85

Logan rolls his eyes then says to me, "About time you showed up." I cock my eyebrow at him. His hands go up in surrender. "Sorry, dude—dick move. So how is she?" he asks as we reach my locker, which is next to Heidi's. Lucy and Cam are there, too, and Dylan, of course. They stop talking, waiting for my response.

"She's not doing too well. I mean, what can you expect, right? She's just having a hard time with the funeral and stuff. I took her to the batting cages yesterday—girl's got good form."

Heidi rolls her eyes at my comment.

"She has a meeting with their family lawyer today," I continue. "I'm going to head back as soon as this UNC shit is done."

Logan raises his eyebrows at my attitude, but the truth is it just doesn't seem all that important right now.

"The funeral is tomorrow at twelve. The gathering is at our house afterward, so I won't be at school again."

"We won't be, either, Jake," Lucy says, holding Cam's hand.

"We'll all be there," Dylan assures me.

Logan pats my shoulder a couple of times before the bell rings, and we all separate to go to first period.

—

The meeting with the UNC guys was a joke. First, they turned up later than they said they would, and it went longer than I anticipated. The training staff is good, and they all seem pretty excited about my being there next season. Some of them hadn't actually seen me pitch in person, so I enjoyed their reaction.

The boys on the team are a different story. I get it. I really do. This is their fourth year on the team for some of those guys, and I get that they're tight with the other players. Now some cocky freshman is going to join the team and may even replace the current starter. Plus the coaches have built up a lot of hype around me, and they take a special trip to some random high school in the middle of Hicksville just to make me feel more comfortable. I'd hate me too, I think. They weren't dicks or anything, but they were far from *welcoming*.

I was finally able to rush home, knowing I definitely missed going to the meeting. Hopefully, it all went well—at least as well as it can go.

When I get home, the house is empty. They must still be with the lawyer. I go to my room and climb into bed so I can maybe get a nap in. I want to text her to see if everything is okay, but I realize I don't even have her number.

Just as I'm about to fall asleep, I hear music. Her phone is on the nightstand, playing "Hey Mickey." She must have forgotten it. I try to ignore it because I don't want to invade her privacy. But it rings again and again . . . I finally roll over to silence the thing and see that it's James—forty-eight missed calls from him, thirteen from Sam, and twenty-three unread texts.

The phone rings in my hand again. "Sam" is displayed on the screen. I try to reject it but accidentally press "accept."

"Hello? Micky?"

Shit.

I put the phone to my ear. "Uh . . . Hi?"

"Oh!" Sam says, surprised. I hear her exhale. "You must be Jake?" She has a thick drawl like her son.

"Yes, ma'am."

"We heard that the funeral will be held tomorrow. I just want to confirm the details with Micky."

I don't know if Kayla wants them there. I'm sure she wouldn't mind his parents, but *him*?

"I'll be sure to let her know you rang, ma'am."

"Okay, then. Thank you," she sighs sadly.

I hang up. I definitely can't sleep now, so I make my way downstairs. Just as I reach the bottom step, the front door swings open and Kayla bursts through. She ignores me as she runs past me up to my room, slamming the door behind her. Lisa, Mom, and Dad are standing at the front door.

"Maybe just leave her for a bit, Jake. I think she needs some time alone," Lisa tells me.

I glance in the direction of the stairs, willing myself to not go up there and demand to know what's happening. I want to hold her and tell her I'm here for her. I head to the kitchen instead, where the grown-ups are talking. I grab an apple from the fruit bowl and lean against the counter. "What's going on?" I ask everyone, taking a bite.

Lisa sighs. "Her parents weren't prepared in case something happened."

"What does that mean?" I ask, looking at Dad.

"There's no money, Jake—even after the house and life insurance payout. It's just enough to cover the mortgage and other debts," Dad explains, shaking his head. "There's enough money to pay tuition on whatever the scholarship doesn't cover. But there's no money left for housing or even textbooks—"

"And she needs to somehow feed herself!" Lisa looks away from the window to me. "I don't know what to do. I mean, she could come home with me . . . My fiancé would say yes if I ask him, but I don't think it's fair . . . She's legally an adult, but she's not ready to be on her own—not with *nothing* . . ." Her voice trails off.

It's quiet for the longest time, all of us staring at the floor. I'm thinking about what we can do to help—if there is anything we *can* do. I push away from the counter, throw my apple in the bin, and head to my room. I get under the covers with her and snuggle, just like she wanted. I don't know how long we stay like that, but I know we both eventually fall asleep.

—

I wake up to her trying to get out of bed, but I hold on to her more tightly and nuzzle her neck. She laughs. It's a small laugh, but it's enough.

"I need to shower," she says, stretching. "I'll meet you downstairs."

Mom is finishing cooking dinner, and Lisa is still here, too. "Where are Dad and Julie?" I ask.

"In the study. They're building the solar system," Mom answers, rolling her eyes. Dad loves helping with these kinds of projects. I remember those days.

I'm getting the drinks out to help set the table when Kayla walks in. She's freshened up. She's barefoot, wearing tight skinny jeans and an olive-green top. The clothes must be Heidi's, because the jeans are skintight and the shirt hugs every curve of her body—just a size too small so about an inch of skin shows between the hem of her shirt and the band of her jeans. I'm staring—more like ogling. I've had my hands all over her, so I know she has curves, but *damn*.

Mom's in front of me. "You have a little drool," she says quietly, playfully wiping my mouth. I swat her hands away and continue pouring drinks into the jugs.

Julie leads the conversation during dinner. She talks about some new dance they're learning. Kayla takes it all in and asks her questions. It's the most I've heard her say to anyone but me. She seems to know what she's talking about, and I wonder if she's taken dance before. She *definitely* has the body for it.

"Hey, Kayla." I clear my throat. "Uh . . . Sam called earlier and asked if you could call her back about the funeral."

Kayla stops chewing and looks at me. "Okay . . . Thank you."

She smiles throughout the entire dinner, making small talk. It's a sudden change in behavior, and I'm not the only one who notices.

"What's going on, Kayla?" Lisa looks at her suspiciously. "I mean, it's great to see you smiling again, but after today—"

"Aunt Lisa." Kayla puts down her knife and fork and sits back in her chair. "I've had a lot of time to think. I can't go to college—not now. It's simply not an option. And I can't stay here anymore. So I'm just . . . I'm done."

FIFTEEN

MIKAYLA

They're all looking at me, waiting for more. I don't have much more to tell them.

"After the funeral tomorrow, I'm done. I'm leaving." I look at Aunt Lisa, who's frowning. "There's nothing left for me here," I say quietly. I look at Jake, who is sitting next to me, and put my hand on his leg under the table. His hand finds mine. "Well, there's one thing, but I don't know if it's enough." I end in a whisper and look down at my plate.

Silence fills the room. When I look up, they're all frowning at me, including Julie. Aunt Lisa is wiping away tears, and Jake grips my hand more tightly.

Nathan clears his throat, and all eyes snap to him. "Listen, Mikayla . . ." He looks at me—*really* looks at me—and I can see the sympathy in his eyes. "You are going to stay here." I open my mouth to protest, but he raises his hand. I let him continue. "You are going to stay here until you leave for college." It sounds like an order. I can see out of the corner of my eye that Mandy is smiling at her husband with a newfound appreciation; she didn't know this was coming.

"I can't stay here," I whisper, looking back down at my plate. "I can't stay here for free at least—let me get a job so I can pay you *something*."

"Mikayla," Nathan says, shaking his head. He sighs, looking almost defeated. "I *have* thought about this, and from the few days I've known you, I can tell you're not going to accept our offer to stay here without working for it. So, will you help me out at the office two days a week? I need an administrative assistant—someone who can file, type, keep things organized—basically all the things I hate. Do you think you can do that?"

I nod, stunned.

"Good, then it's settled. I'll pay you for your time like any other employee, but it's not for room and board. Save that money." I try to interrupt him again, but he stops me. "Save that money for college, Mikayla. We would, however, appreciate it if you could help Mandy around the house. She has a lot of things to organize before Jake leaves for college. You can also be Julie's personal taxi—God knows she needs one for the summer. You can take Mandy's minivan, and she can use my car. I'll finally get to use the company car that's sitting in the office parking garage, collecting dust." I stare at him. "In a few weeks, we'll all sit down and discuss how this arrangement is working out, understood?" He cocks his head to the side, waiting for my answer.

I look around the table. Lisa and Mandy are staring at Nathan in awe, and Julie has her hands clasped beneath her chin, begging me to say yes—like I could say anything else. I look at Jake, who has the biggest, goofiest grin on his face.

"Yes, sir. Understood."

The whole table erupts in claps and cheers, and I find myself missing my family. But it hurts less today than it did yesterday. Being here with them—it's familiar, in a good way.

And I think, for just a second, that maybe my heart can learn to love again.

Sixteen

Jake

We're driving in my truck to the cemetery. Kayla's sitting in the middle, her body tucked into mine like she can't get close enough. I don't mind—not even a little. Everyone else is in the minivan behind us. We're going to skip the usual formalities of a funeral ceremony. I think Mom and Lisa understand that Kayla wants a quiet affair.

When we pull up, I'm surprised at how many people are already there, then I remember that she did lose her *entire* family. I step out of the truck. She follows me, sliding out the driver's side door. I offer my hand to help her out, and she doesn't let go once she's out. She's wearing sunglasses and a simple black dress that Heidi brought over that morning. That girl thinks of everything.

We wait for my parents to park behind us. Julie runs out of the car straight to a bunch of other girls. They must be from dance class, here for Emily. I see that asshole James, and some other kids our age grouped together. They look up when they notice Kayla's here. James starts to walk toward us, but one of the guys pulls him back and says something close to his ear. Good move. I can see his fists ball at his sides as he glares at us.

Lisa moves to Kayla's other side and takes her hand as we walk up to the plots. I'd say there are over a hundred and fifty people here—grown-ups Mom's and Dad's age, some older adults, and kids Emily's and Julie's age. It looks like an entire classroom and their parents showed up. More kids our age are scattered throughout the crowd. Kayla doesn't look up. She hasn't said anything all day or acknowledged anyone. But she hasn't let go of my hand.

When we make it to our seats in front of the three caskets, she begins to shake with sobs. I pull her into me. I notice a group of kids no older than ten lined up in the front row. They're in full Little League gear, some of them holding baseballs and gloves. I look at the large photos of her family propped in front of the caskets and realize it's the first time I've seen her family. I hadn't really wondered what they looked like. Her mom was stunning—she could pass as Kayla's more Asian older sister. Kayla has an exotic look about her, but I had never asked why. And Julie was right—Emily definitely was a younger version of her, and she would have broken many hearts. Her dad was taller than her mom—in the family portrait, anyway. I wonder how tall he was in real life.

I continue to look at the collage of photos. There's one of the whole family and that asshole James, eating at a picnic table on the Fourth of July and laughing. There's a photo of her dad standing front and center with kids all around him decked out in baseball gear. He's holding one of the boys in his arms, who is lifting a trophy. All the kids have huge smiles on their faces—the kind of smile that only kids have, because nothing is ever going to be hard, and they haven't yet experienced pain or heartbreak.

Her dad coached Little League, huh?

Then I see it—a picture of Kayla with her parents. Her mom is heavily pregnant, and her dad has one arm wrapped around her and the other around Kayla. Kayla is dressed in full baseball gear, bat in one hand and a trophy in the other. "MVP," it says. She has a huge smile on her face. No shit.

Lisa begins the ceremony with a short speech. The Little League team then throws their baseballs and gloves into her dad's plot. I even see some police officers paying their respects—including Mendoza and the overweight cop. There are lots of tears and cries, but Kayla stays strong throughout. A few people come over to speak with her, but she mainly nods and tries to smile. She doesn't leave my side.

When most of the people have left, including my family and Lisa, I figure we should head home to prepare for the gathering. I notice a couple approaching us. Kayla notices them, too, and as they walk up she lets go of my hand to give them each a hug. She reaches for my hand again. The couple smiles sadly at Kayla. They look at me and our joined hands.

Kayla clears her throat. "Sam, Henry, this is—"

Sam interrupts her. "Hi, Jake," she says, reaching out her hand. I shake it tentatively. "Kayla has told me so much about you." She smiles warmly at me.

This isn't awkward at *all*.

Henry—James's dad, I'm assuming—shakes my hand, too. "Thank you for taking care of our girl, son," he says and pats my shoulder.

"Uh, it's no problem, sir. She's special, you know?"

"Oh, we know," Henry agrees. "It's a shame our son couldn't appreciate her and keep his dick in his pants."

I stifle a laugh and hear Kayla doing the same.

"Come on, Henry." Sam starts to drag him away. "We'll keep in touch, dear," she says, waving at Kayla.

"Well, that was unexpected," I mumble under my breath.

"Not really. They'd love you, Jake."

—

We head home to the gathering. It already started without us. Fewer people are here than at the ceremony. We join my friends on the back patio. I think Kayla is a bit more relaxed now, because she's keeping up conversation with the several people who come up to her.

A girl I haven't seen before approaches Kayla. "Hi, Mikayla," she says in a mousy voice. "I'm really sorry about your loss." She laughs uneasily. "What a shit thing to say—like you lost something but you'll find it again." She shakes her head.

Kayla laughs. "Amanda, how are you?"

"I'm okay. I'm not going to ask how you are, though."

Kayla laughs again, and it's genuine.

"I just came to say . . . I don't know. Hey, you'll be at UNC, right?"

Kayla looks at me and smiles. "That's the plan. I just have to work out some minor details."

"Cool," Amanda says, nodding her head. "I'll Facebook you my number. We should hang out sometime—maybe go on the prowl for guys who aren't sucky, cheating dickfaces." We all laugh.

"Sounds amazing. I'll call you. And thanks for coming." Kayla smiles as Amanda walks back into the house.

"I like her," Heidi says.

I do, too. But I can't help thinking about what she said about going on the prowl. College is going to be completely different from here. She'll have more friends and attention from other guys. I can't help the jealousy that suddenly consumes me. But what can I do? Lock her in my room the whole damn day?

Then it hits me. Where the fuck is Megan?

—

Everyone has left except my friends. We're talking on the back patio. The sun's gone down so there's a slight chill in the air. I light the little fire pit in the middle of the patio. I don't think my friends will be leaving anytime soon, and Kayla seems to be happy about that since it probably takes her mind off things.

The patio door slides open and Mom comes out with a tray of leftovers. We dig in. Dad brings a cooler and places it near the fire pit.

"Someone needs to be a designated driver—and don't tell your parents. In fact, I didn't even give it to you. I merely placed it in a position that you were able to get to. My story will hold up in the eyes of the law."

Logan opens the cooler. It's filled with beer. "Thanks, Mr. Andrews. You're so my fave person over thirty-five."

My dad chuckles to himself. "And you, Logan, are still an ass-hole," he says, sliding the door closed behind him.

"Burn!" Cam says, laughing.

"So." I nudge Kayla, who's sitting next to me. She stands up to get a napkin full of little things from the tray of food. She saunters back and sits on my lap, leaving her chair empty. I smile to myself. Logan eyes me curiously. I don't care.

"So?" she replies.

"Your dad was a Little League coach?" Everyone is listening in on our conversation.

"Yep—one of the best," she says proudly.

"So that's why you can hit the shit out of a baseball?"

"Yep. I gave it up when I got boobs." She shrugs.

I laugh. My eyes move to her boobs before I quickly force myself to look away.

"Actually, he was a huge baseball fan—and a fan of yours, too."

"What? How?" I ask, because it doesn't make sense.

"Mm-hm," she says, picking up a piece of food and putting it in my mouth. It's hot as fuck that she's feeding me while sitting on me. It takes everything in me not to devour her mouth.

"I actually knew *of* you before I knew you." She pauses, chewing her food. "Dad mentioned you before, so I knew your name but not what you looked like. When I heard your full name, it sounded familiar, but I didn't connect the dots until your mom told me that you were kind of a 'big deal.' Dad actually went to watch your high school games a few times. He said he wanted to watch 'history in the making.' He begged me to go a couple of times, but I was always busy with . . . you know . . ." She trails off. *James.*

"You shouldn't tell him stuff like that, Micky. His head is big enough as it is," Logan says, throwing a bit of food at me.

"Yeah," Heidi agrees. "Baseball and Casey are enough to make his head explode."

Seventeen

Mikayla

I watch Jake stiffen. His expression falls again at the mention of her name. I try to stifle my laugh, but it comes out anyway.

"Okay, someone has to tell me what the deal is with her. Please?" I plead.

Jake starts to talk. I cover his mouth with my hand, and he continues to mumble into it.

"She's a crazy stalker bitch," Lucy offers, taking a sip of water. I guess she's the DD tonight.

"Like, how crazy are we talking here? Writing Mrs.-Casey-Andrews-all-over-her-books crazy, or Mrs.-Heidi-Bieber crazy?" I ask. They laugh, and I see Dylan's jaw tense.

Cam takes a huge swig of beer. "Like, hiding-in-the-back-of-his-truck-after-a-game-*naked* crazy!"

My eyes widen and snap to Jake. He looks down and shakes his head, laughter in his eyes. He removes my hand that was covering his mouth, entwines our fingers, and gives my wrist a chaste kiss.

Logan continues. "That's not all that happened. Tell her the rest, Jake."

I look at him. Oh my God—he slept with her!

"Oh my God, you slept with her?" I gasp.

"No!" he yells, and everyone cracks up. "*No*. What? God . . . No!" he says again, shivering and making a disgusted face.

"Then what?" I ask.

He presses his lips together, refusing to speak. I make an exasperated sound and turn to the rest of them, my eyes pleading for someone to finish the story. Heidi starts to giggle, and everyone joins in.

"What? *What happened?*" *I need to know.*

Heidi calms herself down. "Homegirl proposed to him!" She's struggling to keep talking through her laughter. "She left an engagement ring out on the dashboard of his truck and proposed to him, *naked*, in the backseat—with people all around!"

"No!" I gasp, bewilderment clear in my voice. I look at Jake. He nods slowly. His arm is wrapped around my waist, and he strokes my stomach with his thumb.

"What did you do?" I ask him, but he just shakes his head. I look at everyone else. "What did he do?"

"This is the best part," Cam continues. "He got so freaked out, he jumped out of the car and started to run home. But it was an *away* game! It took him five hours to get back. He left everything in his truck—phone, wallet, gear bag, everything. He couldn't call anyone. He was too freaked to go back in case she or the ring were still there. We didn't drive out to pick up his truck until a week later. He went a week without a car because he was so freaked out."

"That's just one of the stories," Logan adds. "There's, like, a hundred more just as crazy."

I'm laughing so hard now my sides hurt. I'd almost forgotten why we're all here.

Then I remember and stop laughing.

Because today is *not* a laughing day.

I must have stopped rather suddenly, because Jake kisses my temple and says, "You can laugh and be happy, Kayla. They would want you to be." I smile and kiss him on the cheek.

Logan takes a huge gulp of his beer then belches, finger pointing at me and Jake. Heidi and Lucy groan in disgust. "I'm going to ignore this epic, ovary-exploding sexual tension thing you guys have going on and ask a question."

I stifle a laugh against Jake's neck while he rolls his eyes at Logan. "Ask your question, asshole," he says and rubs his nose along my jaw. God, that *accent* and that *voice*. My eyes close for a second. I think my ovaries *will* explode.

"Why does he get to call you Kayla, and everyone else calls you Micky?"

I shrug. "Because my family called me Kayla."

EIGHTEEN

JAKE

It's been a week since the funeral, and Kayla has improved heaps. It'll continue to be tough for a while, I'm sure—years maybe—but she seems to be finding ways to deal. She's worked a couple of days with Dad and has kept busy around the house to distract herself. I go to school only when absolutely necessary—enough to keep Mom off my back. I don't like being away from her.

My graduation ceremony is today, and Kayla's is tomorrow. Her school's guidance counselor came to the house to let her know that her grades were good enough to pass and that she'll still be able to graduate. The counselor also mentioned that she made some phone calls to UNC to make sure that Kayla's scholarship would not be affected under the circumstances.

Dad saw some termites in the garage and has workmen here fixing it. They need to fumigate the garage and the storage room above it, possibly having to fix some of the structural damage, so we have to stay away from there. I've seen how some of the workers eye Kayla when she leaves in the morning to take Julie to school. One guy gawks so much, it takes everything in me to not punch him in the face.

I jog up the driveway after finishing my workout and see Dad talking to the gawker. Dad sees me coming, shakes hands with him, and walks over to me. My eyes don't leave Gawker's—he knows what I'm thinking, because the asshole has the decency to smirk at me.

We walk into the house together. Everyone has taken the day off because of graduation. I knock on my door. No one answers, so I jump in the shower. On my way downstairs, I stop when I hear music and laughter coming from Julie's room. Julie squeals Kayla's name in the middle of a laugh. I smile and knock on her door.

No one answers—the music is too loud. I open the door slightly and peek in. They've pushed all the furniture aside and made a makeshift dance floor in the middle of the room. They're playing "Low" by Flo Rida so loud that the walls are shaking.

Julie is showing Kayla some dance moves, and Kayla's watching intently. Their backs are to me, so they can't see that I'm here. Julie goes to the stereo to replay the song, and they start the routine from the beginning. My sister's good at dancing for an eight-year-old, but *goddamn*, Kayla is *good*. There's a line in the song that is totally inappropriate for JuJu, but the move Kayla does . . . It's almost too much to watch.

Near the end of the song, they do some spinning dance move and see me standing in the doorway. I smile and clap at their performance.

"*Jacarb!*" Julie yells and turns off the stereo. "Don't sneak up on us like that!"

I'm staring at Kayla. She has a sheen of sweat on her body, and she's breathing heavily. She's in yoga pants and a tight-fitting tank, her body on full display. She catches me checking her out, bites her bottom lip, and shyly looks away. *Hot as hell.*

"Jake!" Julie yells again, snapping me out of perv mode.

"What's up, JuJu? That was really good!" I high-five her, and she beams.

Mom and Dad come into the room. "What's with all the yelling in here?" Mom asks, concerned.

"Oh, good," Julie says. "You're all here. Watch our routine! Micky's been practicing with me."

"Oh, no," Kayla says. She's embarrassed in front of my parents. "Maybe wait till it's finished, Julie?" she asks hopefully.

"No! Come on, Micky, please?"

Kayla looks at Julie then at me. A huge smile slowly spreads across her face. "I'll do it if *Jacarb* does it, too."

"Okay, then!" Julie cries and pulls me by the arm into the middle of the dance floor. My parents sit on the bed to watch.

I stand next to Kayla and put my hand on the small of her back, placing my thumb just under the hem of her tank and rubbing gently. Goose bumps break out across her skin. I bend down and whisper in her ear, "You are in so much trouble, missy." She closes her eyes and shivers slightly.

I try to keep up with the dance routine, but I'm a jock, not a dancer. I suck and end up falling in a tangle of arms and legs. Kayla stands over me, laughing so hard she has to hold her stomach. I grab her legs and yank them out from under her. She falls on top of me, and Julie jumps on top of both of us, complaining that we're not taking it seriously.

"Take this seriously!" Kayla mimics her. She starts tickling her, and I join in. My parents, laughing, leave the room.

It's at this moment that I *know*. I don't just think it anymore—I know it. I love this girl. I'm *in* love with this girl.

MIKAYLA

The sexual tension between Jake and me is off the charts. I'm scared I might actually combust at any second—no joke. It doesn't help that we're around each other almost 24/7, always finding ways to not-so-innocently touch each other. It's at that stage where we're pushing each other a little further and further to see how much we can take until one of us cracks. I'm about two seconds from cracking, and if I don't get release soon, I *will* cut a bitch.

Jake's graduation later in the afternoon went smoothly. I met some of his other friends, including guys on his team, and I *stayed the hell away* from Casey. I saw the way she looked at me and joked that I should probably start packing heat. Jake didn't find it so funny.

We're now at a graduation party held at a field near the school. Jake had declined the invitation, but I told him I thought we should go—it would be good for us to get out and socialize with the general population. We're gathered around a bonfire, and I am, of course, sitting on Jake's lap. His usual friends are here as well as a few others.

I'm wearing one of Heidi's dresses. I still don't have the courage to go back to my house. I asked Mandy to pack up my room and all the personal stuff, like photo albums and jewelry, next weekend while we're at Aunt Lisa's wedding, and hired professional movers to take care of the rest. I rented a storage container for whatever isn't damaged. The stuff can stay there until I work out what I'm going to do at UNC. Everything else can go.

Heidi's a size smaller than I am, but she only brought one outfit with her when she came over, so she told me to suck it up and deal with it. It's a navy-blue dress that's tight from the waist down with a looser top that hangs off one shoulder. It's more like something Megan would wear—who, by the way, still hasn't called me. According to Facebook, Meg and James are "in a relationship." I should care, but I don't. Right now, sitting here with Jake, I'm, like . . . James? *James effing who?*

"Hey, look, Jake. Casey's coming over here," I whisper in his ear.

He tightens his hold on me and ducks his head, like he's trying to hide.

"I was just kidding, Jake. Jesus Christ!" I say, laughing.

"That's not funny, Kayla. I'm not kidding—don't do that." He holds his hand to his heart.

I giggle and take a look around. I only see a couple of kids from my school out of the hundreds who are here. "Does everyone go to your school, or is this party also for other schools in the area?" I ask.

"I think it's just ours," Logan says. He's taking a breather from making out with the redhead on his lap. Taking a sip of his beer, he asks, "Why? Are you scared that asshole ex of yours is going to show up?"

I shrug. "Not really. Even if he does, I'm sure Jake will just punch him again."

Logan and Cam spit out their beer simultaneously, and Dylan cusses. Logan glares at me, bug-eyed. "He punched that asshole?"

I nod slowly.

"Which hand?" Dylan asks.

What?

Behind me, Jake raises his right hand, bringing on a tirade of name-calling and questions from the guys. "It's fine!" he yells above them all.

Lucy must sense how confused I am, because she answers my unspoken question. "His pitching hand."

Shit.

I take his hand between mine and kiss the knuckles one by one. I feel him tense at my display of affection then *stiffen* under me. That's my cue to get off him and do something—anything—else.

Nineteen

Jake

I am in too deep—way too deep. I spent the rest of last night with a hard-on, and I don't think it's fully left me yet. This girl is driving me crazy—that dress she wore, then she sat in my lap, laughing, touching, joking, flirting . . . Then she kisses my hand so intimately—my fucking pitching hand. It's by far the sexiest thing a girl has ever done, *ever*. I don't say this to be a dick, but girls have done a *lot* of shit to me.

I throw the covers off my pathetic joke of a bed and stretch. My back is screwed up and my whole body aches. I fold the blankets and shake my head. This thing is definitely not made for a six-foot-two frame. I may attempt sleeping on the floor tonight, because anything's got to be better than this.

I walk into the kitchen—or more like wobble, in my condition.

Kayla's already there. "Your mom left a note. She's at a PTA meeting . . ." She takes in my physical state. "And what happened to you?"

"I don't think the sofa and I are friends anymore." I put on a pout.

"I'll take the sofa, Jake. You can have your bed back. Besides, you can't sleep on the sofa all summer."

"You want to bet?" I ask, cocking my eyebrow at her.

She looks at me for a second then turns away, biting her lip. "At least let me give you a massage," she says quietly.

I laugh.

"I'm serious," she says.

I think about it but shake my head.

"Come on, please? I have to do *something*."

"It's fine, Kayla. I'll see a trainer when we get back from Lisa's wedding."

"It's not fine." She starts to pull my arm to lead me away, but I dig my heels in.

"It's not that I don't trust you." I smirk. "This body is in peak physical condition. I'm *almost* a professional athlete, Kayla. I can't let just *anybody* touch me."

She rolls her eyes at me. "Trust me, I give good massages."

"Yeah?" I eye her. "Says who?"

She looks away and blushes. *James.* I shiver in disgust, but she doesn't seem to notice.

"Look," she starts again, squaring her shoulders. "When James started to really get into basketball, all the training and game time killed him. He'd always complain about being sore, so I researched how to help him—*if* I could help him. One summer, I took classes in physical therapy and sports medicine at the local community college. I learned heaps and actually enjoyed it. For a little bit there, I genuinely considered becoming a sports doctor. I still think about it sometimes."

I let it sink in then shake my head. "He *really* didn't deserve you, you know that, right?"

"I know." She smiles. "I *am* an awesome girlfriend, and some asshole is going to be really lucky one day."

I swear to God I hope that asshole will be me. I motion toward the stairs. "Lead the way, doc."

She smiles and leads me up to my room.

—

Kayla asks me to take my T-shirt off and lay facedown on the bed. She's silent for a beat then asks, "Do you have any lotion or oil?"

"Yeah, there's baby oil in the bottom drawer." I point to my nightstand. The second the words are out, I regret them. That drawer is my sex drawer. It's got boxes of condoms, lube, baby oil, tissues, and porn—yes, *porn*. I hear her open the drawer then chuckle a little.

"What?" I say, trying to hide my embarrassment. "I'm a guy."

Next thing I know, she's sitting on me, rubbing oil onto my back. Her tiny hands knead my aching muscles.

"Jake?"

"Mmm." My face is shoved into the pillow, and her hands feel *amazing*.

"I hope I'm not cramping your style by being here."

I laugh under my breath, but my body shakes. I shift my head so I can talk. "I don't think anyone could cramp my style . . . unless we rewind back to 2002."

She playfully smacks me on the back. "You know what I mean."

"I don't, actually."

"Well, I know there's no shortage of girls who are willing to, uh, partake in certain activities with you." She clears her throat. "I just don't want you to think—I mean, I know how uncool it would be to invite a girl back here and somehow try to make that sofa work."

"Kayla, I don't bring girls home, if that's what you're getting at. So, no, you're not cramping my style by being here. My parents aren't dumb—they know I have sex, or have had sex, I should say. I guess it's just an unspoken rule, you know, with Julie down the hall. I respect them enough to not do that under their roof."

The room's silent for a while. She's still sitting with her parts right on my ass, legs spread, her hands working magic on me. She *is* good at this. Her voice is almost a whisper when she asks, "What do you mean, you've *had* sex? Do you mean you're not doing it anymore—or often?"

I can't believe she wants to talk about this now. I can't handle where she's positioned on me, or where her hands are touching . . . And she wants to talk about sex. My junk is at full attention now. If I think about sex for a second longer, I'm going to come in my pants like I'm thirteen.

"So?" She won't give up.

"You're going to think I'm an asshole." I try to lighten the mood.

"I already think you're an asshole."

"Ha-ha," I deadpan.

"Well?"

"Okay, okay. Well, as you know, we lived in Australia until I was fourteen. I started high school here halfway through freshman year. I was the new kid with the accent, and word had already got around that I was kind of good at baseball, which, apparently, was something girls were interested in. Anyway, once I joined the team, a lot of the older guys kind of took me under their wing. So there was a period of time when it was all parties and alcohol most weekends, then girls were added to the mix. I can't even tell you what my first experience was like. She was older—like, seventeen or something. I guess she just wanted the honor of deflowering me." I stop to make sure she's listening. Her hands are still moving up and down my back, focusing on areas she can tell are tight.

"I sound like a dick, but it's the truth," I continue. "Then there were other parties and other girls. My parents got fed up with it after a year or so. They sat me down and told me that they didn't move all the way back here so I could 'booze up and slut around every weekend'—their words, not mine. They said that we moved so I could focus on baseball, and that was what I should be doing. If I wanted to party, we could have stayed in Australia, and Dad would be earning triple what he's making now. I guess that hit home, and I had to really think about what I was doing with my life. I cleaned up after that. Now baseball comes first. But I'm not going to lie to you, Kayla. It doesn't mean that there haven't been *any* girls since that conversation with them."

Silence.

Followed by more silence.

Then she asks, "Have you ever been in love?"

"I don't know . . . Maybe." *Yes, with you.*

"Did the girls you were with ever expect more from you?"

"No, we were always clear about our intentions before anything happened. In the beginning, there may have been a few who thought that they could be *the one*, but I was never ready for that."

"Did you enjoy it—sex, I mean?"

"Well, yeah, I'm a guy. We don't need much to enjoy it—any hole's a goal. Fuck, that sounded a lot less piggish in my head."

She chuckles then falls silent, still massaging my back. She finally speaks up. "I think I must have really sucked at it. I mean, if what you say is right, it should have been enjoyable . . . Like, it doesn't take much for a guy to enjoy the experience. I wonder why he had to get it from someone else. I must've been so horrible at it."

I feel like an asshole. "Kayla, I didn't mean—"

"No, it's okay," she cuts me off.

I want to turn around and see her face and what emotion she's hiding behind her words.

"The worst thing is," she continues, "he never—not once— gave me an orgasm."

Seriously?

"Maybe," Kayla says, like she's deep in her own thoughts, "there is something wrong with me."

I can't help it—I turn over so quickly, she doesn't even have time to jump off. She's straddling my hips now, and my hard-on is pressed against her. She feels it and for a split second closes her eyes. She opens them and starts to climb off me. I hold her thighs down to stop her. I don't really know what I'm doing—I'm scared she may panic and haul ass out of this house.

Then she moves on top of me.

We both groan out loud. She blushes red, embarrassed by what she just did, and tries to get off the bed again. My grip on her thighs tightens, and my dick twitches. She must feel it, because she moans from deep in her throat and shifts again—just once, but enough. Her head tilts back, and she closes her eyes.

"So, never, huh?" I say, trying to keep my voice even.

She looks at me for a second, still sitting on my hard dick. She looks confused, then understanding dawns on her face. "I've been able to take care of myself, you know." She blushes again and looks away. "But he was never able to—not with his hands or anything . . . Oh my God, this is so embarrassing." She covers her face with her hands.

"It's not embarrassing." I reach up and remove her hands. "So, like, not even oral? None of it?"

Kayla shakes her head. "After awhile I had to start faking it, so he would stop trying. I even planned to see a doctor about it—in case something might be physically wrong down there."

We haven't changed positions, so she's still straddling me and I'm still hard as a rock. "Want to know what I think? I think he's just a selfish asshole who *obviously* couldn't take care of his girl. I should've punched him twice when I had the chance."

She laughs, which causes her whole body to rock against me in all the good ways. She moans again, and I swear I'll come if I hear that noise one more time. I slowly move my hands up her thighs and gently push up against her just once. We stare into each other's eyes. Hers are hooded and filled with lust. If this happens—*when* this happens—planets are going to collide, and the world around us will probably explode.

We slowly start rocking together. It feels incredible—better than being *inside* any girl I've ever been with.

"Jake," she whispers as she continues rocking against me.

My hands creep higher on her thighs until they reach over the back of her shorts to the skin above the waistband. I hook my thumb under the material, silently asking, and she nods slowly in response. I move my hands inside her shorts and under her panties, gently cupping her ass. She sighs at the slight touch, and I swear my dick is so hard it could explode.

I remove one hand, and she whimpers in protest. It may be the sexiest sound I've ever heard. I place my hand on the back of her neck and bring her lips down toward mine. It's early in the morning, so neither of us has brushed our teeth. There's no way I'm going in for a kiss. Plus, if I'm going to kiss her, I'll want to taste her—all of her—and I won't be able to stop. And today, I need to be able to stop. Because I'm afraid that for her it's too much, too soon. And I don't want her to regret anything she does with me.

I kiss her neck. Her torso presses on top of me. With her legs still straddling me, I have one hand on her ass and the other resting lightly on her waist. I begin to lick her skin, and her breathing becomes heavier. She's practically panting, grinding at a faster rhythm. God, she feels so fucking incredible.

Her movements become more rushed, and she starts panting louder. I can feel her heart beating against my chest, and I know she's close. I squeeze her ass more tightly, and with my other hand go for the front of her shorts.

"Jake!" She comes undone almost instantly, and I surprise myself by letting go, too.

"I don't think there's anything wrong with you, Kayla."

Twenty

Jake

Nothing says awkward like coming in your pants while dry humping.

Mikayla

Nothing like a mind-blowing orgasm to keep a goofy smile on your face.

Oh my God. Jake fucking Andrews.

My graduation ceremony is a little dull. It's nothing compared to Jake's—I think my school sucks in comparison. When the person up at the podium finally calls my name, everyone claps—mostly pity claps, I assume. It's a small town, so everyone knows I'm the girl with the dead family. The Andrewses clap the loudest. Jake also does this ridiculously loud wolf whistle that breaks through the air and makes everyone laugh. I also hear Jake's friends shout my name from far back in the crowd. I had no idea they were coming, but I appreciate so much that they're here for me.

I *still* haven't heard from Megan. Zero. Zilch. Nada.

The rest of the students walk. One I've never spoken to before shares a quick speech about the death of my family and how courageous I am. I wish I could listen and absorb it, but all I can think about is Jake and his hands, his mouth, his . . . I'm rubbing my legs together when loud cheers erupt and the students around me throw their caps in the air. *Yay, we're done.* I need to see Jake.

I head over to him and his friends and family. They give me a huge group hug, and Mandy goes nuts with the photos. I pose with everyone individually, and she gets about a trillion of Jake and me. Jake's family then heads home.

Logan's giving me shit about how small my hick school is when Jake walks up to me and puts a protective arm around my shoulders. James sees it and approaches us, sneering. The group steps back, but Logan stays in the same spot. He looks at Jake. "Dude, if you feel like punching him again, just tell me—I'll do it. Don't risk fucking up that hand again, because UNC wouldn't be too happy."

James's eyes narrow then widen in realization. "You're *that* Jake Andrews?"

Jake just shrugs and squares his shoulders.

James looks at me. "Nice job on my truck, by the way."

The group cackles with laughter. "Thank you," I say, smiling like the Cheshire Cat. James shakes his head, looking down. When he looks up, I see a different expression.

"Look, Mick," he starts, then puffs out a breath. "Could you maybe ask your bodyguard here to give us a minute?" He nods toward Jake.

I look up at Jake then back at James. "Nope," I say, making the *p* pop. Jake stifles a laugh next to me, his mouth in my hair.

"Forget it," James mutters and turns to walk away.

"Hey, James?" I call out. He pivots, walking backwards. "How's Megan doing?"

115

He freezes, opens his mouth to respond, then shuts it again before turning around and walking away—for good, I hope.

We say good-bye to the gang—we'll see them when we get back from Aunt Lisa's wedding next weekend. Then Jake and I head home, too. *Home.*

—

A few days later the workers are still going strong, rebuilding the garage. Jake and I are packed up and head out to his truck. We say good-bye to his family on the way out. I thought they might give us a lecture about being by ourselves in a hotel room, but I guess living together at their house is basically the same thing.

When we reach the driveway, I see Travis, one of the workers. He's a nice guy—he always smiles and says hello in the morning when I take Julie to school. He sees me, too, and smiles. "Hey, Mikayla. How are you today, darlin'?"

Jake takes my bag from me and holds it in the same hand as his bag. He grips my hand tightly and pulls me in. He leads me to the passenger side of his truck and throws our bags in the bed. He makes sure I'm seated before closing the door.

But instead of getting into the truck, he walks over to Travis and says something. It looks like a heated conversation, and Travis raises his arms in surrender. When Jake gets in the truck, his face is red, his jaw is clenched, and his eyebrows are drawn together. I don't say anything.

Halfway to the airport, he hasn't changed. Hesitantly, I take his hand in mine, and he seems to calm down a tiny bit. "What is it, Jake? Did something happen with Travis?"

"How do you know his name?" he spits out.

"I don't know. He introduced himself one day." I've never seen him like this, and it scares me a little.

"And you remem—" He whips around and sees my face. He straightens his features. "I'm so sorry, Kayla." He takes a few deep breaths. "I'm just sick of that asshole eyeing you up and down whenever he sees you."

"Jake, he wasn't—"

"Just leave it alone, okay? They'll be done next week."

———

The wedding was beautiful—Mom would have loved it. And the reception was *amazing*. Jake and I drank a bit too much, though, so we stumbled our way to our hotel room. We'd gotten in last night, but after having dinner with Aunt Lisa and her fiancé, we'd crashed and burned immediately after our heads hit the pillows.

We took advantage of the stocked mini bar, and now we're both buzzed, sitting on the floor with our backs against the bed.

"Did you know the legal drinking age in Australia is eighteen?" he says.

"No." I empty the contents of my beer bottle.

"Mm-hm." He fishes through a packet of nuts from the airplane. "It's the same for driving—well, where we were, anyway. It's sixteen or seventeen in some other states."

"Which city did you live in?"

"Melbourne."

"What was it like?"

"We lived in the suburbs, and, believe it or not, it's a lot like home—except there are more traffic lights in Melbourne."

"Were you a bad little boy?" I ask.

"That sounds kind of sexy yet borderline creepy." He laughs.

I smack him on the shoulder, and he pretends it hurt, rubbing his shoulder before continuing. "Nah, I was just a standard little punk. I think the worst thing I did over there was accidentally knock over a pot outside a florist's shop by trying to do sick tricks on my skateboard."

I laugh.

"I felt so bad, I told my mom the minute I got home and begged her to pay for it. She made me apologize to the owner and took it out of my pocket money."

I laugh even harder. "You are so frickin' adorable."

He chuckles under his breath. It's quiet for a moment, and I lean my head on his shoulder.

"Tell me more about it—Australia, I mean. We didn't travel much, so I've never been out of America. We had always planned on going to the Philippines for a family holiday. My grandpa was from there—my mom was half-Filipino."

"I always wondered where you got that amazing color from," he says, rubbing my arm with the back of his finger.

I nudge him. "Tell me."

"Okay, let's see." He contemplates the ceiling.

I stand up to get another beer from the fridge. "Shit," I groan. "We're out of beer."

"What? No way!" He comes up from behind me to look. "Crap. Well, we've got champagne."

I pout. "I can't have champagne without ice."

"To the ice machine!" he announces, one hand on his waist and the other in the air, like he's a superhero. I laugh and jump onto his back. He grabs me around the legs and hands me the ice bucket on the way out.

"We call flip-flops 'thongs,'" he says, turning his head to peek at me out of the corner of his eye.

"What?" I laugh.

"When I was living with my aunt and uncle before we moved back here, a girl invited me to her house for a pool party. The whole class was there. I had taken my flip-flops off by the side of the pool,

so when I was ready to get out I asked this girl, who was smokin'
hot for thirteen, to hand them to me—except I said, 'Chuck us me
thongs!'"

I throw my head back in laughter so hard, he loses his balance
and has to steady us.

"After that, people kept teasing me that I wore thongs—which
in Australia is called a G-string, FYI. Anyway, it took me a good two
months to convince people that I didn't wear *thongs*, and that I was
asking for *flip-flops*."

I'm glad he's holding on to me, because if he weren't, I'd be rolling around on the floor.

"Mikayla, is that you?" I look up to see Aunt Lisa's mom smiling at me.

I climb off Jake's back and give her a hug, trying to hide the fact
that I'm buzzed—or wasted. I'm probably closer to wasted. "Hi,
Mrs. Jennings. What a lovely ceremony!"

"Oh, yes, dear, it was. It was nice to see you smiling. Did you
have a good time?"

"Yes, ma'am, I really did." I smile at her.

"That's wonderful! Your parents would be so happy." She looks
at Jake. "And this is your boyfriend?"

"Oh, he's not—" What is he? I look at him. He's eyeing me,
waiting for my response with a goofy expression on his face. I laugh
a little and take his hand. "This is my Jake," I say proudly.

Jake glances at me sideways and smirks. He reaches out and
shakes Mrs. Jennings's hand. "Nice to meet you, ma'am." He holds
up the ice bucket. "I'll get the ice and meet you back in the room,"
he says to me before walking away.

When I return to our room, I notice that the ice bucket is filled
and sitting near the bottle of champagne on the little dining table. I
can hear the shower running. *Weird.* I sit on the edge of the bed and
wait for him to come out.

When he does, my jaw drops. He's shirtless with just sweat-pants on. They ride so low on his hips, I can see the band of his boxer briefs peeking out. He has a towel in one hand, drying his wet chest. The steam from the bathroom pours out through the open doorway, and he shakes his head to get rid of some of the water.

My mouth goes dry, and I itch to run my fingers over his stomach. I sit on my hands so I don't get too tempted. My eyes roam down his body. He has to know what I'm doing, because he hasn't moved since he walked out and noticed me. I must be wasted, because I'm positive that time stops—the second hand of the clock must have decided that I deserve some luck and is pausing to let me stare at this masterpiece of a boy. I rub my legs together, trying to ease some of the tension down there.

He finally moves and sits down next to me—so close that his bare arm is rubbing on mine. I can feel his heat at my side. It's not the only place I'm feeling heat.

I'm ridiculously horny beyond belief.

I'm too ashamed to look at his face. And I don't know how he's reacting to my stare-athon. In my mind, I must look like a giant St. Bernard with sloppy drool dripping out of its mouth, panting and whimpering like it needs to lick the giant bone inches from its face.

Jake can be my giant bone. Oh my God. *Bone.*

I should lick him.

On his chest.

No! I'm not *that* wasted. But is he? Maybe he wouldn't remember if I gave him just one lick.

I turn to face him, my eyes on his chest. *Do it . . .*

"Kayla?"

"Mmm?" I'm almost there.

"If you keep staring at me like that, I'm going to have to ask you to take your shirt off so we're even."

Twenty-One

Mikayla

I snap to reality and jump back a bit.

I was *two seconds* away from licking him.

Laughing to myself, I run past him into the bathroom, so I can steady my breathing and get some space. I look in the mirror, but all I see is that St. Bernard. I laugh out loud this time.

"What's so funny in there?" He yells so I can hear him through the door.

"I was totally going to lick you!"

"What?!"

What the fuck? Why did I just say that?

"Nothing!"

When I finally emerge from the bathroom, he's lying on the bed with his legs on the floor, like he flung himself backwards from a sitting position. He's got one arm over his eyes. He hears me come out but doesn't move.

"I'm, like, in a euphoric state of buzzed right now," he mumbles. "How are you holding up?"

"Me too, but I think I'm a little worse off." I sit on the bed. "Hey, Jake?"

"Mmm?"

"You need to put a shirt on."

He doesn't say anything—he just gets up, goes to his bag, and throws on a T-shirt. He then walks over to the champagne, pours two glasses with ice, and hands one to me. Half an hour later, we're on the floor again, laughing.

"Let's play truth or dare!" I cry, like it's the greatest idea in the world.

"Or," he says, holding his finger up like he has a better idea, "I could braid your hair while we watch *Hannah Montana*. That would be swell."

"I'm serious." We're way past buzzed again.

"I'm serious, too, Kayla. You don't need to play games. If you want to fool around, just say it," he jokes, reaching out to grab a boob. I swat his hand away and giggle. He feigns disappointment. "Okay. Ask me anything, and I'll tell you the truth. The same goes for you, too, though, okay?"

"Done." I nod. "Me first. How many girls have you slept with?"

He moans and rolls his eyes. He pours himself another glass of champagne and says, "Shit, I've got to hit the gym tomorrow."

"All right, Captain Deflect-o, answer the question."

"I don't know." He shrugs. "Between thirty to fifty, I guess."

I scrunch my nose and give him a disgusted look.

"Don't look at me like that, and don't judge me—I was a different person then," he says defensively.

"A different person? Maybe five or six different people—that would make it less piggish."

He chuckles. "My turn. I dare you . . ."—he pauses for dramatic effect—". . . to let me touch your boobs."

"Er, I'll take truth, thanks," I say, laughing.

"Damn it!" he spits out, faking anger. "Okay. Is it true that . . . you want me to touch your boobs?" He starts reaching out for a grab.

I swat his hand away again and laugh out loud. I fight a mental war against my physical urges, because the last thing I want is for us to do something we can't take back—especially when we've been drinking. With a sigh, I say, "You kind of turn into a horny creeper when you're drunk. This game's over." I crawl into bed, and he follows.

We snuggle under the covers and I nestle my head on his chest. He puts his arm around me, his hand on my waist, and kisses my forehead. We're both a little sleepy-drunk.

"I was just kidding about the boob thing, Kayla," he says through a yawn.

"I know."

He's silent for so long I don't know if he's fallen asleep. His breathing is even, and his chest rises and falls rhythmically.

"Hey, Jake?" I whisper, hoping not to wake him if he has already fallen asleep.

"Mmm?"

"Have you ever been in love?"

He sounds very tired when he answers. "You've already asked me this."

"Yeah, but I didn't get a proper answer."

"Yeah, you did, and it's all you'll get. Good night, Kayla."

"Hey, Jake?"

"Yeah, Kayla?" He's drifting off.

"I more-than-a-lot like you."

He's quiet for so long again that I don't know if he heard me. Then he says, "I more-than-a-lot like you, too—so much more-than-a-lot."

—

True to his word, Jake gets up early the next morning and goes to the hotel gym. I meet him there about an hour and a half later. I feel guilty about all the dessert and alcohol I've had over the last couple of days and figure I should do something about it.

When I get there, I see Jake in his workout clothes lifting weights. His arms, tanned and defined, flex and unflex with every movement. I'm not the only one who notices. A group of women who look a few years older than us are pretending to stretch in front of him. I know what they're really doing, and it pisses me off.

The truth is, Jake's at a whole other level.

Jake Andrews: the *could-be* pro baseballer.

There are boys, and then there are men. Even though we're the same age, I still feel like a little girl next to him.

James is a big dude—he's a jock, too—but we were high school sweethearts. With him I felt like we were on an even playing field . . . while he felt like *playing* the field. I roll my eyes at the thought.

I'm in the real world now.

And in the real world, there *are* no Jake Andrewses for me.

I suddenly don't feel like working out anymore.

I want to go back to the hotel room and be the frumpy, stupid little girl I am. As I turn to leave, Jake sees me and calls out my name. I stop and wait for him. He puts his weights down and walks in my direction—but not before a *more* than stunning blond blocks his path. *Great.*

He crashes into her and almost knocks her over. He has to hold her up, one hand on her arm and the other on her waist. "Whoa," he says, "are you all right?"

I see her eyes widen at his deep voice and accent. She puts a hand on his chest, rubs up against his side, and on tiptoe whispers in his ear. She's tiny, so he has to bend down to hear what she's saying.

After a couple of seconds, his eyes widen and he raises them to look at me. He's still bent over, listening to whatever Slutbag has to say. After what feels like hours, Slutbag straightens up and hands him a piece of paper.

Her phone number.

Of course.

He takes it with a nod and puts it in his pocket.

My heart drops to the floor and into a pool of my idiotic, childish jealousy.

I can't stand to see any more, and I'm sure the lump in my throat is a sign that I'll soon burst into tears. And if I do—*when* I do—I sure as hell don't want to be here.

I'm heading to the exit when I hear him yell my name again and ask me to wait.

But I don't.

I can't have him see me like this.

I walk faster, but he's catching up to me. He calls my name one more time, but I don't turn around.

"Kayla!" he grunts, grabbing my arm and forcing me to turn and face him. He takes in my face. "Hey, what's wrong?"

"Nothing," I spit out and cross my arms like a six-year-old. I stare daggers at him.

A huge smile slowly creeps across his face. He straightens up and also crosses his arms. He winks at me. *Winks.*

"What are you smiling about?" I almost shout.

"You're jealous," he says matter-of-factly. He's got a huge grin smeared all over his beautiful, smug ass of a face.

"I am not." *Brat.*

"Are so." He nods.

"Am not!" I stomp my foot. *Brat. Brat. Brat.* "I have no reason to be." I can't help pouting.

"Yeah, you do," he says, putting his arm around me and turning us toward our room.

I look up at him with a questioning expression, and he looks down and kisses my forehead. "Why should I be jealous?" I ask.

He shrugs. "Because I'm *your* Jake," he says, "and you're *my* Kayla." He smiles, fishing in his pocket for the piece of paper. Once we're in the room, he throws it in the trash.

He's *my* Jake. And I'm *his* Kayla.

I like it.

I more-than-a-lot like it—so much more-than-a-lot.

Twenty-Two

Jake

When we get back home, the house is empty, so we decide to crash in my bed for a few hours. It's early evening when we wake up. We can hear people chatting downstairs.

I slowly peel Kayla off me and stretch out. When I sit up, I almost shit myself—Julie is sitting cross-legged at the end of my bed, watching us.

"JuJu! What the fu— I mean, how long have you been here?"

Kayla is awake now, sitting up with sleepy Bambi eyes and her hair all messed up.

I look back at Julie, who's still staring at us. "Are you guys going to get married?" she asks.

"What?" I say, exasperated.

"My friend Michelle's dads do everything together. But she says they're sad because they can't get married. Are you guys going to get married?"

What the fuck? I look at Kayla. She looks shocked. I turn back to my sister. "What are you saying, JuJu?"

"Well, you and Kayla do everything together, so you should get married. Michelle says her dads can't get married . . . So why do they do everything together?"

I don't know what to say. I look at Kayla for help.

She smiles at Julie. "Because they're in love, just like your mommy and daddy."

Julie thinks for a second then shrugs. "Cool. You guys want to play *Rock Band*?"

I blow out a huge breath I didn't know I was holding. "Sure, go set it up. We'll be down in a minute."

After she leaves the room, I flop back onto the pillows. "Jesus Christ," I breathe.

Kayla looks down at me from her sitting position.

"Crisis averted, thanks to you," I tell her.

She chuckles under her breath. I grab her around the waist and pull her toward me for one more quick cuddle before we have to make our way downstairs.

After an hour of *Rock Band*—which Kayla rocks, by the way—Mom calls us for dinner. We answer questions about our weekend and the wedding. Julie apparently did really well at her dance recital, and Mom spent a bit of time at Kayla's house—well, her old house—gathering her personal things.

After dinner, Mom gets up and plops an entire apple pie in front of me—the whole thing. I stare at her curiously, but she continues around the table, handing out other items. She gives Kayla a stack of dessert bowls, Julie napkins, and Dad silverware. She has a gigantic tub of ice cream.

What the hell?

"We're going to have a picnic, kids," Dad says, standing up. I look around me. Julie is beaming, and Kayla just shrugs. Everyone stands and walks out of the dining room, carrying their items, so I follow. We step outside, and by this point I'm in complete WTF mode.

Kayla comes up to me and murmurs, "Hey, they're *your* family."

We walk up the stairs next to the garage that lead to the storage room above. They must have finished fumigating or whatever. When we get to the top of the stairs, Mom holds the door open for us. I step in and freeze, shocked.

Mikayla

I'm pretty sure my body has forgotten how to breathe or function at all. I feel something wet on my arm and look down. Tears—I'm crying and I didn't even notice. I look at Jake and he smiles. I look at Mandy and Nathan. They're watching me, hopeful. I hand the bowls to Jake and walk over to Mandy. I pull her in tight before hugging Nathan, too. Then I move to my bed.

My bed—from home. It's the same cast iron white frame that squeaks when I sit down, with the same comforter and pillows . . . And there's the baby blanket my mom knitted when she was pregnant with me.

"How did you . . . ?" I look at Mandy.

"I had a lot of help." Mandy shrugs. "Actually, Logan and the guys helped move the stuff in with Dylan's truck. The girls did the painting and decorating. Nathan was busy with Julie's recital and work, so . . ."

I look at Jake. He puts his hands up in surrender. "I had no idea."

"You guys," I say, my voice breaking. I look at each of them, my eyes begging them to understand what my brain can't voice.

"Let's eat!" Nathan announces.

And we do—on the floor of my new bedroom, which is *exactly* the same as my old one. I even have my own bathroom. And they placed everything where it was in my old room—the dresser, night-stand, and lamps . . . even my desk and MacBook.

We're scarfing down the apple pie and ice cream when I notice a photo frame on my nightstand. I stand up mid-chew and walk over to it. There's space for four photos in the frame, but only three are filled. One is a family portrait—one of those lame posed shots with the standard watercolor-blue backdrop. The other is a candid shot of Mom, Emily, and me, laughing. I swallow. It was taken at one of Dad's Little League games, when a player accidentally junk-shot him with a bat. It was cruel to laugh, but his reaction was hilarious. One of the moms caught it on camera and gave us a photo of it. The third one is a picture of Jake and me at my graduation. I don't remember its being taken. It must have been when I ran up to him after it was over. He wrapped me in his arms and lifted me off the ground, spinning me around. His arms are wrapped around my waist and my hands are around his neck. He's got his cap on back-wards, and I'm looking down at him, beaming, while he's smiling back up at me. I remember wanting to kiss him so badly at that moment.

I tear my eyes away from the frame and look at Mandy. Tears falling, I tell her, "Thank you."

I can see she's holding back her own tears. "I just thought . . ." She has to stop to clear her throat and take a deep breath. She holds up a camera and motions around the room. "Maybe you might want a photo with—"

"With my family?" I beam through my tears. "I definitely need one of those."

A sob breaks through her laugh as she holds up the camera, and I get a new family portrait to last a lifetime.

"I'm thinking that I far from more-than-a-lot like you, Mikayla Jones," Jake says, and the flash goes off.

Jake

I always knew my mom was an amazing woman, but I never knew just how amazing until now.

We head back into the house after dessert. Kayla insists on cleaning up after dinner, so I go upstairs to shower. I'm glad to have my own bed back, but I don't like that she's so far away, either.

I must have been in the shower for a while, because she's all done by the time I come downstairs. Mom tells me she's in her room. As I open the door to head outside, Mom yells out my name.

"We don't need to have a talk about stuff, do we?" she asks, sitting on the sofa with my dad.

"What stuff?" I ask, hoping they elaborate. Because as much as my parents are awesome, talking about sex makes them *so* uncomfortable.

Mom starts to blush. Dad mutes the TV and looks at me. "Just remember that Julie lives here, too, and, um, wrap it before you tap it." Dad chuckles.

"Nathan!" Mom screeches, slapping him on the chest.

He grabs her in his arms and kisses her—like, full-on making out. It's not the first time I've seen them do that, but still . . . *gross!*

"All right, guys, I'll leave you to it," I say and head out to her room. I knock on the door.

"Jake?"

"Yeah, it's me."

"Come in."

"Who were you expect—" I cut myself off when I see what she's wearing. She's freshly showered and in her pajamas—bright-red boy shorts and a matching tank.

Instant semi.

"Well, I didn't really want anyone else seeing me like this." She motions up and down her body. Damn right, no one else will see her like that!

She moves to her dresser and fishes through a little wooden box. I lie down on her bed. She turns around and sees me there. She looks confused, eyebrows drawn together, thinking . . . or remembering?

Then it hits me. I'm lying on the bed that she's probably had sex with James on hundreds of times.

I jump up and make some lame grunting noise. When I look at her, she's glaring at me with a "What the fuck?" look on her face.

"What's wrong?" she asks.

My jaw hurts from clenching it at the thought of her and James together. "I just don't really feel like lying on the same bed that you and that asshole ex of yours had—"

"Oh!" she gasps, surprised. "We never—I mean, he never . . . Well, not that . . . Oh, God!"

"You've never had sex on this bed?" I ask incredulously.

"No, we never even fooled around on it, I promise. You're safe." She laughs.

"Thank God," I sigh in relief and lie back down. "Then why were you looking at me like that?"

"I've never seen a boy on my bed before. It was just . . . I don't know." She blushes and looks at the floor.

"Come here." I motion next to me. She lies down on her side and moves my right arm so she can nestle in the crook. I stay on my back, her head resting on my chest. A comfortable silence fills the room.

I'm almost asleep when I feel her hands move, her breath blowing out as she sighs. My other hand is resting on my stomach, and she moves hers so that our fingertips are touching. She spreads her fingers and pushes her palm against mine. We look at our hands.

Our skin is only lightly grazing—a soft touch, yet it feels so intimate, like we're more than what we are. I know I want to be more—more than this.

I intertwine my fingers with hers and touch something I haven't felt before. I pull our hands closer in and look. She's wearing a diamond ring and a wedding band on her ring finger and another wedding band on her right thumb. "Are these your parents' rings?" I ask quietly.

"Huh? Oh yeah, they are. I probably shouldn't be wearing them—like it's disrespectful or something. But it makes me feel closer to them."

"It's not disrespectful at all, Kayla," I whisper, kissing her hair. "If anything, it's beautiful. Those rings are a symbol of their love, and so are you. I bet when they put those rings on each other's fingers, they didn't have a clue they'd create someone as special as you."

She smiles sadly. "Have I told you how they met?"

I shake my head.

"Mom was twenty-one, and Dad was eighteen. He worked part-time delivering flowers. One day he delivered some to Mom, and she signed for them. But they weren't for her. When she read the card and realized he had delivered them to the wrong address, she rang the company. Dad had to pick them up and redeliver them to the right address, but not before getting her number. That night, he called her and they spent hours on the phone, talking about anything and everything. Mom actually had a boyfriend at the time, but apparently he was an asshole. He worked the night shift, so she set her alarm for the morning. Around the time she knew he got home, she called him and broke up with him. Two weeks later, Dad pretty much moved in with her. They fell in love instantly, Jake. It was like he went to the wrong address on purpose.

"Mom used to always tell the story when I was little. My friends' parents would read *The Little Mermaid* and *Snow White* to them, but my parents told me my very own fairy tale. That's what Mom called it—their fairy tale. I believe in it, too—that instant, intense love. It's fate."

She sits up to look at me. Tears brimming in her eyes, she tries to talk through the lump in her throat. "I believe in happily-ever-after." She looks at me with so much emotion, I hope to hell that I'm reading her right—that the look she's giving me is telling me everything I want to know. She believes in fate, in love—in *us*, forever.

She stands up and walks to the window. This room never had windows before—it was just storage. Dad must have had them installed. She opens the curtains and stifles a laugh. "Have you seen this yet?" she asks, turning around to face me.

I try to figure out which way we're facing. I come up behind her and look outside. Her window faces the window in my room. The garage is detached from the house, but not by much. I could easily climb out my window and jump the space between the two roofs. "My dad totally did this on purpose."

"Your dad is so my fave person over thirty-five."

Twenty-Three

Mikayla

I turn away from the window, and he is *right there*. My chest presses against his. When I look up, he's staring at me, his eyes filled with desire.

"You know," he says, placing his hands on my waist and shifting us slightly to my left. "We never really talked about what happened the other morning."

My eyes move away from him. I can't face him anymore.

He takes one step forward and pins me against the wall, lifting my chin with his finger so I have no choice but to look at him. He raises an eyebrow.

I squeak.

He smiles. "Kayla," he whispers. His head falls to my shoulder and his lips lightly graze my skin. He opens his mouth and his tongue slightly darts out to touch me. My skin breaks out in goose bumps, and I shiver—but not from cold. His hands are on my waist again, his thumbs moving up and down on my stomach, just under my top. I close my eyes and take a deep breath, biting my bottom lip to stop myself from pressing my mouth against his.

When I open my eyes, he's watching me. He pushes himself against me, and I can feel how much he wants this—how much he wants me. He kisses me along my neck to my jaw and near my mouth, but he stops himself from kissing my lips. He groans as his hands dip into my shorts and under my panties, gripping my bare ass.

"Kayla," he sighs.

I wrap my legs around him and grind on him in an effort to release the tension. I kiss his neck and under his ear, gently biting his earlobe. He groans again. I avoid his mouth like he did mine. I kiss along his jaw to his collarbone. I want more—I need more.

I reach for the hem of his T-shirt, and he helps me lift it over his head. His body is leaning into mine, keeping me pinned against the wall. My hands are everywhere at once. I caress his back and his rock-solid chest, his muscles straining from his neck down to his arms. He definitely has an athlete's body—he's not a beef-head but perfectly toned and fit, every ridge in his abs defined and a smattering of curls leading to that perfect V that goes lower to his . . .

I kiss his chest, gripping his back with my hands. My fingers hold on to him so tightly, my nails dig into his back, almost breaking his skin. I find his nipple and take it in my mouth. He grips my ass more tightly and lifts me up, moving us to the bed. He lays me down—and that's when the panic sets in.

Being in this room with him is just too much. The memory of my parents surrounds me, and I wonder what they would think if they knew what was happening right now.

I pull back slightly and wait until he's looking at me. "Jake, I can't—we can't . . ." My hands are still wrapped around his neck, and he hovers over me, arms on either side of me like he's about to do a push-up. "We can't do—"

"It's okay, Kayla." He kisses my forehead. "We don't have to do *that*. I mean, I don't want to—not yet. But, please, just let me touch you. I think I'd die if I couldn't . . ." He searches my face for an answer. I nod.

His head dips down to kiss my chest, moving lower and lower until he reaches the swell of my breasts. He moves one hand to the hem of my top and lifts it over my stomach and my breasts. I sit up and help him remove it, and I instantly lean into him, skin-on-skin. The heat from his skin envelops me. He hasn't seen me topless before, and I'm afraid. He gently lowers me. I move reluctantly and lie still, watching him take me in—how his eyes roam from my face to pause on my breasts. "God, Kayla, you're so fucking beautiful," he whispers and lowers his head. His mouth is on my nipple, licking and gently biting while his other hand softly caresses the other breast.

I've never, *ever* felt like this—this wanton need to combust. I've never felt like my body was being worshipped before. It feels like Jake can't get enough. The minute I feel his hand under my shorts, I lose all control. I spread my legs further for him, and he makes a moaning sound that vibrates through my nipples straight to my core. I grip his hair and beg him without words to *please don't fucking stop*. When his fingers find what they're looking for, a loud moan escapes me, and he has to stop working on my breasts to tell me to be quiet. "Shh. Jesus Christ, Kayla. You're so fucking wet."

I grip his head harder and push him back down to my tits. I need him there. He laughs a little to himself before continuing. His fingers are moving inside me, working their magic. I feel something building in the pit of my stomach, and I'm scared and amazed at the same time. This has never happened before, not with anyone, and it feels so much better than anything else.

He pulls away, and I look down at him. His eyes on mine, he squeezes my breast in his other hand then runs his glistening bottom lip along my nipple. *So fucking hot.* That's all it takes for me to explode all over his fingers. I thrash wildly, screaming his name over and over—so loudly that he has to cover my face with a pillow.

Once I've come down, I remove the pillow and slowly open my eyes. He's lying next to me, still shirtless. He leans over and smiles. "So . . . You're a screamer?"

"I had no fucking idea, Jake—not until you." I shake my head in disbelief.

"Good answer," he says. He stands up and walks to the bathroom, his hard-on tenting his pants.

"Where are you going?"

"To take a really cold shower, or take care of myself. I haven't decided yet." He walks backwards into the brand-new bathroom, built just for me, turns, and closes the door behind him.

I go to my dresser and grab the baby oil. I enter the bathroom and notice his shocked face as I make the decision for him.

TWENTY-FOUR

MIKAYLA

The summer days go by quickly. It's already been a few weeks since we got back from the wedding. I work two days a week with Nathan, and he pays me like we'd discussed. Personally, I think he overpays, but what can I do? Jake works out and trains every morning, but the afternoons are relaxed and lazy. I drive Julie around as agreed, and we hang out with Jake's friends when we can.

Out of respect for his family, we haven't had any more moments. But it's not *just* that. I think we're both just happy to be around each other and haven't talked about taking things further. I don't know about Jake, but I'm waiting to see how things go when we leave for college. It might be completely different once we're not together all the time.

When I get home, I grab my MacBook from my room and settle into a chair on the back patio. A few minutes later, I hear the door slide open. "What are you doing?" Jake asks, stepping out.

"Browsing online for apartments and jobs near campus." I glance up from my computer.

He looks at me for a beat before sitting in the chair opposite me. "You can't do student housing?"

"You have to pay for the year in advance, so, no, I can't. I'm hoping there's some cheap shared housing nearby. Whatever job I get will hopefully pay enough to cover the rent. Plus, I've got to consider how close everything is to bus stops, because I won't have a car."

There honestly aren't too many options out there, especially this close to the start of the school year. I don't tell Jake because I know he'll worry—and, really, it's not his problem, as much as he would like to make it his.

"What about you?" I ask. He hasn't even mentioned where he'll be staying.

He stares at me, an emotion I can't decipher on his face. I try to hold his gaze, but it's so intense, I have to turn away. "I haven't yet decided what I'm going to do," he finally says.

"Seriously, Jake? School's around the corner—you better decide. There aren't many options available."

He smirks at me. "Kayla, I'll be fine. I—" He points his thumb at himself. "I'm kind of a *big deal*. I'm sure whatever I decide, they'll somehow make it work."

"Okay . . ."

The back door slides open again, and Julie comes out. We're going to the mall today. I think she's been bored out of her brains. It's hard to remember what summers were like when I was her age, having to depend on others to get me around. I close my computer and stand up to leave.

"Where are you guys going?" Jake asks, standing up, too.

"Out!" Julie snaps. "And you, *Jacarb*, are not invited."

"What? Why not?" He actually sounds annoyed.

I nudge Julie a little. "Come on, Julie. He won't take no for an answer. Just let him tag along. Please?" Honestly, I just want an excuse to spend time with him.

"Fine! I'll be waiting in the car. Don't take too long." She pivots on her heel and walks away.

"Jesus Christ," Jake huffs, adjusting his cap. "What's her problem?"

I shrug.

JAKE

The mall. Yay. (Sarcasm.)

Julie's been in a bad mood since we left the house. I don't know what her deal is, but she better snap out of it, because her little brat attitude is pissing me off.

Kayla's over at one of those skill-tester machines, trying to cheer her up by winning something for her. But she doesn't win, and Julie's now kicking the shit out of it.

I walk over to her and pick her up to face me. "What the hell is going on, JuJu?"

"Shut up, Jake. Don't call me that! That's a baby's name, and I'm not a baby!"

I roll my eyes and set her down. "Okay, *Julie*. Want to tell me what's going on?"

"You! *You* are what's going on! *You* are not supposed to be here. This was supposed to be *my* day with Kayla, and you ruined it!"

Kayla's eyes go big, and she bends down to Julie's level to speak to her softly. I can't hear what she says. "Give us a minute?" Kayla asks me.

If this is Julie now, I'm glad I won't be home for the teenage years. "Have all the minutes you want," I say and walk off, shaking my head.

While waiting, I notice a few girls from school walk past me and wave. I nod back. Then I realize they're Casey's friends, and my eyes dart around like a maniac's, looking for her. If she's here, I'm getting the fuck out—Casey is no joke.

Luckily, Kayla and Julie walk up just before I have a panic attack. Kayla takes my hand. I love it when she does that in public. It's like an unspoken agreement that I'm hers and she's mine. Even though we haven't messed around since that night a few weeks ago, nothing's changed.

"Julie has something she would like to say to you."

Julie steps in front of me and crooks her finger. I bend down to listen to her. "I'm sorry," she whispers and wraps her arms around me. Thank God she's back to normal—another crisis averted, thanks to Kayla.

We walk around the mall with Julie in front of us. "So what was the deal with her?" I ask Kayla, bringing her hand to my lips and kissing it quickly. I can't seem to keep my hands and lips off her. If we can't be intimate in the way I want, I'll take whatever I can get.

"She's just growing up. She wanted us to spend some girl time together today. She thinks she needs a training bra and wants to start wearing makeup." Kayla giggles.

"What?" I yell.

Kayla nudges me and tells me to shut up. Julie turns around and eyes us suspiciously. She keeps walking when I fake a smile at her.

"She's frickin' eight years old, Kayla!"

"I know. I'm just going along with it to amuse her. Trust me, okay?"

"Fine. But my eight-year-old sister better not end the day looking like a whore."

"Oh my God!" Kayla laughs out loud. "I can't believe you just said 'eight-year-old sister' and 'whore' in the same sentence."

"Shut up! I'm not kidding."

We walk around for a bit longer before Julie decides to walk into a store. I don't pay attention until we're inside, and I'm surrounded by lingerie. "What the f—"

A hand covers my mouth. "Shut up, Jake," Kayla whispers fiercely. "Just play along, please."

"Fine, but I'll wait outside."

They come out half an hour later. Julie has a small bag with some Disney princesses on it. Okay, so the store must cater to girls her age, too. Kayla is holding a bigger bag—a nice paper one with a ribbon tied on top. I stand and walk up to her. I try to take the bag from her so I can see what she bought, but she swats my hand away. "What?" I ask, feigning innocence.

She rolls her eyes. "You can't look."

"Why?" I ask, suddenly a little pissed off for no good reason. "Who's it for, Kayla? Who's going to see it?"

"Jake." She comes to a halt and squeezes my hand so I stop walking, too. Julie continues a little ways ahead of us. "It's for you," she whispers. "Not for anyone *but* you. I don't want you looking at it while Julie is here. It's, uh, too mature and not suitable for girls her age."

My eyes widen, and a smile pulls at my lips. I'm suddenly not feeling so annoyed anymore.

"You're an ass," she says, swatting my shoulder and walking away.

I walk up to her and take her hand. "I can't wait!" I whisper in her ear, and she laughs.

—

After lunch, Julie says she's too tired to walk. Kayla offers to carry her on her back as a joke, but she does it anyway. My two girls look pretty damn cute.

"Kayla, get on Jake's back!" Julie cries out, laughing.

"I don't think so, sweetie. We'd break his back."

"No way! Jake's, like, the strongest man who ever lived. Come on, Jake!"

"You have to pay your ticket to get on the ride," I tell her, a stupid thing we used to say when we were kids. I stand next to her, and she gives me a kiss on the cheek.

"Now your entrance fee, little lady," I say to Kayla, putting my face in front of hers.

She straightens up, readjusts Julie, and kisses me on the lips—just once, softly and quickly. She was so quick, I didn't even register what was happening until it was done. She smiles a small smile, a faint blush creeping up her face. She then jumps on my back.

It's the first time our lips have touched since the limo ride that first night. In the couple of times we've fooled around since then, we've never kissed. Even though this kiss was the furthest thing from sexual, it was still intimate—and purposeful. She knew it would mean something. And it did—it meant everything.

We only walk a few feet before I hear my name being called. I slowly let go of Kayla and Julie and turn around to see Aunt Jenna and Uncle Jim walking over to us. Julie gives them both a hug, and I shake hands with my uncle and kiss my aunt on the cheek. She steps back and sees Kayla. She notices my taking Kayla's hand and smiles.

"Aunt Jenna, Uncle Jim . . . This is Mikayla." I make the introductions.

"Oh!" Aunt Jenna's eyes widen slightly. "Oh, Mikayla, Nathan's told me so much about you." Then to me she says, "I didn't realize she was your—"

I feel Kayla tense next to me and I interrupt my aunt.

"Yeah, she's *my* Mikayla." I smile, looking at Kayla, and I know I've said the right thing because she beams at me. Holding on to my arm, she quietly tells them, "It's a pleasure to meet you both."

"They're the aunt and uncle I stayed with when I came back for six months from Australia. Uncle Jim here is the reason I have so many offers on the table."

Uncle Jim laughs, shaking his head. "Jesus, kid, you've got a big head."

"I'm kind of a *big deal*, didn't you know?" I joke. Kayla laughs next to me. I love hearing her laugh.

After the small talk is over, we say our good-byes. As we're heading out the exit, Julie gasps, "I have to go to the pharmacy! I need tampons." I stop in my tracks. "Just kidding, *Jacarb*!" Julie cries and races outside. Kayla kisses my cheek.

"I'm so ready to get out of this place," I tell her.

—

I haven't been able to get the sexy underwear out of my mind. It's close to midnight, and it's all I can think about. As soon as we got home, Kayla holed herself up in her room. She didn't even come down for dinner, saying she had job applications to fill out and a bunch of research to do.

I climb out my window and knock on hers. She opens the curtains after a few seconds and lifts the window. I pull myself in and sit down on her bed.

She stays in front of the window. "What's up, Jake?" she asks. It's dark in the room, so I can't see her face.

"Nothing . . . I was just thinking about you."

"Oh." She hasn't moved from her spot. She's as far from me as physically possible.

"Did something happen?" I ask. Something is definitely wrong. She hasn't been the same since we left the mall.

"No. Why would you say that?"

"Well, normally when I'm around, you're always right next to me, if not on me . . . Now you're all the way over there." I try to sound concerned, but it comes out sounding more pissed off than anything.

"Jesus Christ, Jake. Sorry I'm not jumping your bones 24/7." She raises her voice.

Something is definitely up, and I have no clue what's going on. I try to calm down before I open my mouth again, because if I keep talking I'll say something stupid. I *really* don't want to do that.

"Kayla, if something's going on, you'd tell me, right?" I move to switch on the lamp on her nightstand so I can see her face. Her cheeks are all red, her nose is running, and her eyes are bloodshot.

Before I can stand up, she saunters over to me. She stands between my legs and places her hands on my shoulders. My arms instinctively go to her waist. I look up at her. "I'm okay, Jake," she says. "I've just had a bad evening. I promise. I'm sorry."

I lean my head on her stomach. I kind of feel like a dick. "Want me to stay tonight? I can come back soon—not like anyone would really care." I wish I knew how to help her.

She shakes her head.

Something is definitely up.

I leave her alone in her room and hope that tomorrow will be a better day.

Twenty-Five

Mikayla

"Micky!"

I drop what I'm holding. It falls to the floor.

I look up to see Logan walking toward me.

He stops in front of me. He looks at my face, the floor, then the shelf I'm standing next to. Then he does it again.

All this happens in about two seconds.

To me, it feels like years.

From the moment I heard my name called, a thousand emotions came over me—panic, regret, sadness, confusion, humiliation, anger, disappointment . . .

The biggest one, though, was fear.

I was scared shitless.

Logan bends over and picks it up. He stares at it for a second or a minute—a hundred fucking years. It doesn't matter.

It will still be a pregnancy test.

As he puts the item back on the shelf, I feel tears form in my eyes. A sob escapes me, and I fold over. He wraps me in his arms and leads me outside, whispering comforting words. He opens the door of his car for me, and I get in.

Once he's settled in the driver's seat, he puts the key in the ignition but doesn't turn it.

Moments of silence pass.

Then he faces me. "You're pregnant?"

"I don't know." It's barely a whisper.

"So you haven't taken the test yet?"

"No." I start to cry. "Please, Logan. You can't tell anybody about this. No one—especially Jake. Please."

"Mikayla, I wouldn't. It's not my story to tell." He tries to smile, but he doesn't quite follow through.

The car is silent apart from my sobs. I didn't even think about the possibility—not for a second—until Julie joked about tampons yesterday. James and I were sexually active in the weeks leading up to prom night. I was meticulous about taking the pill. It's 99 percent effective, but I'm *two weeks* late. I didn't even notice. How could I be so stupid? Nothing scares me more than the thought of being a teen mom. What the *fuck* am I going to do?

"My dad's a doctor," Logan finally says. "I can take you to him now, just to be sure. It'd be confidential by law. No one will know, I promise."

I nod and look out the window. He starts the car and reverses out of the spot.

—

Dr. Matthews is the complete opposite of Logan. He's gentle and soft-spoken, with a tiny build, slight comb-over, and glasses. He's heard about the situation with my family. I see the sympathy in his eyes, and I know it's genuine.

A urine and blood test later, I'm actually able to breathe again. They took a blood test just to double-check, but all signs point to negative. Apparently, my body just kind of flaked out on me. Dr.

Matthews says that skipping cycles or being late is common when the body is under a lot of stress or trauma.

Thank God.

I thank Dr. Matthews, and we get into Logan's car. I then realize how long I've been gone. I need to pick up Julie from her friend's house, which is on the other side of town from where I left Mandy's van. Logan offers to go with me to pick Julie up then drive me back to collect the car.

"Thanks so much for this. I can't tell you how much I appreciate it. I would normally have Megan in times like this. It's just . . ." I trail off.

"Have you spoken to her yet?"

"Nope, not a single word."

It turns out that Logan's house is around the corner from Julie's friend's, so after we pick her up, he wants to stop by to pick up his gear. He has plans to meet Jake at the cages soon.

"Hey, Julie," Logan says, looking at her in the rearview mirror of his Mercedes convertible. The top is down. "Knock, knock?"

Julie giggles. "Who's there?"

"Wooden."

"Wooden who?"

"Wooden you like to know."

Julie cracks up. It's one of those jokes that's so dumb, it's hilarious—like "Why did the kid fall off the swing? Because he has no arms!"

We're all laughing like idiots when we pull into Logan's driveway. A familiar truck is already there. I look at Logan, wide-eyed. He holds his hands up in surrender. "I didn't say a word—I swear it."

We look at the truck and see Jake step out.

His fists are balled at his side.

Jaw tense.

Eyes filled with rage.

149

He's pissed.

Beyond pissed.

"You girls stay here, okay?" Logan says before hopping out of the car.

Jake

I'm sitting in my truck, about to text Kayla to meet me at the cages because I miss the shit out of her, when I hear a car pull up and people laughing. I turn and see Logan, Kayla, and Julie.

What in the *actual* fuck.

I hop out of the truck, and it takes everything I have to not run up to this asshole and punch him. I couldn't give a shit about my hand. It's the last fucking thing I care about.

Logan approaches me, hands up. "Whatever you're thinking right now, quit. It's not what you think—not even close."

"Then start talking, asshole." I shove him so hard on the chest, he falls back a few steps. I hear Julie squeal in the car, but I don't give a shit. "Explain to me why the fuck you're playing family with my girl *and* my sister?"

"I can't," he says, shaking his head and looking down.

"What the fuck do you mean you *can't*?"

I'm in his face now so he'll look me in the eye when he tells me he's been screwing the girl I'm in love with.

In love with. Shit.

"I can't, dude—it's not for me to say."

"What the fuck does that even mean?" I push him again, harder this time.

"Quit pushing me, asshole! I'm two seconds away from pushing the fuck back."

Rage consumes me. I'm so fucking pissed, I don't even know what to think. How the fuck can they do this to me—and around Julie?

"Julie, wait!" I hear Kayla yell. Julie jumps out of the car and runs into the street. She doesn't look before crossing, and a car has to brake at the last minute to avoid hitting her straight-on. She screams, and Kayla runs over to her and picks her up in her arms.

"Get in the fucking truck, *now!*" I yell at them.

Julie sobs harder. Kayla carries her over to the truck. "Quit yelling at her! She's scared!" Kayla shouts back.

"I don't give a shit! Just get her in the goddamn truck!" I scream at them.

"No!" Julie shrieks. "I don't want to go anywhere with you! You're an asshole!"

She's never spoken to me like this before, but I've never acted this way in front of her. In fact, I've never acted this way at all. I breathe in and out a few times, eyes closed, trying to calm down. When I open them, I see Kayla crying, holding Julie in her arms, and whispering soothing words in her ear.

"I—I'm sorry, JuJu," I stammer. "Just *please* get in the truck."

"We get it, we're going," Kayla says. She looks at Logan for a second and tries to convey a message with her eyes.

What the *fuck*.

I'm done with this shit.

TWENTY-SIX

JAKE

Julie cries the whole way home. It's the only sound in the truck the entire ride.

When we get home, Kayla carries Julie into the house and up to her room. I go to my room and slam the door. The frames hanging in the hallway fall and hit the floor. I hear Mom at the bottom of the stairs cry out, "What the hell?"

A few minutes pass before my bedroom door opens. Something flies in the air and hits me square in the head. I pick it up. It's Kayla's phone. I look up at her.

"You better call your *best friend* and apologize for being such an asshole. Then you better go see Julie and start making it up to her big-time, because that little girl is a mess, and you're the asshole who did that to her." She's fuming. I've never seen her this angry—not even when she caught James and Megan together. *Fuck.*

She turns to leave. I jump off my bed and run to her, grabbing her arm to force her to look at me.

"*What?*" she growls.

"*What the fuck is going on?*"

"What the fuck do you *think* is going on, Jake?"

"You tell me! You were the one playing happy-little-family with my sister and Logan. Did you have a good old laugh together? What were you two doing? Talking about how stupid I am—how *stupid Jake* has no idea what you guys are up to?"

"That's what you think—that we're fucking behind your back?"

"That's what it looks like to me!"

"He's your best friend, Jake! There's no way—"

"So fucking what? Megan was *your* best friend!"

Her expression falls instantly. Tears immediately pool in her eyes, but she's quick to wipe them away. "Call Logan," she says, before turning and slamming the door behind her.

MIKAYLA

I ended up having to Facebook-message Lucy to pick me up and drive me back to the mall to get Mandy's car. I didn't tell her anything, and she didn't ask any questions.

When I get back to the house, I hear Jake and Julie in the backyard. I look through the gate and see her holding a baseball bat. He's pitching balls slowly at her, encouraging her while she laughs. He's trying to make up for it.

He should. He's an asshole.

—

I'm lying in bed when I hear tapping at my window. I get up, open it, and without saying a word get back into bed.

Once I'm under the covers, I feel the bed dip next to me and hear him place something on my nightstand. My phone.

"I called Logan."

"Good."

"He didn't tell me anything, though."

"Good."

"Are you going to tell me what's wrong?"

"Have you quit being an asshole?"

"Yes."

He tries to get me to flip over so I'll look at him. I turn to face him, and he brushes the hair out of my eyes. "I'm sorry, Kayla, for what I said about Megan and the way I acted. I don't know what came over me. The thought of you and Logan, or of anyone else . . . It just—"

"Jake, stop." I sit up so I can see him properly. "Logan saw me buying a pregnancy test." Jake's eyes bug out for a second before I reassure him, "I'm not." I wave my hands in the air. "I just thought I was. I was late, and he saw me buying a test. I panicked, and he took me to see his dad, who confirmed I wasn't. I had to pick up Julie from her friend's, so he took me to get her because Mandy's car was still at the mall. Julie's friend lives one street over from him, so he drove home to pick up his gear before he was going to drop us off at the car. That's when you came in and acted like an asshole. *Asshole!*"

He's silent. I continue. "He was going to meet you at the cages after he dropped us off. He was just there for me, that's all." I pause for a minute. "Wait . . . He didn't tell you?"

Jake's shaking his head, taking it all in. "He said it wasn't his story to tell, and if I wanted to know I had to hear it from you." He blows out a breath, puffing out his cheeks. "Fuck, Kayla. I really am an asshole. I was a dick to both of you. And I scared the shit out of Julie. Why didn't you tell me? Was that what last night was about?"

"Yeah. I didn't think about it until we were leaving the mall, then I wigged out and I didn't know what to do. I didn't tell you because I wanted to be sure first. I didn't know what I was going to do if . . . you know."

"So you're not—for sure? Like, 100 percent?"

"Yeah, Jake." I nod. "I'm sure."

He breathes out a heavy sigh, and we sit in silence for a long time. "Can I stay with you tonight? Please, Kayla?" he barely whispers.

I scoot across the bed and lift the covers. He takes his T-shirt off and gets in. We hold each other, not wanting to let go—not even for a second. We look into each other's eyes intently.

Talking without speaking.

Feeling without touching.

"Jake?"

"Yeah?"

"It's just you. It's *only ever been* just you. It will *always* only ever be just you."

He kisses me—a quick kiss on the lips. But it has the passion of a thousand kisses and holds the power of a thousand promises.

"*So* much more-than-a-lot," he says before we fall asleep in each other's arms.

Twenty-Seven

Jake

After that night of the pregnancy scare, or whatever it was, Kayla and I have been a little off. We still talk and are close, but it's, like—I don't know—like our planets aren't aligned or something. I was an asshole to all of them. I apologized to Logan, and he gets it. But still, I feel like a dick. I should have been there for her. Instead, I went all Neanderthal on her and fucked it up.

I finish at the gym with Logan, Cam, and Dylan. They're meeting up at some club tonight—one of those where you can get in at eighteen. Dylan's cousin is the bouncer, so we'll be able to get drinks, too—no problem. Obviously, they invited Kayla to come with us. I don't know if she'll want to, but I do know I'm not going without her.

I head to her room as soon as I get home. "It's open," she yells out after I knock.

I walk into her room. She's lying in bed with Lucy's e-reader. "Hey," I say shyly, not looking at her. It's bad enough that things have been off between us, but her lying in bed like this . . . I don't know if I can handle it.

"What's up?" She hasn't taken her eyes off her book. She and Lucy really *are* book best friends, whatever the hell that means.

I clear my throat, because, truthfully, her lying in bed is making me nervous. "The guys are all going out to this club tonight, and they wanted to know if we'd come?" It comes out like a question.

She puts her book down and looks at me. "Jake, I really don't feel like it. You can totally go, though."

I'm still standing by the door. I haven't moved closer to her—it's too damn tempting. "It's cool. Honestly, I'd rather just stay with you," I tell her, because it's the truth.

She smiles a small smile and seems to change her mind. "I have two chapters left; then can we go?"

I smile and nod.

Then we just look at each other.

No one says anything.

I realize I should probably leave her to her reading, but I don't want to go. She must somehow know this, because she rolls her eyes slightly and lifts the covers on one side.

It's an invitation.

And I'm sure as shit going to accept.

I know a huge grin is plastered on my face, but I don't care. I walk over to the bed then realize I'm still in my gym gear. I probably smell like sweat-covered asshole. "I think I should take a shower first," I tell her.

"Okay," she says and continues to read.

I get in and out of the shower in 1.3 minutes flat. As I'm drying off, I remember that I don't have any clothes.

Shit.

I can't get back into my sweat-covered-asshole clothes, so I put the towel around my waist and think. If I leave this room, I can go down the stairs and outside, then through the house to my room . . . But if my parents and JuJu are home, then I'll have to explain why I'm stepping in from outside in nothing but a towel. I could climb out the window, jump between the roofs, and hope that my window is open. This sounds like a better plan, unless my neighbors see and call the cops because a frickin' creeper is on the roof of the house in nothing but a towel.

I go for option A, because surely it makes more sense.

I step out of the bathroom, and she looks up at the sound. She does a double take when she sees me. Her eyes go wide, and her mouth opens a little. Her breath catches, and she starts to blush. I stand there for a few seconds. Internally, I'm fist-pumping the air, celebrating.

Because I'm a douche bag.

When she finally looks away, we speak at the same time.

I say, "I don't have any—"

She says, "Top drawer of my dresser—"

Then we laugh a small, nervous laugh.

I walk to her dresser and open a drawer. I see the boxers and a plain white T-shirt that I gave her the first night she stayed with me. While I dress—boxers under towel, T-shirt on, towel off—I feel her eyeing me. When I'm done, I look at her, and she looks away too quickly.

More internal fist-pumping.

After I'm dressed, I crawl under the covers with her. It's warm from her body heat, and I'm a little cold—okay, not really, but whatever excuse to be close to her. She's back to reading her book, facing the other way. I try to get settled. I can see the red still coloring the tips of her ears. I just want to be near her. I come in close to her and spoon her. She tenses then relaxes a little. Once my arms are around her, I hear a small moan escape her. I hope I didn't imagine it.

I must fall asleep holding her, because I'm woken up by her turning in my arms. By the time I register what's happening and open my eyes, she's looking right at me, inches from my face.

Mikayla

God, he looks so frickin' good, it should be illegal.

He's got those tired, sleepy eyes, and he's blinking, trying to focus. When he finally does, his lips turn up at the corners and his voice is scratchy. "Hey, beautiful," he says. And I swear to God I *swoon*.

I move to get out of bed and start getting ready.

"In a minute—wait." He tightens his arms around me and nestles in the crook of my neck. I wrap my hands around the back of his head. The position is so intimate—like we're more than whatever it is we are, more than this. For a second, I close my eyes and imagine that this could be our life.

But only for a second.

His breathing changes, and a tiny moan escapes him. He runs his nose up my jaw toward my mouth, and my breath catches. He moves his hand on my waist lower, down to my hips, past my ass, and onto my bare thighs. I'm only wearing boy shorts, and I don't think he knew because the second his fingers skim my skin, he sucks in a breath, holds it, then lets it out so frickin' slowly, it warms my neck. His hands tighten on my thigh. He pulls my leg over his so his hardness is touching me, and I can tell how badly he wants me. My eyes close, and his breath shortens. I thrust against him just once so he knows that I want him, too.

So fucking bad.

In the next second, his mouth is open and on my neck, and I feel the heat from it creating heat somewhere else. Our joined parts are moving together slowly, intimately, almost imperceptibly. I feel my body tingle with the sensation and throw my head back. He moves his mouth down to my collarbone and the swell of my breasts, and he's sucking and licking, and, oh God, I want him so fucking bad. I want all of him—right now.

I moan out loud from the pleasure of him and what he's doing. "Holy shit, Jake. What are you doing to me?" I breathe, because I can't control what comes out of my mouth when he does these things to me.

He tenses in my arms and pulls away—all the way, as in, out-of-the-bed away. I miss him instantly. He stands up to his full height, and his hands go down to his boxers to adjust himself.

Hot.

He clears his throat and looks away. "Jesus Christ, Kayla. I'm so sorry. I got carried away." He starts to walk away. "We should get ready and head out," he mumbles before leaving my room.

What the fuck just happened?

JAKE

Half an hour later, I've showered again—a cold one this time. I hear a knock at my door. I freeze mid-greet—Kayla's standing on the other side, and the cold shower I just had suddenly seems pointless. She waves then stands with her hands behind her back, waiting for me to say or do *something*.

But all I can do is stare.

She's wearing a light-blue dress with a wide neckline, so one shoulder and part of her upper arm is exposed. It's loose fitting, with a drawstring tied around the waist, and stops just past her ass—literally just enough to cover her goods. She's wearing a little makeup, mainly around her eyes, and she smells like coconuts. It's crazy sexy, but it's not *meant* to be. It's just Kayla being Kayla.

She chuckles, which brings me out of my trance. I turn to unplug my phone charging on the nightstand and take the opportunity to adjust myself. *Again.*

—

When we get to the club, my friends are already there. The guys do the bro-hug-and-cheek-kiss greeting, then we settle into the booth they reserved for us.

While walking through the club, I saw more than a few guys check her out. I couldn't help but put my arm around her and draw her in, because it's the Stone Age and I'm a caveman. She didn't seem to mind, though—not even a little bit.

An hour later, we're all buzzed. Logan found some chick to hang off his arm. She's sitting at our table, cooing at him while he talks to us. It's kind of weird, but whatever. A Ludacris song comes on, and Heidi makes the girls get up and dance. I watch Logan mouth the words to the song. Apparently, he went through a Ludacris phase in middle school and acted like he was black. I wish I'd been there to see it.

The song's pretty dirty—something about people's fantasies— and the girls start dancing kind of dirty, too. Dylan gets my attention and nods at the dance floor. I get what he's saying. We get up and walk over there, standing like jealous creepers about five feet away from the girls in case any asshole wants in. Cam stayed at the booth, saying Lucy could hold her own. I've seen Lucy drunk a few times. She gets loud and nasty and cusses like a sailor. It's pretty damn funny, because it's the complete opposite of who she is.

The girls are into it. Kayla's dress moves higher with every move and clings to her perfect ass. I know I'm a dick—but I'm also an eighteen-year-old guy. Dylan notices a guy eyeing Heidi. The guy starts to approach her, but Dylan moves forward just enough to catch his attention, and he backs away. Dylan doesn't say much, but his presence sure does.

Three songs later, all of us return to the booth. I rest my arm on the seat behind Kayla. She moves closer to me so our sides are completely touching, and places her hand lightly on my leg.

A few minutes after we sit down, a bartender brings a drink over, and places it in front of Kayla. It's some bright-green drink in one of those shakers. Her eyes widen for a second, confusion on her face. I stare at the drink, eyebrows drawn together.

What the fuck?

My gaze moves from the drink to her. She's looking at me. Who the fuck would buy her a drink when I'm sitting right here? Did she talk to some asshole while I had my back turned, or when she was out on the dance floor for, like, a minute, before I got there? She must sense what I'm thinking, because she shakes her head. It's a small movement, but I see it.

Just as she's about to ask the bartender who got her the drink, he points to someone a few tables away. He's sitting with a bunch of other guys around our age. I don't recognize any of them. Understanding dawns on her face, and, slowly, a smile pulls on her lips. She looks down at her hands, almost shyly. She then picks up the drink, takes a sip, and stands up.

She walks over to the guy without a word.

Logan pulls his mouth away from his girl for the night. "You know that asshole?"

"No. Do you guys know who he is?" I ask mainly Cam and Dylan.

Dylan speaks up. "Looks familiar, but I can't place him."

The whole time she's talking to him, I'm watching like a creeper. They talk for a while, both smiling at each other. Then he leans down and says something close to her ear. Her expression immediately changes. She looks almost sad, but when he pulls back she nods a few times. He rubs her upper arm.

I'm so close to standing up and punching this guy for touching her.

When she makes her way back with drink still in hand, she doesn't say anything—not one fucking word. She just acts like nothing happened. No explanation as to who that asshole is or what they talked about. Nothing.

—

The shit with Kayla and that guy pissed me off, so I take it out on myself. I drink, and drink . . . and drink.

By whatever the fuck time it is, I'm beyond buzzed and a little more on the drunk side. I'm at the bar, ordering *another* beer. I haven't spoken to Kayla since she came back from talking to that asshole.

"Jake, is that you?"

I turn around to see Madison, this girl I went to high school with. Her dad's the baseball coach. She's a cool girl—knows her shit when it comes to baseball, which is all we've ever talked about. She's cute, but she's in no way even close to as cute as Kayla.

"It *is* you!" she squeals and runs up to give me a hug. She's obviously drunk—her face is splotchy and her breath reeks of alcohol.

I hug her back, but it's more like holding her upright. "You okay, Madison? Had a bit to drink, have ya?" I chuckle. Her arms haven't left my neck, and I'm doing my best to keep her up.

She moves closer to me. Maybe she isn't drunk—maybe she just wants to be close. She says, "I was hoping I'd see you before you left for college. I've always wanted to fuck you, Jake Andrews."

My eyes bug out, and I try to pull her off me. But her mouth attacks my neck, and the one second she's there feels like hours.

It was only a second, but a second was all it took. When I look up, I see Kayla. She's watching us. In her head it must have played out completely wrong, because she looks at me with tears already in her eyes.

She then turns and walks away.

And all I do is watch her.

TWENTY-EIGHT

MIKAYLA

Seriously—fuck my life. There's only so much shit I can take before all the fucked-up things in my life consume me.

After I manage to stop the tears and clean myself up, I take a few deep breaths and open the restroom door.

Jake's standing by the restrooms, leaning against the wall with one foot up and his hands behind his back. He's looking down at the floor. When he hears the door open, he looks up, and a sad smile creeps across his features. I try to smile back, but I don't know that it shows.

I start to walk back to the others, but he grabs my arm and starts to say something. Guys coming out of the men's room walk toward us, and Jake has to push us against the wall so they can get through.

So here we are. I'm leaning against the wall with him in front of me.

When the guys pass, he doesn't step back. I let him stand right where he is—so close we're almost touching. He's resting one hand against the wall next to my head, and the other hangs by his side. He reaches up and cups my face gently, and I can't help leaning into him slightly. He shifts his body closer so the fronts of our bodies are pressed together.

He dips his head so his mouth is close to my ear. I can hear him breathing over the noise of the club. "Whatever you're thinking, quit. It wasn't what you think." Then he lightly takes my earlobe in his mouth. It's enough to make my knees weak and my body give out.

But he's on me, holding me up as his lips move from my ear to the spot just behind it and down to my neck. I reach up to grip his hair. He lowers his hand that was cupping my face and moves it down my side, past my waist and hips to my bare thighs. He lifts my leg so it's around him and he's in between me.

Leaning against a fucking wall.

In a fucking club.

With people all around us.

I forget what my name is, because I'm so goddamn turned on right now, and I know he is—I can feel he is. My head falls back slightly and I moan, because being with him like this is *so* intense, physically and emotionally.

He takes that as an invitation, and his kisses get less gentle and more extreme. He's licking and sucking—hard, like he wants to leave his mark, like he wants the world to know I'm his. And I am—his, I mean.

Just when I'm about to bring his mouth to mine, because I *need* to kiss him, and we've never, *ever* kissed like that before—

"Holy shit!"

Jake immediately lets go of my thigh and cups the back of my head to pull me into his chest.

He knows I'm embarrassed.

I turn slightly and peek under his arm to see who interrupted. Some guy I don't know is standing frozen just outside the men's room. The doors open and two other guys walk out and bump into the back of him. The smell of weed pours out behind them.

"Jake fuckin' Andrews," one of the guys sing-songs.

Jake nods at them, no emotion on his face.

"Holy shit, dude," the other says, his eyes roaming over me. "You got fire!"

Then all three walk past us, patting Jake's back on the way out and laughing to themselves.

Jake pulls me back to look at me. "You okay?"

I nod, blushing a little. "What does 'you got fire' mean?"

He laughs, shaking his head. "It means they think you're hot."

JAKE

We spend another hour or so at the club, but I'm beat from waking up at five in the morning, so we catch a cab home.

I walk her up to her door, but I don't want to leave her. I don't want to spend the night apart.

"So . . . good night," she says through a yawn.

"Good night," I tell her, pulling her in so I can kiss her temple. I don't make a move to leave, though. I know I'm in way over my head with this girl, but I can't help it.

She smiles a little before looking down and opening her door, but she doesn't close it. She goes into her bathroom, and I stand outside, waiting. She opens the bathroom door, dressed in pajamas, and climbs into bed. She doesn't look at me or say a word the whole time.

I take that as an invitation and walk in. I stand on the opposite side of the bed and strip to my boxers. I get into bed with her. We lie on our backs, looking up at the ceiling. She reaches down and takes my hand in hers under the covers, our fingers entwined.

I can't get tonight out of my head. I think about that asshole and wonder who the fuck he is and what he was doing buying my girl a drink. I let out a sigh.

She must know what I'm thinking, because she says, "Jake, if there's something you want to ask me, just ask."

"If you know I want to ask, why don't you just tell me?"

It's her turn to sigh. She looks at me. "I don't like playing games, Jake."

I return her gaze. "Then don't."

We shift to face each other. We're inches apart, but our bodies aren't touching—only our fingers are still entwined.

"His name's Andrew. He went to my school—he's James's best friend. He bought me the drink because he knows I love it. He introduced me to it."

"Why didn't you just tell me?"

"Because I wasn't sure how you'd feel if I brought up James. Besides, you didn't ask."

"What did he say to you?" I move the hair from her face and tuck it behind her ear. "You looked sad for a moment there."

"He said that he was sorry about what happened that night. He said that just because his best friend is a dick doesn't mean that he is. I was sad because he said that he'll miss me when we go off to college. We were friends, too, you know? It shouldn't have to end because James is an asshole."

I take a deep breath in then huff loudly. "You should have just told me."

"You should have just asked," she replies.

It's quiet for a few moments. Then I say, "I don't know that it's my place to ask. I mean, do I have a right to ask?"

"Who was the girl, Jake?"

"She was no one."

Silence.

"She's this girl who went to my school. She's the coach's daughter. She threw herself at me, but I stopped it as soon as I knew what was happening. I swear it."

She sighs and moves closer to me, burying her face in my chest. I hold her. "You have the *right* to ask, Jake. But you have no *reason* to."

Twenty-Nine

Mikayla

"So Lucy's all up in this girl's face, picks up a random drink from one of the tables, and throws the contents on her," Cam says, laughing.

"What did she say after that? It was so fucking funny," Logan joins in, trying to remember.

Apparently, after we left the club some girl was at the bar next to Cam, trying to get him to notice her. When he brushed her off, she grabbed his junk—not in a bad way, but in a . . . seductive way.

"Oh yeah!" Logan laughs. In a high-pitched voice, fingers snapping, he mimics, "'My man would never touch you, you fucking slut! You're so fucking ugly, it's like your face caught on fire, and someone tried to put it out with a goddamn fork!'"

We crack up. We're at Lucy's cabin, drinking around a bonfire. It's good times.

"I was so turned on," Cam says.

Lucy just sits quietly.

"And she knew it, too," Cam continues. "She turns into this animal when she knows I'm turned on. She blew me in the car on the drive home!"

"*What?*" Heidi yells, a disgusted look on her face.

The boys all cheer for Cam, and I stifle my laughter against Jake's neck. I feel his body shake with that deep, throaty chuckle I love so much. I look up at him but his cap is in the way. I flip it backwards so I can get closer to him, and he smiles at me. I glance at Lucy. She's not saying anything—she just looks down and blushes. It must be true.

After the laughter dies down a little, Logan sighs. "I can't wait to get the fuck out of this hick town."

We all look at him. His eyes are red, his lids are droopy, and he's been slurring his words the last hour. He's obviously beyond buzzed, but he hasn't stopped drinking. I asked Jake if we should cut him off, but he assured me that Logan knows his limits.

"I just get sick of being the seventh wheel, you know?" He's still looking down, and we watch him curiously. It's a big deal when Logan has something serious to say, so we listen. "I mean, even before Jake met Micky."

I tense, but Jake squeezes my hand reassuringly.

"When Jake was single, it wasn't like he was on the prowl or anything, but he didn't care, you know? It was never about girls with him. I just . . . I don't know. Sometimes, I watch all you guys, and I want that. I know I'm an asshole, but it's not like . . ." He shrugs to himself.

We eye each other. I guess we never thought he felt this way.

"I see you guys together—how you get each other, how you want to be around each other all the fucking time—and you're there, you know, through all of it. I finish my days and I got no one to go to. Nobody gives a shit if I have a bad day or not." He sighs out a heavy breath. He looks at the sky and runs a hand through his hair.

"I know I sleep around, but it's not like I haven't been looking. I just haven't found anyone who makes me feel *anything*—not the way you all feel about each other. I guess I'm just wasted . . ." He trails off.

Everyone is quiet. What *do* you say to that?

"Want to walk with me?" Jake whispers in my ear.

I nod, and we slip away. We end up sitting cross-legged on a dock that I didn't know existed. We face each other, the moon the only source of light.

"Your friends are great, Jake."

"Yeah, they're good people. They like you."

I smile to myself, because I like them, too.

He reaches out to take both my hands in his. His fingers play with the rings on my right hand. He lifts my hand to his lips and kisses my ring finger, like it's the most natural thing in the world for him to do.

"So what Logan said was crazy, right?" he says.

"Yeah, I guess so. But not everyone finds someone they want to be with this young—even if it's for a little bit, you know?"

He agrees. "It must suck for him to not have someone."

A comfortable silence falls over us for a few minutes, both of us looking elsewhere. Then he laughs a little. "You know, my parents still make out like teenagers sometimes. I've seen it."

"Really?" I ask. "That's so *cute*."

"You mean *gross*?"

We look at each other. "No, Jake," I say quietly, shaking my head. "I mean cute. Can you imagine finding someone you can't keep your hands off of?"

He laughs. "Yeah, Kayla, I actually can." He's looking straight at me.

"Then, like, twenty years from now still feeling the same way? Can you *imagine* how good that would be?"

He's still staring at me, concentrating on my words. "Yeah, Kayla. I can imagine exactly what it would be like."

His gaze is so intense.

Like looking into the sun.

I have to look away.

He stands abruptly and pulls me up with him. We sit down at the edge of the dock, our feet in the water. He sits behind me, with me between his legs, and we look out over the water. "It's nice out here," I say.

He wraps his arms around my waist and folds his hands on my lap. "Mm-hm," he murmurs, resting his chin on my shoulder. I feel his nose behind my ear and hear him inhale deeply.

"Did you just sniff me?" I ask, giggling a little.

"Yep," he says, the *p* tickling my ear. "You smell so good, Kayla." He moves my hair to one side and rubs his nose along the back of my neck a few times. Then he kisses me, and I shiver under his touch, goose bumps breaking out on my skin. He kisses me softly and slowly, his mouth moving lower down the middle of my back to the edge of my tank top then back up again. His mouth finds my shoulder, and he licks my skin. I don't say anything. It takes everything I have to try to keep my breath even and avoid moaning in pleasure. It's so erotic. He's hard as a rock behind me, and I can feel it through his shorts, pushing against my ass. He moves his hands to the inside of my thighs and, palms flat, slowly pushes my legs further apart, my short denim skirt shifting higher.

I tilt my head back at the thought of what he's going to do and can feel the wetness soaking through my panties. I want him to touch me—any part of me—so badly. He moves his left hand higher on my stomach until it's just under my breast and shifts his right hand up my thigh. My body shakes with anticipation. He softly cups my breast, and I groan from the feel of it. His fingers graze the outside of my panties right *there*. He strokes me a couple of times through the material before he stops and exhales heavily.

"Fuck," he mutters, more to himself than to me. "You're soaked, Kayla."

"What do you expect?" I breathe out. *"You're* touching me."

He groans softly then moves my panties aside to slip a finger in. My mouth instantly goes dry, and I begin panting, my chest heaving.

"Shit," he growls, removing his hands. I whimper at the loss. "Kayla," he says hoarsely, his hands on either side of him now.

It takes me awhile to find my voice and calm down. "Mmm?" I finally get out. I turn my head to the side. His face is within an inch of mine—he could whisper in my ear.

"I think . . . I think that maybe I'm falling—"

"Yo, asshole!"

Logan.

"Fuck," we both say.

THIRTY

MIKAYLA

"It's official. I'm going to be a homeless, jobless college student," I moan, picking at my fries. Jake and I are sitting at a picnic table near the concession stand at the batting cages. His friends came with us to the cages, too. "Maybe I should defer for a year and work full-time to save up some money?" I ask, more to myself than anything.

He looks at me for a while. "You don't have any other choice? Surely there's financial aid or something."

"It's too late for that. College starts in a month." I'm sad. I've looked into my options, and they're all dead ends.

Lucy and Cam come to sit with us. Heidi is watching Dylan bat while Logan pitches to him. He's no Jake.

"What are we talking about?" Cam asks, stealing one of my fries. I shove the whole thing at him. I'm too depressed to eat.

"About how I'll experience college while living on the street, panhandling for cash." I pout, watching the others at the cages.

"Why don't you just—" Cam starts before cutting himself off.

I turn back to him, and he's looking away. I look at Lucy and Jake, but they won't look at me. "Why don't I just what?" I ask them.

"Um, I was going to say . . ." Cam stumbles over his words for a while, obviously trying to think of something to say. "Stripper! You could totally be a stripper."

Lucy smacks her palm on his forehead. "You, my dear Cameron, are a pig!" He flinches and rubs his forehead. Everyone chuckles for a bit.

"You guys may laugh now, but I might end up having to do just that," I say.

Jake stops laughing instantly.

JAKE

"Hey, so there's something I need to talk to you about." I lightly kick Kayla's bare leg. It's late afternoon, a couple of hours after we got home from the cages. She's lying on a towel in the grass in a white bikini, hot as hell.

She sits up and moves her sunglasses to the top of her head. I sit down in front of her with my legs stretched out and pull her toward me so she's straddling my legs. She's close enough so I can look at her and maybe touch her a little, but not so close that my junk is touching hers. She looks at me and waits.

I take my cap off, run my hand over the back of my head, then put my cap back on backwards so she can see me better. "I, uh . . ." I blow out a breath.

"What's wrong, Jake? You're all nervous and sweaty . . . What's going on?"

"So, my grandma," I start to say. She leans back a bit, confused about where this is going. "She started a college fund for me when I was born."

She relaxes a little.

"Anyway," I continue, "Mom says Grandma came from a family with old money, whatever that means. The money was there for me when I finished high school, but I got a full scholarship, so obviously I don't really need the money for college."

"Okay . . ." She looks so damn confused, it's kind of adorable.

"My parents said the money was mine for me to use however I want. They gave me a few options: put it in the bank, donate some, invest some . . . But they really thought I should buy a house near campus. That way I wouldn't live on campus, distracted by the 'college life,' as they called it—no frat houses and stuff. They know that I want to focus on baseball and may get sidetracked like I did before, and they trust me enough to let me live on my own. Plus, after I graduate, I could rent it out and make a killing. But at the end of the day, they left it up to me what I did with the money. They would have been fine with my blowing it all in Vegas . . . Okay, maybe that's taking it a little too far."

She still looks confused. "So . . . Are you saying that you bought a house?"

"Dad looked at a couple of houses, and one weekend we toured them together. So yes, I ended up buying one, Kayla—I bought a house. It's a cottage—not a condo or anything. It has three bedrooms, a porch, and a little backyard. It's pretty decent." I look at her and wait. "Say something," I plead.

"Um . . . Good job? I don't know what you want me to say. That's awesome, Jake."

"But you didn't answer me."

"Did you ask a question?"

Oh yeah. She has no idea where I'm going with this.

"Will you move in with me?" I ask, looking straight at her.

"*What?* I can't do that, Jake. It's your house, and you need to focus on baseball—that's why you bought it, right?"

"I bought it thinking that Cam and Logan would live with me. But they want to live the college life," I say, rolling my eyes.

"If you *really* want me to live with you, why are you asking me now?"

"Because I don't want you to be a stripper!" I blurt out.

"What?" she says through a laugh.

"Truth is, I wanted to ask you a long time ago, but I didn't want you to think I was asking with, like, other intentions in mind." I shrug. "I didn't want you to feel like we had to be in a relationship. If I asked too soon, you'd think it was just my pity talking and say no. But your pride would later get in the way when you'd realize there were no other options and you'd flake out on college altogether and become a stripper, and I *really* don't want that—"

"Jake, stop!" she says, giggling.

I'm rambling like an idiot. The thing is, I really want her to move in with me, even if we live in separate rooms. I just want to be around her all the time any way I can—*forever.*

"Are you sure?" she asks cautiously.

"More sure than anything, ever."

"Okay, then." She smiles.

"Okay? As in okay, you're going to move in with me?" I'm so hopeful that a huge toothy grin spreads across my face.

She nods a few times, smiling back.

"You, Mikayla Jones, have just made me *so* happy." I pull her closer to me. She's straddling my waist now—in her bikini. I grab her ass once and kiss her forehead. I want to do more, but she pushes me away and stands up.

"We have so much planning and decorating to do," she says excitedly, walking backwards. "When can we go see it?"

"We can take a trip tomorrow, if you want. But I can show you photos of it on my computer right now."

"Well, come on, then—show me." She turns around and marches toward the house.

"Sure," I yell out. "I just need a minute," I add, holding up a finger.

She stops and looks at me quizzically. I point to my dick. She laughs out loud, shaking her head and walking through the sliding door.

I got it bad.

THIRTY-ONE

JAKE

After my dick settles, I head up to my room to get my MacBook and show her the pictures of my house—*our* house. When I get there, though, I see that she's already sitting on the bed, still in her damn bikini. I don't look at her too long, because I know I'm already hard again and I haven't even touched her. Kayla—in that bikini, with so little between us, on my bed—*kills* me.

I try to keep my breathing even and not trip over my own feet as I walk over to my desk. I sit down and open my MacBook then turn around to tell her a bit more about the house.

But when I turn, she's right in front of me, my eyes level with her tits and her nipples poking out through her bikini top. She sits on my lap and turns us so we're facing my desk again. She's wearing virtually nothing, and I'm in workout shorts, the material so thin I'm *sure* she can feel me. She makes a strangled moan as she makes herself comfortable—on my dick.

I rest my chin on her shoulder and click around on my MacBook to bring up the photos. Her hair smells like roses. It always smells like roses. I run my nose along her jaw, breathing her in. She sighs and moves on me, moaning so quietly you'd miss it if it weren't the only sound in the room.

I have to clear my throat a few times before words even come out. "So, this is the house from the outside," I start, trying so hard to keep my mind from going where it's going.

"Uh-huh," she says, but her eyes are closed and she's breathing heavily.

My mouth goes dry. I click to the next picture. "And this is the kitchen . . ."

"Mm-hm." Her eyes are still closed, her lips parted. She's almost panting, slowly moving on me.

I open the next one. "And this is—"

She grabs my hand, cutting me off, and lowers it to her stomach . . . lower and lower until it's down her bikini bottom, and I'm touching her. "Fuck," I grunt into her shoulder as she starts riding my fingers. My dick is so frickin' hard, I could swing it and hit a home run. She starts moaning and moving, and I can feel her wetness on my palm. I start to kiss her neck, but she abruptly stands up. I look at her confused.

She sits back down, straddling me on my chair. She tries to kiss my neck and rip my T-shirt off at the same time while still grinding on me. I'm so fucking close, I can't handle it. I hand her my cap and remove my T-shirt. She puts my cap back on backwards. "Keep this on," she says huskily.

We stare at each other for a minute before she starts running her hands over my chest, her delicate hands taking me in. I move my hands up from her waist until my thumbs touch the bottom of her breasts. I rub her nipples through the thin material of her bikini.

She moans and her head falls backwards, giving me perfect access to her neck. I start kissing it, licking and sucking . . . I move lower and lower until her nipple is in my mouth, and she's grinding on me, moaning with every movement. I move my hand under the front of her bikini, but she grabs it and opens her eyes. My mind's so buzzed with lust, I have no idea what's going on.

Holding my hand, she whispers, "Lock your door, Jake."

I roll us in the chair over to my door and lock it. In a second she's on her knees in front of me, pulling my dick out of my shorts.

"Kayla." I don't know if I actually say her name, but I know I sure as hell think it. Before her head dips, I stop her. "Are you doing this because I asked you to move in with me?"

She laughs. "No, Jake. I'm doing this because I want to—I've wanted to for so long. Because you turn me on so much, because being around you all the time is driving me fucking crazy. And because I so much more-than-a-lot like you."

Then her mouth is on me and around me, and there are fireworks in the room, and my heart's stopped beating. My toes curl, and my fingers are in her hair, and she's moaning, and I'm groaning. Then I'm two seconds away from exploding, and I warn her but she won't stop. The world flashes white, and somewhere in the distance violins play and angels weep, and she's taking it all until it's over. I finally look down to see her Bambi eyes watching me—she's licking her lips and it's the sexiest thing I've ever seen in my entire goddamn life.

My mouth is so dry, I can't speak even if I wanted to. She stands up and walks to my window. Before I realize what's happening, she's halfway out.

"Wait!" I yelp, like I've just learned how to speak for the first time.

"What's up?" She smiles innocently at me.

"You can't just leave," I say, pulling on my shorts and walking over to her. "I have to reciprocate."

"Oh, you will," she says, winking at me, "but not today."

Then she's out the window, jumping onto the garage roof and climbing into her bedroom.

Mikayla

Once I'm in my room, I get under the covers and double click my mouse, the whole time thinking of Jake's face when he let himself go. Jake Andrews is definitely swoon-worthy. I should write a book about him.

THIRTY-TWO

JAKE

The day after Kayla literally, and legitimately, blew my mind, we visited my house. She fell in love with it instantly—almost as quickly as I fell in love with her.

She suggested that we use her family's furniture that's in storage. Honestly, I can't care less what's in there, as long as she is. I tried numerous times to reciprocate, but she wouldn't let me. I was, however, able to cop a feel every now and then.

MIKAYLA

College starts in two weeks, so there's a bonfire party in a huge field tonight. It's the last blowout before we all leave for college, and people from about five different schools will be there.

I was a little wary when we first discussed it, because James and maybe Megan—who I *still* have not heard from—will more than likely be there. But Jake and his friends assured me that it won't be a problem, and if it is, they'll go Chuck Norris on his ass.

So that's where I find myself—sitting in a huge field around a bonfire. Whoever set this up is a genius. There's a dance floor at one end of the field for dancing or groping or whatever, with a DJ keeping that area entertained. Lots of people have parked their cars and trucks and have their own bonfires and music going—including us.

All of Jake's friends—who he tells me I should start calling *our* friends—are here, along with some other guys. That creeper from the batting cages is here, too, still staring me up and down. His name's Derek. Jake noticed but hasn't done anything about it—*yet.*

"Hey, Micky!" Logan yells from the bed of Dylan's truck. "I got your jam for you!" There's an iPod dock in the bed of the truck, and he's been playing with it most of the night, our own personal DJ. "Hey Mickey" comes blasting through the speakers. Heidi squeals and jumps off Dylan's lap. She grabs me and Lucy, and we dance with her in the middle of our group. We dance like idiots, because—let's be honest—we're about two beers away from being completely wasted. Most of our dance moves consist of that monkey dance from 1956. Good times.

As the song winds down, Heidi stops dancing and nudges me, cocking her head in the direction of the dance floor. I look up and see James walking toward me, head down and hands in his pockets. By the time he reaches us, the music has stopped and Jake is on the edge of his chair, waiting to make a move.

"Hey, Micky," James says shyly, looking at the ground.

I realize, seeing him like this, why I liked him in the first place. When I met him, he was the shy new kid with a Texan accent and that southern hospitality.

"Hi, James. How are you?" A small smile appears on my face. I feel like the situation is resolved—like I've accepted it for what it is. He hurt me and can't take it back, but that's okay, because I've moved on. I'm over it—I really am. There's no point in hating him, because it's so much harder to hate than to love someone.

He laughs. "I've been better." He looks up at me, and there's so much sadness and regret in his eyes that for a second I let my heart break for him—but only for a second.

"Listen," he starts to say. He looks around at my friends, who are watching his every move. "Is it all right if we talk somewhere?" I see Jake move from the corner of my eye. "I just think that maybe we should talk and say good-bye—for closure, I guess." He looks back at the ground.

I turn to look at Jake. I know I don't need his permission, but I still want it, out of respect for him and for us. He stares back for a few seconds before nodding almost imperceptibly.

I turn back to James. "Okay," I say softly.

James looks up at me then at Jake. "Thanks, man. I'll have her back in a minute. Just one dance."

He walks ahead of me toward the dance floor. I look over my shoulder once to see Jake glaring at us, jaw clenched and eyes narrowed. I wait while James walks up to the DJ and talks in his ear. When he comes back, he stands in front of me and lightly rests his hands on my hips. I look back at Jake, but he's no longer watching us. I place my hands on his upper arms, making it clear that this is in no way intimate.

The DJ changes songs. "Bruno Mars?" I ask James.

"'When I Was Your Man' has kind of been my anthem for the last couple of months," he says, sighing a little.

That makes sense. "How's Megan?" I ask.

"I'm not sure. You're better off asking her new boyfriend, but you'd have to travel to LA to do that," he huffs.

I look at him, bug-eyed, waiting for an explanation.

"Yeah, whoever was going to be her roommate at UNC brought her brother with her when they met up. I guess they hit it off, because two days later she packed up her life and followed him."

He laughs, but it's a sad laugh. "I didn't even know until two days after she left."

"Sucks, doesn't it?" I say, more with understanding than with malice.

"Not really," he says, surprising me. "I was never in love with Megan."

It's quiet for the longest time while the song plays. His anthem.

"I really am sorry, Micky, for what it's worth. You were the greatest thing that ever happened to me. You were my life." I start to interrupt, but he stops me. "No, I know I didn't express that enough to you, and I'll forever hate myself for that. But you need to know that I loved you so fucking much. I still do. Whenever I thought about my future, it always included you." He pauses and takes a few breaths.

I'm crying silent tears, because I know—I know what he's talking about. I had felt it with him, too.

"You were the one walking down the aisle toward me," he continues, "and you were the one raising our kids. I always smiled to myself when I thought how you were going to be there for me every night when I got home from work, in your study writing your books. We'd have a few kids, a decent house. It was perfect in my mind. *You* were perfect. You *are* perfect, and I threw it all away, because I'm such a fucking asshole, and I can't take it back." He starts sobbing, his head on my shoulder. "I can't take it back, and I can't have you back, and none of this . . . this life I have . . . is worth it without you. I fucked it all up . . ." He trails off.

I pull myself away. "I should get back. They're probably wondering where I am."

He nods, wiping his tears away with the back of his hands. "I'll walk you back."

—

When we get back to the bonfire, I sit down in my chair, a little emotionally exhausted from the whole thing. Logan takes a seat next to me.

James eyes him for a second then nods. "Matthews," he greets him.

"Asshole," Logan replies. He turns to face me. "I got a song for you, Micky." He presses the remote for the speaker dock, and "Everybody Knows" by Dustin Tavella starts playing. I chuckle to myself, because the chorus is about your boyfriend cheating and being a douche bag. Heidi and Lucy get up to dance, and James just shakes his head. "You're kind of a dick, Matthews," he grunts.

Logan sits back in his chair, crosses one foot over his knee, and links his fingers behind his head. Like a boss, he says, "And not a single fuck was given."

Everyone except James bursts into laughter. I shouldn't laugh, but it *is* funny.

—

After a few minutes, I realize Jake isn't here. I scan the crowd and see him talking to a girl—a ridiculously beautiful girl. My jealousy kicks in and I try not to stare, but I can't help it.

They're standing as close to each other as possible without actually touching. Slowly, he raises his hand to tuck a stray piece of hair behind her ear. She grabs his hand and squeezes it for a second, smiling up at him. When she lets go of his hand, he puts it in his pocket—probably to stop himself from ripping off her clothes and having his way with her.

He sure isn't having his way with me.

I close my eyes and inhale deeply, the buzz from the alcohol slowly making its way to my brain.

"Hey, Marisa's here!" the creeper Derek announces.

Everyone looks at Jake and *Marisa*. Lucy and Heidi then look at me, and I just shrug—because, really, what can I do?

"She looks more hot now than ever," Derek says, "if that's even possible."

The ache in my heart tightens just a little bit. "Who's Marisa?" I ask. I have to know.

"His girlfriend," Derek answers.

"I wouldn't say she's his girlfriend . . . She *was* . . ." Cam looks at me curiously.

"They were just starting to get their shit together. What happened?" Derek muses out loud. "They were supposed to go to prom together, right? I remember the whole school talking about it for weeks beforehand."

Heidi clears her throat. "She had to go to a modeling thing in New York last minute." She eyes me with an apologetic look on her face.

"That's right!" Derek crows. *Asshole.* "The star rookie and the supermodel—it's like a match made in heaven."

At that, I stand up and walk away—away from that asshole, away from Jake's friends, and away from Jake and this whole fucking night.

THIRTY-THREE

MIKAYLA

I'm sitting on a log in the woods, sobbing like a twelve-year-old girl, because my stupid crush likes the hot chick. What did I expect? Jake Andrews is at a whole other level, so of course he gets supermodels.

"Hey," a timid voice greets me. I look up to see Heidi and Lucy walking toward me.

"So, that's Jake's girlfriend, huh? Or ex?" I sniffle.

Heidi nods. "Ex."

"Jesus, she's not attractive at all. He could have done so much better," I scoff, my voice laced with sarcasm.

They giggle a little.

"At least tell me she's stupid or horribly mean, or that she used to be fat or something. Anything!" I beg.

Lucy spits out, "I wish I could, Micky, but that fucking bitch has it all—ten out of ten in everything. She's super smart—like, Harvard smart. She's nice to fucking everybody. And she's always looked like she belongs on the cover of a fucking magazine. I hate it so much! If I could get away with it, I'd fucking cut a bitch for you."

My eyes widen, and a small laugh escapes me.

Heidi shakes her head. "She's a mean drunk."

"And a profane one, too," I add.

Quiet fills the air for a few minutes.

"Look," Heidi says. "Lucy is right—she's actually a really nice girl. But he doesn't like her in the way he likes you."

I think for a minute. He has never mentioned her—not even once. If she hadn't been out of town that night, and she'd been his date to prom, then where would that have left me?

"You should get back to the party," I tell them. "I'll be fine. I just need a few minutes to clear my head."

"You sure, bitch? It's our last time to party before we're all thrown into the real world. Don't let fucking stupid shit get you down . . ."

I love drunk Lucy. I laugh and nod, and they leave.

Five minutes later, I walk back through the clearing toward our bonfire. Jake is in his seat, and Marisa is there with him—not *with* him, but she's sitting in the circle, while Derek drools over her.

Great.

I sit on the bed of the truck. I don't take my spot next to Jake or on his lap, because it just doesn't feel right anymore. Logan hands me a beer. I see Jake eyeing me, but I don't care. He never mentioned her—not once in the last three months. All I am to him is some stupid girl he took pity on and now can't get rid of.

And he has a supermodel ex-girlfriend. I need more beer.

Logan cuts me off after my third in ten minutes.

Valid.

———

I've been sitting in the back of the truck for I don't know how long, and I can see James watching me. His friends, who were also my friends, are about twenty yards from us. He can see me, and I can see him. But he's *watching* me, and I've seen him get up and grab no less than fifteen beers in the last hour. He must be wasted—and he never gets wasted, ever. His head dropped forward between his shoulders, he can barely sit up straight. This is not like him at all. He's going to pass out, and none of his drunk friends are going to take care of him when he does.

I jump down from the truck and head toward him. Even an asshole like him deserves to get home safely. As I walk past Jake, he grabs my hand. I turn and see his confused face, but I shrug his hand off and march forward. I don't really know why I'm pissed at him, but I do know that if *she* were his date that night, there is no way I would even know who Jake Andrews is.

I stand in front of James and kick his shin gently. He looks up at me, his bloodshot eyes almost fully closed. When he sees it's me, he straightens up a bit and tries to act less drunk.

"Mikayla," he slurs and gets up from his chair. Surprisingly, he doesn't act as drunk as he looks. "Have you come back for me, baby? Have you forgiven me? Please say yes."

"No, James, I just—"

"I'm so glad, baby, so fucking glad," he interrupts, throwing his arms around me and lifting me, spinning me around.

"James, put me down, shit!" I yell. He does, and I start walking away, back to my group.

He follows. "Mick, I'm sorry. I don't know what the fuck—just wait, please."

I make it halfway before he catches up to me and grabs my arm, forcing me to turn around. "I'm sorry, Mikayla. I'm so fucking sorry." Tears are running down his face faster than he can wipe them away. "God, you're so fucking beautiful, I just love you so much." His voice is strained.

And then . . .

He reaches into his pocket . . .

Pulls out a little black velvet box . . .

And starts to get down on one knee.

The second I see the box, my eyes snap shut—I can't watch this happen.

Not when I hear him get down on the ground.

Not when I feel his hand take mine.

And not when I hear him say, "I asked your dad and everything, so I got this for you the day before prom."

THIRTY-FOUR

JAKE

Logan and Cam are holding me back as I watch that asshole get down on one knee, with a fucking ring in his hand, and ask the girl *I* love to marry *him*.

And I can't do shit about it.

Kayla's eyes are shut, and when she opens them, she says something to him. James stands up, wiping his face. She says something else, and he looks at the ground, nodding. Then they leave.

They walk away from this party and leave.

And I have no idea what the fuck just happened.

—

It's three in the goddamn morning, and Kayla's still not in her room. I should know, because that's where I am, waiting for her.

Like an abandoned fucking puppy.

Finally, I hear a car door slam and rush to look outside. It's Kayla. She pays the cabdriver and starts to walk upstairs. She has to know I'm here, because the lights are on.

She opens the door and pauses when she sees me. She then walks past me, like I'm not even fucking here. She gets in the shower. Five minutes later, she's dressed in pajamas and crawls into bed.

"Are you going to marry that asshole?" I ask, because I need to prepare myself for the moment when she breaks my heart.

"No, Jake, I'm not."

Thank God.

"So what the fuck? You just leave and don't bother calling? You didn't bring your phone with you. Where were you all night, Kayla? Did you *fuck* him for old times' sake? Just one last hurrah?"

She starts crying, and I know I'm being a dick. I calm myself down a little. "I really want to feel okay about all of this. But I don't know what's going on. You have to tell me."

"What? Like you tell me?" Kayla spits out.

"What do you mean?"

"Marisa?"

Fuck.

"You didn't tell me you had a supermodel girlfriend who was supposed to be your prom date. Instead you end up with me, the stupid girl whose boyfriend had been screwing her best friend for two years and was too fucking clueless to know. You take pity on me and hang out with me. Then my family is murdered, and I have no one, so now you're stuck with some strange girl sleeping in your fucking bed, taking over your fucking life, and you can't get fucking rid of me." She wants to yell, but she's keeping it together.

"She wasn't my girlfriend," I whisper.

She laughs. "That's it? That's all you have to say?"

I start to speak, but she cuts me off. "We talked," she says, exhausted. "James and I talked. That's *all*. He had asked for my dad's permission to marry me. I didn't know. I wanted to know what my dad had said to him, because I need a memory of him—of them, my family. Because I'm starting to forget them . . ." Her voice breaks as tears begin to flow again, and a sob overcomes her entire body. "I feel like I'm starting to forget them, Jake—like they're fading away, and I don't want that. What your mom did with this room for me . . . I felt like they were here with me. I could smell the memories in my blankets and clothes. But they're all going . . . The memories are fading, and sometimes . . ." She stops to close her eyes and take a breath. "Sometimes, when I close my eyes, I can't see my family anymore. But I don't want to forget them. He helped me remember, Jake. That's all."

I crawl into bed with her and tuck her head under my chin. "You'll never forget them, Kayla. They'll always live in your heart."

It's quiet for the longest time as she cries quietly in my arms. When the sounds of her crying stop, and I think she's fallen asleep, she whispers, "Jake, after we move into the house, I'm going to find a job, then I'm moving out. I can't be this broken girl anymore."

I don't say anything, because what can I say? It's the last thing I ever wanted.

Thirty-Five

Mikayla

It's moving day.

It would be an understatement to say that things have been awkward between Jake and me since the night of the bonfire party. Now we'll be living together until I can save up enough money to move out. I want to tell him that it's not because of him—it's because of me. I don't want to think that our circumstances are the only reason we feel the way we do for each other—*if* he feels anything for me at all.

I had hired movers to take some of the furniture from storage to the house. Mandy was at the house to oversee it all. After I said a very tearful good-bye, and a billion thank-yous, to Mandy and Nathan, I went upstairs to say good-bye to Julie.

She'd been in her room most of the day. I guess she wasn't very happy about our leaving. I had gotten close to Julie over the last couple of months. She didn't replace Emily, but she came pretty close.

I wanted to give her a special gift, so I had written a fairy tale for her and gotten it professionally illustrated. It was about a little girl who was a princess, of course. She wore a cape, because she believed that one day she'd be able to fly and dance in the clouds.

Her older brother, the Prince, was a *secret* superhero who went around at night saving the world—in his baseball gear, of course. His powers came from his right hand. He would raise it to the sky, and the sun would beam down on it. His hand held the strength of a thousand men.

The Queen and King, her parents, were also heroes—but not your normal everyday ones. They were the kind of hero who loved and cared for those who didn't have anyone else to love and care for them. Julie loved the story, and when Mandy and Nathan read it, they loved it, too.

We're now in the car. It's a two-hour drive to Jake's house, and we're driving in silence.

Awkward as hell.

"So," he says out of nowhere, surprising me and making me jerk in my seat a little. "Julie showed me the book."

"Oh, yeah?"

"It's beautiful, Kayla—really. You're something else, you know that?" He says this without taking his eyes off the road.

More silence.

I guess he can't take the quiet anymore, because he plays with his stereo until the Bluetooth connects with his phone. And then . . .

"What Makes You Beautiful" by One Direction comes on.

My head snaps up. His eyes are wide, a blush creeping to his cheeks. "Holy shit!" I cry out in laughter. "One Direction, Jake? Really? What happened to you in the last two weeks?"

He laughs—a good, all-out, carefree laugh. I miss it so much. And God, I miss *him* so much. "Shut up!" he says, looking at me sideways. "It must have been on a compilation I downloaded, or JuJu probably put it on there!"

"What? Your eight-year-old sister took your phone and downloaded One Direction on it? For what? For the times she has your phone and you don't?" I'm laughing now, tears in my eyes.

"I honestly don't know how it got there. I swear it." He laughs again.

By the time we get to the house, we've listened to the song no less than twenty times. We now know most of the words and have half a dance routine made up for it. Thank you, One Direction, for breaking this awkward tension. If for nothing else, I will always remember that one song for bringing back the most important person in my life.

THIRTY-SIX

MIKAYLA

It's not enough that I have to live—and deal—with Jake Andrews. Now I have to put up with Jake Andrews in *college*. And that Jake Andrews is at a whole other level that I didn't even know existed. Everyone around me definitely downplayed the hype around his coming here, because he *is* a big deal. I can't go anywhere without his being stopped every two minutes. Everyone wants a piece of him—and I mean *everyone*.

I thought that Marisa chick was hot, but she's nothing compared to the women here. And I say "women," because that's what they are—older, more experienced women. From the couple of college parties I've experienced in the last two weeks, I *know* he can have any girl here.

Which is why I choose not to go to many parties at all.

I'm still that frumpy, stupid, jealous, insecure little girl I was at the hotel.

In our home, he's *my* Jake, and I'm *his* Kayla. We hug, hold hands, talk, and laugh. We don't kiss, and we haven't taken things further than innocent touching. As hard as it is, we *have* held back.

But the minute we step out that door, I shut down. I don't want to be known as the girl who hangs around Jake Andrews—the one he saved one tragic night and cared for when no one else did. And I don't want the other girls to see me as competition, because I was that girl with James and Megan—and there are way too many Megans in college. Only this time, it would hurt so much more, because what I feel for Jake, when I let myself feel it, is a thousand times heavier than what I felt for James . . . which means the heartbreak would hurt a thousand times more, and I don't think my heart can handle any more pain. So out there, in the real world, I don't let myself feel the love I have for him, because I really, truly, and deeply love him.

And I'm so fucking scared that I'm not enough. That I'll never really be enough for him—*my* Jake.

A few days after we moved in, I landed a job at a video store. Yes, those still exist. It's shit pay, but they work around my schedule. And when it's not busy, I get to read and do homework, so it works out perfectly. I'm saving the money I earn so I can hopefully move out soon. I want to start working on finding out who I am without Jake, so *if* the time comes, I can give him *me*—all of me.

Meanwhile, contrary to how our relationship ended, James is being a good guy. We did plan on going to college together, so I see him around campus and catch up with him every now and then. He's the only one—a piece of my past—who understands and remembers my family the way I want to. He was a big part of my life, and for four years he was part of my family. He loved them, too, and for a while he felt too guilty to grieve them the way he should have. Girls ogle James when I'm with him, but it doesn't bother me at all. Truthfully, James is a good-looking guy—but only to those who have never laid eyes on Jake Andrews.

JAKE

Every fucking day I have to wake up to her in her short shorts and tight shirt, hot as hell in the morning with her tired Bambi eyes.

Every day she's here, and I can't have her.

To have to be around the person you love, and not be able to *love* them, is the hardest thing to do.

I hate college. I hate the never-ending pressure to be this hotshot. I hate the constant recognition from everyone because I can pitch a decent game. I hate the stupid, endless string of college parties I'm pressured into going to, and I hate the attention from all the other girls, when I only ever wanted just one—and she won't have me. I hate the stupid classes and the stupid commitments, because they all keep me away from her. I'm so fucking close to throwing in the towel and going pro. But I don't, because I know she won't follow me.

And none of this shit makes sense without her.

Sometimes I see that scared little girl I saw when we pulled up to her parents' house that night. I hate that she ever has to feel like that. I want to shut out the world around us and have us just be the way we are behind closed doors, where no one else can dictate who we are and what we feel. I just want her—*my* Kayla.

Occasionally she'll have lunch with that asshole James. I hate it so much, because he gives her something that I can't. He gives her memories of her family and the times they shared. I hate that he loved them and I never can. I hate that they shared moments together and I never will. I hate that he taught Emily how to ride a bike, and I'll never even get to meet her. I hate that I'll never get to ask her dad's permission when I propose to her (because I plan to one day). I hate that he's allowed to miss them and I can't, and I hate that he hurt her.

But I can't hate *him*, because he brought her to me.

She says she still wants to move out—something about finding herself without me around. I keep my mouth shut, because I know it's important to her, but I just don't get it. I don't understand why she wants to find herself without me there, when I plan on being a part of her life *forever*—when I love her so damn much, it hurts.

THIRTY-SEVEN

MIKAYLA

I hear the front door swing open and Logan's and Jake's voices. I caught the bus to go home so I could get ready for work. My shift starts in fifteen minutes.

"You tell her then, asshole," Jake says. He's pissed.

I run out of my bedroom, hopping on one leg while I pull my other boot on. "Keys?" I say to Jake with my hand out. As Jake gives me his car keys, I look at Logan. He has that cat-that-ate-the-canary look. "Tell me what, Logan?"

"It's nothing." He shrugs.

"Logan here opened his big fat mouth and told the team I live off campus in my own house. So guess what? Now we're stuck hosting a team 'get-together' tomorrow night." Jake speaks for him.

"Oh," I say. That's not so bad. "I'm working until ten tomorrow night, but I think I should be able to crash at Lucy's," I tell him, going through my purse to make sure I have everything.

"What?" Jake says. "I don't want you to not be here. This is your house, too, Kayla. I don't want people to think this is party central."

"Chill the fuck out, dude. It's not a big deal," Logan reassures him.

JAKE

It's the night of the stupid "get-together." Kayla left for work a couple of hours ago, wearing a light-gray sweater dress and cowboy boots. I let her take my car so she didn't ride the bus like that. Then I made Logan drive me around to help me get ready for the party.

Logan wanted a full-on blowout. I threatened to call the whole thing off when he begged to invite his entire frat house. *Fuck no.* So it's just the guys from the team with their girls and our group.

Logan borrowed a few kegs from someone in his frat, and Lucy and Heidi organized snacks. I really wasn't up for this. I just wanted to spend the night at home with Kayla—maybe try to persuade her to let me reciprocate. God knows we need to do *something* about the tension in this house. I can't even jerk off because she might hear or know somehow. I've been taking a lot—and I mean *a lot*—of cold showers.

About two hours into the party, she walks in wearing that gray sweater dress and those cowboy boots, looking as hot as I've ever seen her. The guys cheer, and a couple of them even make their way over to her. I watch how she reacts. I don't know if she's still interested in what we have. I know how I feel. When she moves out of this house like she's planning to, she'll take a huge part of me with her.

She waves shyly and gives a few of the guys a little hug—nothing that I need to worry about. She sees me leaning against the kitchen counter and saunters over, smiling. I grab a beer and hand it to her. "Hey," she says, giving me a quick kiss on the cheek. She then turns and joins the party.

MIKAYLA

I walk into the living room. Jake watches me, leaning against the back of the sofa. He drinks his beer, his eyes never leaving mine. I stop in front of him and look up. He places a hand on my waist. "I'm heading to bed. I'm exhausted. I'll see you in the morning?"

He nods. He then takes my hand and leads me to my room. He closes the door behind him and stares at me. "You need to lock your door tonight, Kayla. Please?"

I nod. He leans in and kisses my temple before leaving the room. I lock the door after him.

JAKE

A few of the guys ended up crashing at the house, because they were too wasted to drive home. We're all early risers because of our strict training schedule, so I make coffee and toast and leave a box of cereal out for them before they go. They're respectful and quiet, because they know Kayla's sleeping.

They're sitting at the dining table, munching, when Kayla walks in wearing her pajamas, which are tiny boy shorts and an ever tinier tank. She's not wearing a bra. Her eyes are still half-shut, and her hair is all over the place. She's mumbling something under her breath as she shuffles over to the coffeepot. She pours herself a cup and lazily walks over to me. She leans the front of her body against mine and reaches up to give me a kiss on the cheek. "I'm cold," she murmurs, still half-asleep.

"Uh-huh," I say, rubbing my hands up and down her arms and glaring at the guys over her shoulder. "Maybe you should put more clothes on, Kayla." It sounds like a request.

"Nope," one of the guys says. "She looks fine just the way she is."

Kayla squeals and tenses in my arms. I can't help the chuckle that escapes me. She moves my body to cover hers, but first she pinches my nipple and twists it, which really hurts. "Jake, I hate you! Why didn't you warn me that people were here?" She holds me like a shield as she walks back into her room. Once she's in, she pushes me out the door then slams it shut.

"Lucky bastard gets to wake up to that every morning," one of them says.

"Asshole," someone agrees.

I smile to myself and pick up her coffee. I knock on her door, and she opens it slightly, face flushed from embarrassment. I hand her the coffee and kiss her on the cheek. "You look beautiful this morning."

THIRTY-EIGHT

JAKE

I hear the front door open and slam then a squeal of frustration. I rush out of the study and run to the entryway. Kayla is standing there, drenched from head to toe and covered in mud.

"It's storming outside! What are you doing?" I almost yell at her, like she's a disobedient child.

"I had to get home from work! This car drove past me when I was walking from the bus stop and splashed all this water and mud on me. Then a dog ran after me, and I got scared and hid in some bushes, which landed me in more fucking mud."

"Where the hell was your phone? You should have called me!"

"It's dead!"

I roll my eyes. It's always dead.

She starts to move away from the front door, but I stop her. "What are you doing? You can't walk through the house like that. You'll get mud everywhere!" But I'm laughing now, because she looks so frickin' grumpy and adorable.

"Jake." She says my name like an annoyed moan. "What do you want me to do? Strip outside and walk through the house in my underwear?"

I raise my eyebrows at her.

"Don't be an idiot," she says. "What should I do?"

"Wait here," I tell her and run to the bathroom to turn the shower on. I make sure the temperature is just right before I go back and throw her over my shoulder. She squeals in surprise. When we get to the bathroom, she shifts like I'm going to put her down, but instead I stand her up in the shower—fully clothed, shoes and all. She screams while I laugh.

Then she has my shirt in her hands and pulls me in with her. She laughs while I scream—a manly one, though. I'm not a fucking pussy.

Then we're both laughing. And I realize it's been a long time since we both laughed like this. We look at each other. She breaks the stare by throwing her head under the shower spray. She tilts her head back, and the water streams over her face and down her hair. Her lips are partially parted.

We're in a confined space with nowhere to move. We're both soaking wet, and she's *so* fucking hot. I try to clean out some of the mud from her hair. Her breath catches when she feels my hands on her. We're facing each other under the water, her body pulled into mine, because the space in the shower gives us no other option.

Then she peels off her dress. She's in a bra and panties, and that's *all*. "Dirty dress," she says and shrugs by way of explanation, throwing the dress out of the shower onto the bathroom floor.

I clear my throat and try not to look at her tits.

Or her legs.

I try to keep my hands at my side so I don't touch her—balled into fists so I'm not tempted.

"You're all dirty, too," she says, pointing at my clothes.

I look down and see mud on my T-shirt and shorts from carrying her in here. I take them off and stand under the water in my boxers. She can see I'm hard but tries to play it cool. I see her chest rising and falling with her breaths, and I know she's as turned on as

I am right now. We're testing each other and seeing how far we can take this before someone snaps—most likely my dick. I'm not going to crack, though. I need to make sure that if I touch her, she's going to want it. I don't know what the hell she wants. She's only made clear that she's leaving. So I stand there, eyes on her, not moving.

She turns around to face the stream of water and starts to wash herself. I study her back unabashedly, because she can't see me. My fingers are itching to touch her. I close my eyes tightly. I make a sound, but I can't tell you what kind. I imagine my pushing her against the tiles, ripping her panties off, and being inside her. I imagine the noises she would make, and I swear I almost come.

This is bad—really fucking bad.

When I open my eyes, she's facing me. She takes her bra off, and my eyes are glued to her tits like I'm ten and this is my first titty mag. She brushes her palm against the head of my dick lightly, but I feel it—my dick feels it—and it jerks under her touch. I almost pull back, but she does first. She turns the hot water off, and cold water fills the shower. I yelp under my breath and jump out of the stream.

"You need a cold shower, Jake." She gets out, grabs a towel, and leaves the bathroom.

—

By the time I'm done, she's dressed and on the sofa, ordering food and looking through DVDs to watch.

She hears me walk in. "Hey," she says almost shyly. "I ordered Chinese. Is that okay?" She wants to act like nothing happened. *Fine.*

"Um, yeah. I'm actually heading out now, though." Lie.

"Oh?" she says, surprised and a little confused.

"Yeah, uh . . . I have a date." Lie. Lie. Lie.

Her face falls. She looks away, but I can see her swallow and wipe her face quickly.

I run to her so fast, I almost trip over myself. I squat in front of her. "Kayla, I was just fucking around. I'm not going out on a date or anything. I was being a dick. I'm sorry. Please don't cry." I try to wipe her tears, but she swats my hands away.

"You're an asshole," she says through a sob.

"I am," I agree.

It's quiet for a few moments, then she grabs my face in her hands. She makes sure I'm looking straight at her. "Please, Jake. Don't do that."

I lean into her touch. She's biting her lip. I glance from her eyes to her mouth and back again. I wet my lips. Her eyes follow my tongue.

"Do what, Kayla?" I need to know how she feels and what she wants from me—if she wants to be more than this.

MIKAYLA

His tongue darts out to lick his lips, then his teeth bite his bottom lip. I watch it play out like it's in slow motion. I have to close my eyes and concentrate on breathing.

"Kayla?"

My eyes snap open. "Huh?"

"Do what, Kayla?" he asks again.

I think about how to answer, as though it will determine whether I live or die.

I look at him and see the concern in his face. I love him—like, *love* him. I want him to know that, but not yet. Because I need him to love me back—*all* of me.

"Don't hurt my heart, Jake," I say quietly.

He drops his head for a second then stands up and sits down next to me. He takes me in his arms and kisses my temple. "I'm sorry, baby. I'll never hurt you again, I promise."

THIRTY-NINE

JAKE

She's lying across the sofa, reading a book on her e-reader. I guess Lucy let her keep it. I'm supposed to be watching ESPN, but I can't take my eyes off her legs. She's wearing her standard pajamas: tiny boy shorts and matching tank. Her feet are fidgeting, her toes curling and rubbing against each other. Her chest moves up and down from her steady breathing. She's not wearing a bra, and her nipples are poking through the material. I want so bad to put them in my mouth and taste them.

She's holding her book in one hand while the other rests on her stomach, her little finger tucked just under the band of her shorts and her tank top riding up her waist. She begins to move her little finger side to side under her shorts, her legs slowly rubbing together. She makes a low moaning sound.

I want so bad to be inside her.

Mikayla

I'm supposed to be reading my book, but I can feel Jake watching me. His gaze is locked on my legs and stomach. His eyes burning with lust, he licks his bottom lip then bites it. It's so fucking hot. I can't stop looking at his face, just like he can't stop looking at my body.

I squeeze my legs tight, thinking about how he makes me feel—how he can make me come like no one has before. A moan escapes me before I can stop it. If I weren't so afraid of my feelings, I'd tell him to fuck me right now.

He moves his hands slowly from his lap to the band of his shorts. He reaches into his shorts, grabs his dick, sits up slightly in his chair . . . and adjusts himself. I close my eyes, breathe in and out, count to ten, then excuse myself to bed.

Once I'm under the covers, I frantically Mikayla myself. It only takes a few seconds before my release, because in my mind they're my hands wrapped around him, not his, and I'm bringing him to my entrance so I can scream his name over and over.

As I'm coming down from the haze, I realize my throat is scratchy—I actually *was* screaming his name.

A second later, I hear the shower running.

FORTY

MIKAYLA

"I need a new job, and I definitely need to buy a car," I huff, closing the front door behind me.

Logan and Jake are sitting on the sofa, watching ESPN, but turn when they hear my complaining.

"You look like shit, Micky," Logan observes.

Jake punches him hard in the arm.

"Thanks, asshole." I glare at Logan. "You would, too, if you had my day."

"What happened?" Jake asks on his way to the kitchen. I sit down on the sofa, and Jake sits down next to me, handing me a beer. I take a sip. He pulls my legs up on his lap, takes my boots and socks off, and slowly massages my feet. It feels like heaven. If Logan weren't sitting right there, I don't know where this moment would end up.

"First," I say, "some smelly sleaze-bucket customer was convinced I was in a porno." I pause as Logan laughs. "He had the DVD and kept trying to show me the back of it. I couldn't convince him I'd never been in one, so he kept pushing for me to play it on the screen so he could double-check. He was pushy as hell, and it was so uncomfortable. Luckily, a TA from one of my classes was there, and he asked the asshole to get out. My TA stayed for a bit afterward to make sure he didn't come back."

"What the fuck?" Jake growls. "Why didn't you call me? Who was that asshole?"

Logan laughs harder.

"My phone's dead—"

"Your phone's always dead! Start charging it!" Jake yells.

I pout, but it's true—my phone's always either low on battery or dead. "I don't know who he was—just some random asshole I haven't seen before," I say.

Jake stares at me for a moment. I stare back until Logan interrupts my thoughts. "And second? You said that was the first . . ."

"Some creeper on the bus licked my elbow! Legit licked my fucking elbow. He got off at the same stop, and I swear I thought he was going to follow me home. So I ran. Hence I look like shit."

Logan's all-out laughing now. I start to laugh as well.

Jake looks pissed off. "It's not funny. Why are you laughing?"

"Come on, Jake," I say, nudging him. "If it happened to anyone else, we'd all be laughing."

His features relax a bit. "You're getting a car as soon as possible, Kayla."

"Speaking of getting a car, I brought my laundry to my favorite girl in the world." Logan tries his panty-dropping smile on me.

I look at him and chuckle. "That has got to be the worst segue since the beginning of time." I get up and head to the laundry room, so I can get started.

I hear Jake smack the back of Logan's head. "You gotta quit doing that shit. She's not your mom."

"I don't mind!" I yell, halfway down the hall. "It makes me feel needed."

Logan laughs then says loud enough so I can hear, "Dude, you should tell her how much your dick needs her." Logan yelps in pain, then I hear the front door opening. "Just bring my stuff to the party tonight, okay, Micky? You're coming, right?"

"Yeah," I yell. Lie.

The front door closes, and Jake walks into the laundry room. "So we're going to the party?" he asks, spinning his cap backwards.

"You can, but I'm not."

"But you just told him—"

"Jake, Logan's mind works like a five-year-old's. He wouldn't take no for an answer, but I doubt he'd even remember if I were there or not."

He moves closer to me—so close I can smell him. "But what if I want you there? What if it's me who's asking, and you *know* I'll remember if you're there or not?" He places his hands on my waist and presses me against the dryer.

The atmosphere has suddenly switched.

Goose bumps from his touch break through my skin, and my breathing accelerates. It's been so long since he's touched me like this, and I need him to do . . . something, so my body doesn't hate me.

I lean into him slightly, my breasts lifting, and he knows it's an invitation. He dips his head to my shoulder, his lips on the bare skin. Moving so slowly and softly it's painful, his tongue slips out a tiny bit and moves higher up my neck to my jaw and ear. "I heard you last night," he whispers.

He moves his tongue lower, back down my neck to my collarbone. He bends over me so he can kiss the swell of my breasts. His hands go lower down my waist to my hips and thighs, until they meet at the bottom of my dress. Slowly and softly like his tongue, he moves his hands back up the bare skin of my thighs under the dress. It's so erotic, and I'm so turned on, but I haven't made a sound.

Then he cups my ass gently, and I almost cry out with need. He slowly moves his fingers just under the material of my lace panties, and he groans when his hands hold my bare ass. His mouth is on my breasts, slowly kissing me everywhere. I'm panting, my mouth dry and eyes closed, feeling everything at once. God, I want him so fucking bad . . . The thought makes me moan out loud.

He uses his teeth to pull my dress and bra down so my breasts are hanging out over them. His eyes are filled with lust as he stares up at me. He groans once, his eyes rolling back. Then my nipple is in his mouth, and he's grabbing my ass more tightly. He's sucking and licking like he can't get enough, and *I want him inside me.*

He pulls down my panties. They drop to the floor, and I can feel the coldness of the air on my wet heat. He puts his hands on my waist and lifts me onto the dryer, his mouth not leaving my breasts. His palms on my inner thighs, he spreads my legs for him. He stands in between them, and I can feel his hardness through his sweats. We grind against each other, my head thrown back and my chest lifted for him to devour.

His mouth leaves my breasts and goes lower. He kisses my stomach through the material of my dress. I know what he wants to do, and I want him to do it so bad, but . . . I grab his head in my hands and tell him, "Not now, Jake. Not like this." His mouth returns to my breasts, then he pulls back. I whimper, and he puts his fingers inside me. He moves them in and out, circling around, and I'm moaning, so fucking close.

I can feel the build-up. I know I'm being loud, but I don't care. He looks at me and laughs, because he knows I'm a screamer. But I cut him off by pulling his sweats down just enough so I can grab his huge, rock-hard dick in my hands. I stroke him up and down, and he moves in and out. I'm so wet and turned on, and he knows I'm about to come because his fingers work faster. I feel him harden slightly more before we both go over the edge. We breathe into each other, waiting to come down from this amazing feeling. We hold on until the buzz fades.

We never even kissed. We have *never* kissed.

When we're finally calm, Jake says, "I missed you so fucking much."

FORTY-ONE

JAKE

I persuaded Kayla to come to the party with me. I'm so glad, because tonight I want her with me. I want to be able to hold her and let everyone know that she's mine. She's wearing a short green dress and those cowboy boots, and it's hot as hell. We *almost* didn't make it here. She had to keep tearing my hands off her.

When we get to the frat house, there are hundreds of people already there. I have my girl under my arm, and she seems happy, which makes me happy. We sit down with our friends in front of the karaoke stage, laughing because the people who think they are good actually suck. It's hilarious. She's on my lap, drinking her third or fourth beer, and she's giggling while watching someone onstage. My hands are on her bare legs, and her arms are wrapped around my neck. I rub my nose along her jaw, and she shivers every time I do it. I love it.

"Hi, Jake."

Oh *fuck*. I don't even look up because I know who it is. I grip Kayla more tightly. She's trying to hold back a laugh, and I can feel her body shaking with the effort.

"Hi, Lacey," she says, her voice syrupy sweet.

"It's Casey," she snaps.

I flinch and Kayla feels it. She giggles again. I close my eyes, freaking out, because Casey is mental. I know I'm a macho asshole, but I can admit that I'm scared when she's, like, within a five-billion-yard radius. Kayla reaches up and strokes my head like a baby, which actually helps. My hands try to creep higher up her bare thigh, but she swats them away.

Casey hangs out with us for ten full minutes, pretending we're best friends. I keep my eyes closed and my head buried in Kayla's neck. Then Casey leaves, and I can breathe again.

"She seemed nice," Matt, one of Logan's frat brothers, comments. Everyone stifles a laugh.

"Yeah," Kayla says. "Her face and conversation say 'I'm nice enough,' but her eyes say 'I have eight dead bodies in the basement!'"

Everyone cracks up, and I kiss her on the temple like I used to. I missed her so much. I never want to be apart from her again.

—

Some guy is waving at me from across the room. I have no idea who he is, so I just smile. He looks at me awkwardly then eyes Kayla on my lap. "You know him?" I ask her.

She looks up and smiles when she sees him. "I'll be right back," she says, getting up and walking over to him. He eyes her as she walks toward him. I almost stand up, but Logan reaches for my arm and pulls me back down. Who is this kid, and how does he know *my girl*?

I shake my head and nudge Logan with my knee. I'm about a ten on the buzzed scale and about a five on the wasted. I jerk my head, and Logan looks over at them. He smiles. I want to punch his smug face.

"That's Phil or Will . . . Something like that," Logan says.

"And?" I ask, wanting more information.

"And that's all you get. Why? You jealous?"

I look at him. "Quit being an asshole—you know I'm jealous. Who is he?"

"You're not allowed to be jealous, because, from what I know, she's not your girl, is she?" he asks, his eyebrows raised, begging me to say something stupid, like declare my love for her or something. He's not getting it—not today.

"Who is he, Logan?" I'm not in the mood for this shit and he knows it.

He sighs. "He's Maloney's brother. I've seen him around the house a few times. He's not a frat brother, though. He's, like, a higher-education type, junior maybe senior, on his way to med school or something. That's all I got."

Med school? I'm the high school jock, and he's a med school student. Great. I'm *fucked.* I stand up and walk to a better position where I can watch them.

"Don't be an asshole, Jake," Logan warns, but I don't care.

MIKAYLA

Some girl in the corner of the room has been eyeing Jake the whole night. I don't know who she is, but it's pissing me off. I'm sitting on Jake's lap when she comes over to our group. She takes a seat on Matt's lap. He looks startled for a second then places his hand on her thigh.

She never takes her eyes off Jake the whole time.

Jake doesn't seem to notice or care. But I do. If she were a guy, I'd junk-punch her for sure. After thirty excruciating minutes of her trying to seduce him from across the room, I've had enough. I stand up to leave, but Jake tightens his hold on me. "Just ignore her."

So he has noticed.

"You think it's okay for her to sit there and look at you like that? It's making *me* uncomfortable, Jake," I whisper so only he can hear.

"And you think it's okay to talk to some guy I don't know about whatever the hell you guys were talking about, and the whole time he's gawking at you like he wants to eat you?" I can hear the anger in his voice.

"Jake, he was not—"

"I'm a guy, Kayla. I know what he was thinking."

"Jake, who's your friend?" Tramp-tits asks, interrupting us. I look at her and narrow my eyes.

Jake sighs next to me. I look at him. "Christy, I'm trying to have a conversation with my girl here," he says, shaking his head.

"I didn't know you had a girl," Tramp-tits says. He ignores her and looks back at me, trying to return to our conversation.

I continue. "I thanked him for being there today. He was the TA I told you about. He mentioned there's an apartment in his building that—"

"*What?*" Jake yells then softens his tone. "You mean to tell me that that asshole just *happened* to be at your work today, and now he's telling you about apartments *near* him?"

I open my mouth to say something, but Tramp-tits interrupts *again*. "Is something wrong, Jake? Anything I can help with?" she coos innocently, batting her eyelashes at him.

That's when rage consumes me, and something I never knew existed takes over. I stand up. Everyone around us falls quiet, waiting for what's about to happen. Logan and Jake are on their feet, ready. I stalk over to her to get in her face. Lucy and Cam—I didn't even know they'd arrived—are right next to me.

"Quit eye-fucking him!" I spit out, pointing my finger in her face. "I'm right fucking here. Do you know how *disrespectful* that is?" I fume, motioning up and down my body.

"Yeah, you fucking slut!" Lucy yells. Cam laughs and throws his arm around her.

"I'm so fucking sick of girls like you, thinking it's okay to want what's not yours to have!"

"Fucking whore!" Lucy yells. She's drunk. I love drunk Lucy.

"Calm down, bitch," Tramp-tits says. *Bitch?*

"Bitch?" Lucy and I repeat.

"Yeah," Tramp-tits repeats, standing up. "I'm not the only one who's looking at him, so why do you care?"

"Because he's fucking mine!" I growl. "And if I so much as see you look at him again, the next thing you'll be gawking at is my fist coming toward your face! Got it?"

"I swear to God, Micky," Lucy snarls. Cam's pretending to hold her back, amused by her drunken state. "I'll cut a bitch for you. Just let me go, Cam. Let me go!" she yells, trying to fight his grip.

Tramp-tits walks away, and we burst into laughter. I don't know how it went from heated to hilarious—probably because of Lucy and the fact that we're all drunk.

Jake puts his arm around my shoulders. "I'm so turned on right now," he says.

—

Jake later surprises everyone by getting on the karaoke stage. He stands there with a mic in hand, a blush creeping to his cheeks. Looking down, he clears his throat then speaks into the mic.

"This is, um . . . This is for my girlfr—" He cuts himself off when he sees my eyes bug out, because I'm not his girlfriend—not yet. It wouldn't be fair to him, because I'm not ready. But I'm also not ready for him to move on.

"I mean, *my* Kayla. Just, um, *mine*." He has a little smile on his face, and it's so frickin' adorable. Then the music starts . . . and we all laugh.

It's One Direction.

He starts to sing. It's so sexy, because his accent is in full force. I want him with everything I have and hope that one day I can give him all of it.

—

When we get home, I go straight to the bathroom and start getting ready for bed. He comes up behind me and kisses the bare skin on my shoulder. He kissed me so lightly, for a second I thought I had imagined it.

"Kayla?" He's looking at me in the mirror.

I close my eyes. "Mmm?"

He turns me around and kisses my forehead. He places his hands on my waist and lifts me up onto the counter, his chin leaning on my shoulder. He spreads my legs and stands between them, but he doesn't make a move to do anything else. He looks at me like he's seeing me for the first time and tears pool in his eyes. I have no idea what he's thinking or feeling, so I spin his cap backwards and take his face in my hands. "What's going on, Jake?"

He clears his throat and looks away.

"Jake?" I ask again.

He speaks so softly, I almost don't hear him. "I know we haven't spoken about it, but things haven't been the same between us after that night at the bonfire party." He clears his throat again. "Are you still mine? Are you still *my* Kayla?"

I don't know what to say to him.

I don't know if I am.

But I know I don't want to be anyone else's.

"If you still want me," I whisper.

He sighs, relieved. "I more-than-a-lot want you."

JAKE

"Can you sleep with me tonight?" I ask her.

"What?" Her eyes are huge.

I chuckle. "Not like that—just sleep. I miss you in my arms so much, Kayla. I just want you near me."

"Okay," she says, smiling. She sits down next to me on the edge of my bed. We're both a little quiet now—thinking, I guess. It will be the first time we'll sleep together since the bonfire party.

"Kayla." I clear my throat. "I need you to do something for me."

"Anything," she whispers.

"I know that you said you wanted to move out. You have your reasons, and I respect that." I pause and take a few breaths, because I don't want to sound angry when I say the next part. "But please, don't move near that guy. I just don't trust him, and he obviously wants you—"

"Jake—"

"No, Kayla. I know you're naive when it comes to these things, but he does, and you're—"

"Jake, stop. I'm not going to. I know how you feel, and I wouldn't do that to you. I respect your feelings, and I would never do anything that would make you question mine."

I take her hand and kiss her palm. I'll never understand how some jerk-off had her and treated her like shit. I'm going to be the luckiest asshole in the world when she finally lets me love her.

FORTY-TWO

JAKE

When I open the front door, I see Kayla sitting at the dining table, a shoe box, a bazillion magazines, and craft supplies in front of her.

"What are you doing? Decoupage?"

She eyes me curiously and starts to laugh.

"What?" I say. "Mom went through a craft phase when she was pregnant with JuJu. Seriously, though, what are you doing?" I drop my gear bag near the front door and walk over to her.

She's cutting pictures out of a bunch of teenybopper magazines—Justin Bieber, One Direction, and some dudes from those vampire movies and the show in which kids kill each other. I look at her for a long moment. She stares back. "You're not going on a stalker road trip with Heidi, are you?" I ask seriously. She laughs.

I walk to the fridge to pull out a bottle of water. I sit down on the chair next to her, and she gets up and sits on my lap. We haven't spoken about what happened the night of Logan's frat party. We haven't made anything official yet, and we still haven't kissed properly. The kissing part is quickly driving me crazy. I don't mind everything else. We sleep in my bed every night, and we more-than-a-lot like each other. That's enough for me for now—but not forever. Soon, we're going to have to talk about it.

I put my hand on her waist, and she wraps her arms around my neck. I kiss her temple.

"What are your plans for tomorrow?" she whispers.

"Spending the day with you?"

She smiles, but it doesn't reach her eyes.

"What's going on, Kayla? Did something happen?"

She slides off my lap and sits back down on her chair. She picks up the scissors and starts cutting the magazines again. She's quiet, and I let her be. I know this side of her. She's working up the courage to speak, so I wait.

"It's Emily's birthday tomorrow," she says quietly, putting down the scissors then looking up at me, tears filling her eyes. I pull her chair closer to me then lift her up and cradle her like I used to.

"We have this family tradition. Every year on our birthdays, we'd sit down and make ourselves these boxes." She points to the shoe box. "We'd stick pictures on them of things that reminded us of that year—guys, movies, songs, anything we were into at the moment. We'd leave an opening at the top, kind of like a mailbox, and store them in the pantry. Whenever someone did something worth remembering, or something nice, or they made you laugh, we'd write it on a note card and put it in their box. It could be anything, really. I remember one year I put in Emily's box that I saw her picking her nose and eating it." She laughs sadly. "We started the tradition when I was about five, and we started to make Emily's when she was about that age, too."

Tears are running down her face, and I wipe them away with my fingers. I try to breathe through the lump in my throat, because I don't want her to see me crying. I don't want her to know how much my heart is breaking right now, too—how much I wish that I could fix this pain she has to carry everywhere, every day.

"Then each year on our birthdays, we'd open our box and read the notes. It was like a year's worth of surprises and memories at once. We always opened them at our birthday dinner and go through them one by one. It didn't matter if it lasted for hours. We laughed and cried through every single note." She's quiet again as she remembers.

"It sounds like an amazing tradition," I say, squeezing her tightly.

"It was only for Dad, Emily, and me. Mom didn't get one," she continues.

I have to clear my throat. "Why not?"

"Because, Dad said, we should treat Mom like every day is her birthday. She did so much for the family, and meant so much to us, that we should appreciate her every second of every day. Dad made her a special box out of plastic, and we'd write notes to put in it. Because there were so many, she got to read them once a week. A lot were from Dad, reminding her how much he loved and appreciated her. Some were from Emily and me. We used to write stupid things, but we always meant them—like 'Thank you for washing my baseball or dance gear,' or 'Thank you for encouraging me or helping with my homework.' She was an amazing woman, and Dad was right. She did so much for us. I'm glad she got to know once a week how we felt." We're both crying now, not looking at each other but past each other. I'm trying to imagine her life while she's remembering it.

"We kept the old ones from previous years in the garage. The fire took them all. That son of a bitch took so many years of love, memories, and laughter away from me." She starts to sob as the anger consumes her. "I fucking hate him, Jake. I hate him so much. And I don't understand why—why he couldn't just let them go. My parents wouldn't have done anything if he'd just let them go. It's not like . . ." She sniffles and has to take a few deep breaths. I just sit there and let her feel, because she's never spoken about it all like this before. She's been sad and hurt, but she hasn't been angry. "It's not like he turned around and there they were, so he just started shooting. It was one shot each, straight to the head. He must have known what he was doing."

She's crying on me now. The tears soak through my sweater as I hold her. It's all I can do until both our tears stop. I pull away so I can look at her. Her big brown Bambi eyes look back at me. "What can I do to help?" I ask.

She sniffles and hands me a bunch of magazines. "Go through these and cut out anything you think a ten-year-old girl would like. I'm going to make some tea."

MIKAYLA

When I bring the tea back to the table, Jake isn't there. "Where are you?" I yell at the rest of the house.

"Hang on, I'll be there in a sec!"

I sit down and wait for him.

"How about this? Can we stick this on?" He comes in and hands me a photo of me and our friends at my graduation. I'm standing in the middle with him and Logan on either side of me. Jake has his arms around my waist, and Logan has his around my neck. The rest of our friends crowd around us. Everyone is making stupid faces—crossing their eyes, sticking their tongues out, making rabbit ears. Cam is pretending to hump Lucy. Jake and I are just looking into each other's eyes with huge goofy grins on our faces.

"I thought . . . Never mind, it was a stupid idea," he says, starting to walk back down the hall.

I stop him by grabbing his arm. "Jake, it's a beautiful idea."
"Yeah?"
"Yeah." I take the photo from his hands.

"Think she would have liked us?"

I think about this for a while. "Yeah, Jake, she would've liked our friends. You, though—she would've *loved* you."

Just like I do.

JAKE

I hear knocking on the door.

We're in my bed, and Kayla is wrapped around me. It's perfect.

I hear more knocking on the door.

Kayla moans and holds on to me more tightly. I hold her, too. She's so warm.

More knocking.

Fuck. I may have said that part out loud.

I jump out of bed, pull on sweats and a hoodie, and walk out of the bedroom, leaving Kayla to sleep the morning away before we go to the cemetery.

More knocking.

"I'm coming!"

Shit. It's James—at *my* front door.

"Hey." He looks behind me.

"She's asleep, asshole. What do you want?"

He rubs his face then raises the flowers he has in his hand. "Here," he says.

"Um, thanks?" I respond, taking them.

He thrusts his hands in his front pockets. "This is so fucking awkward."

"No shit," I deadpan.

He huffs, his cheeks puffing out. It's cold outside, and I really don't know what he's doing here, so I start to close the door.

"Wait," he says. "I know it's Emily's birthday today. Every year for their birthdays, her dad would buy them flowers—tulips, to be exact. Emily got pink, Micky got yellow, and Denise got red." He's looking down and shaking his head. I study him, brows knitted together. He looks up. "Kevin accidentally delivered tulips to Denise . . . That's why . . ." He trails off.

I think I understand what he's saying. "Why are you telling me this?" I ask him.

"Because you're it now." He shrugs. "You're everything to her."

I nod and thank him before closing the door.

When I return to the bedroom, she's sitting up. She sees the flowers in my hand, and her eyes widen with understanding. "From James?"

"Yeah," I sigh, handing them to her. "But from now on, they'll only ever be from me." I kiss her on the temple before jumping in the shower.

FORTY-THREE

MIKAYLA

We spent most of last night writing on note cards to put in Emily's
birthday box. Some things were goofy and funny, and some things
were heartfelt and sad. Jake put a few of his own in, but he wouldn't
let me see what was on them.

Now we're at the cemetery. It's the first time we've been here
since the funeral. I know I should visit more, but it hurts. Jake gives
me a kiss on the temple then walks back to the truck to give me a
few minutes alone with her. I feel a little strange talking to no one,
so I just place the box on her headstone and sit with her for a bit.
Before I leave, I reach into my pocket for the letter I wrote after Jake
had fallen asleep and slip it into the box.

Dear Emily,
First off, I love you and miss you so much. You would have
been ten today. It's a little hard to write about things you've
done, like we used to do, so I guess I'll just write about what we
would talk about if you were still around.

I don't know how these things work, but I'm sure you know
now about James and Megan, and don't worry, I'm okay.

Emily, I met a boy and fell in love—so deeply in love, it hurts. His name is Jake. He's super cute, and you would have loved him. You all would have. Dad already kind of did. He is absolutely everything books tell you that boys should be. If you were still here today, I would tell you to never settle for anything less than the Jake Andrewses of the world. Because they exist—and not just in fairy tales.

I have new friends, too. You would love Heidi. She loves Justin Bieber almost as much as you do. They all care about me—like, truly care about me. They were there for me when no one else was.

It hurts to know that you'll never have the feelings or experiences everyone should have, like falling in love for the first time or having your heart broken. You'll never have a first kiss or butterflies on your first date. A guy won't hold your hand for the first time or hold you in his arms. You'll never know the feeling of telling a guy you love him, or his telling you.

The worst thing is that you'll never know the feeling of falling—falling in love with someone. And I don't mean love—I mean *love*-love. Mom-and-Dad love. The love that's so instant and intense and easy, it feels like all the world's forces collided and fate gave you a push, and you're there, in front of the person who's now a part of you. The world spins and your heart explodes, and you want nothing else at all in the entire universe as long as you can be with that one person all the time. When you're not, you think about him until your mind is consumed, and it's almost like you're suffocating and drowning . . . But in a good way, because your love is all around you.

God, I can't even begin to tell you . . . I just wish that you could have felt it, too.

So that when you found your Jake Andrews, you would know.

You would know what it feels like to stand in front of your forever.

Love,

Kayla

JAKE

Emily,

If you're half the person your sister is, I would have loved you, too. You're super cute. I would have had to work with your dad to beat off all the future guys.

My sister Julie says that you're one of the funniest people she's ever met. That's saying a lot, considering she knows me. Ha-ha.

1D are *so* much better than J. Biebs.

Don't worry about Kayla at all. I promise to take care of her always. She's my everything. And I love her so, so much.

Love,

Your future brother-in-law (fingers crossed),

Jake

MIKAYLA

"So, is there anything else you guys did for her birthday?" Jake asks as he turns the key in the ignition and waits for the truck to warm up.

"Not really. I mean . . . Megan and I used to take her for ice cream, then we'd have the family dinner, where we'd do the box reveal."

"So, ice cream, then?" He smiles at me, pulling me closer to him on the seat and kissing my temple. "And we can go hang out with my family."

I smile and nod.

At the ice cream shop, Jake pays and we sit down in a booth. "Do you miss her? Not Emily—Megan, I mean. Do you think about her?"

I think for a second. "Yeah, you know what? I really do. I mean, we were best friends since, like, fifth grade. I always thought that losing her would be like losing a limb. I think eventually I would have forgiven her, like I have James. But I don't think I can now. I mean, where the hell has she been? Not one phone call, no texts, Facebook, e-mail, nothing. Even when my family died. Nothing."

"Did you ask James why she wasn't at the funeral?" he asks.

"No, because I don't think there really is a suitable reason. Do you?"

"Not a single one."

———

As we're driving home after visiting Jake's parents, I see a rental sign in front of an apartment block. I ask Jake to stop so I can take a look around. By now I've saved up enough money for a security deposit and first month's rent. The location is good. It's close enough to campus so I can catch a bus, and hopefully I'll soon have a car. The apartment itself is pretty awful—Jake's house looks like a five-star hotel in comparison. But with some furniture and decent decorating, I might be able to make it my home.

We left early in the morning to go to the cemetery, then spent most of the day at Jake's parents' house. The two-hour drive there and back has us beat, too, so we crash as soon as we get home. We've spent every night in Jake's bed since the frat party. He *still* won't kiss me, though, and I don't know why.

When I come out of the bathroom, he's sitting up in bed, shirtless, with the blankets bunched at his waist. I get under the covers, lay my head on my pillow, and look up at him. He looks down at me and smiles—but it's a sad smile. I smile back only a little, because I'm trying to decipher the hurt in his eyes. I stare at him, and he stares back. It seems like we try to communicate without talking for a long time.

I don't know what he's thinking.

I know it's not good.

I almost don't want to know.

The longer I stare at him, the sadder he looks—until eventually tears start to fill his eyes and he has to look away.

I swallow the lump in my throat.

I don't want to talk.

I don't want to ask him what's wrong.

Because I'm scared now. This is the moment when it all ends—when he tells me that he doesn't want me here.

Or want me *at all*.

I feel pain in the back of my eyes and throat and behind my nose from trying to hold in the tears that are bursting to get through. I refuse to listen to him. I don't want to hear what he has to say, because the second the words come out, it will all be over. I will have nothing left—not one fucking thing.

He clears his throat once, and I close my eyes. I wish all the wishes in the entire frickin' world that this is not happening. "What are we doing?" He says it so quietly, I almost don't hear him.

I let out the breath that I didn't know I was holding. "What?" I squeak.

"I'm sorry, Kayla," he says.

I move to get out of the bed, too embarrassed to be so intimate with him when he tells me that we—whatever it is we are—are done.

"Whoa, where are you going?" he asks, holding on to me. "We need to talk about this."

I panic and escape from his grasp. "I can't." I close my eyes, because I don't want to see his beautiful face. "I don't want to hear it, Jake, please. I just don't want to," I beg him and run to my room across the hall.

He follows me. "What's going on?" He sounds worried. I can't look at him.

"I'm just—I'm sorry, okay? I know what you're going to say, and I don't want to hear it. I just don't. I can't. Not today, Jake, please." I'm almost hyperventilating, kneeling on the floor by my bed.

"What are you talking about, Kayla?" He pulls me up and puts his hands on my face to make me look at him, but my eyes are shut tight. I refuse to look. "Kayla! What do you think is happening here?"

"Jake, please." I surrender to the pain and fall to my knees again. He kneels next to me. "I don't want to be a desperate, broken girl who needs you. That's why I want to find somewhere else to live. But I waited too long, and now you don't want me here, and I'm sorry. I'm so, *so* sorry."

I'm a sobbing mess; the tears are flowing so quickly, I don't have time to wipe them away. My head is pounding, and my heart hurts so much I'm sure it's going to break. I rest my chin on my knees, my hands wrapped around my head. I wish the world would leave me alone for just one minute, so I can gather the strength to get up and face it.

I don't know how long I sit there crying. Once the tears have dried up, and I've quieted down, I finally get the courage to look up. He's there, watching me and waiting—for this stupid little girl to calm the fuck down so he can get this shit over with. I start to cry again.

"Stop!" he cries. His tone is forceful enough that I listen. "What the fuck have I ever done to make you feel like I don't want you here? Or that I don't want you at all?" he asks, hurt and confused. "God, Kayla. I kept my mouth shut because I knew it was important to you to be out on your own or whatever. But it's not what I want! Not for a fucking second. And you should know that without my having to say a goddamn word. You should *feel* that. Have I not shown you how I feel about you? Have I not been clear in the way I act toward you? I don't know what else I could have said or done without actually coming out and saying the words." He positions us so I'm straddling him and wraps his arms around me. We can't get any closer. "Kayla, it was you who wanted to leave, not me. You're the one who wanted to find somewhere else to live. It was never me."

I don't know how to explain this to him so he understands that it's not about him. I close my eyes and exhale a steady breath. When I open them, I look straight into his deep-blue gaze. "I want to make sure that I'm strong enough on my own without you. Since that night, it's been only you. You're my entire world. I need to learn to stand on my own and be my own person, but I can't do that here."

"Why not?" he pleads. His face is so close to mine, our mouths are almost touching. I want to kiss him. I look at his lips then at his eyes. He must know what I'm thinking, because he licks his lips just a tiny bit. I close my eyes so I'm not tempted, because this is *not* how I want our first real kiss to happen. "Just try. Please?" His voice breaks.

I look at him.

Really, truly look at him.

And I fall in love all over again.

"Please, Kayla. Just give it until the new year. Promise me?"

I nod.

He picks us up off the floor and carries me back to his bed. He holds me, and I hold him.

"God, Jake, I more-than-a-lot like you."

"Kayla, I passed that stage a long, long time ago."

FORTY-FOUR

JAKE

It's been a week since we went to Emily's grave, and a week since that night we . . . I don't know what that night was, but it did bring us closer together. I guess we needed to have it out.

Also, Kayla is a little girl when it comes to insects and rodents.

She saw a mouse and a cockroach and demanded that pest control fumigate our house. Apparently, we have to be gone for two nights, so she suggested heading back home for the weekend. But I, being the gentleman that I am, booked us a weekend at a hotel. It's nothing swanky, but it's something different, and I think we need it.

"I hope you're not planning on getting lucky tonight." She elbows me as I take our bags out of my truck.

"I asked for extra pillows just in case," I say smugly.

She gasps, her mouth wide open in shock. I laugh so hard at her reaction, I have to stop to catch my breath.

Once we're in the hotel room, I kick myself for not bringing any alcohol. I know we don't need any to have a good time, but it sure doesn't hurt. I tell Kayla that I'm going to go down to the bar to see if I can charm them with my good looks and "panty-dropping smile." (Her words—*definitely* not mine.)

She says she's going to hop in the bath.

I say I'm staying.

She pushes me out the door.

Fifteen minutes later, after talking to the bartender (who happens to be a baseball fan) and meeting up in some sketchy alley, I'm back in our room. She's still in the bath. "Having fun?" I ask her, trying to sneak a peek. The bubbles are so high, I can't see shit anyway.

"Mm-hm," she murmurs, eyes closed. "We should totally get a hot tub for your house."

"That can *totally* be arranged." I smirk at her. "Can I get in?"

"Yep." She pops the *p*. "I'm getting out now, anyway." She stands up, completely naked and dripping wet. I stand there frozen with my jaw on the floor, my eyes outside my head and my mouth foaming.

Instant hard-on.

By the time my brain catches up to my dick, she's already drying off and putting a robe on.

"Wait." I'm acting like I'm twelve and have never seen a naked girl before. Truthfully, I only act like that with Kayla. I have to clear my throat a thousand times so something—anything—would come out. "What are you doing?" I almost yell at her, because I'm pathetic and have no control over anything at the moment. "Take that off. Get back naked. Hurry!"

What the fuck did I just say?

She chuckles at me, pushes me out of the bathroom, and locks the door behind her.

I rest my head against the bathroom door, waiting for her to open it and come out, so I can tell her to get naked again. I need to see her again.

She opens the door, still wearing the robe. I practically rip it off her—or at least try to. But my brain and body don't work, because all the blood has rushed to my dick. She's laughing at me and pushes me away so I calm down a bit. But in my head, I'm a six-year-old kid who didn't get the Teenage Mutant Ninja Turtle action figure I wanted, and I'm going to plead for it every hour until I get what I want. Because I'm a brat, and I need to see her naked.

Once I've settled down a bit, we open the champagne I brought, fill glasses with ice—the way she likes it—and start drinking. It's not long until we're slightly buzzed.

"Did you have a pet kangaroo in Australia?" Kayla asks.

I spit out my drink, because it's one of the funniest things I've ever heard.

"What?" She laughs. "What's so funny? Did you?" she asks through a giggle.

"No," I say flatly. "We did *not* have pet kangaroos. They do *not* roam the streets or backyards like everyone thinks. In fact, the only time I saw a kangaroo was at the zoo."

"Oh," she says, still giggling. "Then why would everyone think that? It doesn't make sense."

"No shit."

"I'm tired," she says, stretching. Damn it, now I know we won't be fooling around.

"You ready for bed?" I ask, walking over to my bag to get my phone charger.

"Almost," she whispers behind me. I hear something soft drop to the floor.

When I turn around, her robe is around her ankles, and she's wearing hot-pink matching lace underwear. It's almost see-through *everywhere*. The pink complements her darker skin, and I swear to God my dick is about to explode.

"Holy shit," I breathe.

She laughs shyly, her cheeks red and her face hiding behind a curtain of hair. I walk toward her slowly, because her body deserves to be taken in from top to bottom. When I finally reach her, my mouth is dry. I can't take my eyes off her. I'm inches away from her, so close that I can feel her body heat radiating. I reach out, but my fingers stop millimeters from her. "I don't know what to touch first," I tell her.

She closes her eyes and says softly, "I don't care, Jake. Just touch me."

MIKAYLA

I feel like he's everywhere at once.

His hands.

His mouth.

Everything.

Everywhere.

He lifts me, his hands on my ass, and I wrap my legs around him. He groans when our parts collide. I can feel him, and I'm sure he can feel me. He carries me to the bed and lays me down. He stands above me, and for a few seconds that feel like hours he looks at me. His eyes wander over my body, and I'm almost ready to cover myself. I'm so self-conscious—it took so much courage to wear this and *be* this in front of him.

"God, Kayla. You are so damn beautiful." With a crooked smile, he asks, "Is this what you bought that—"

I nod. I bought it at the mall with Julie.

"It's about fucking time I got to see it."

I laugh as he rips off his T-shirt and pants, leaving on his boxers. Then his body hovers over mine, and I can feel skin on skin, a guttural moan escaping me before I can stop it. He's kissing my neck, his hands all over the place like he can't get enough.

He leans back, his weight on his elbows. Our parts are joined together, my lace panties and his boxers the only barrier. He looks up at me. "As much as I love what you're wearing, and that you're wearing it for *me*, I'd prefer that you didn't have anything on." I nod.

Slowly and effortlessly, he unclips my bra and removes the straps from my shoulders, kissing my skin. Once it's off, he hovers his body lower, kissing my bare stomach and curling his fingers around the band of my panties. He has to be able to tell how turned on I am and how badly I need him.

Slowly—so slowly—he pulls down my panties until they're on the floor. He sits on his heels and looks at me, his eyes roaming all over my body. He comes back up and lies on his side facing me. I'm on my back, head turned to face him. He moves hair out of my face then rests his hand on my stomach.

"Shit, Kayla. I'm going to regret this," he breathes.

"Regret what?" I ask. He starts to move his hand lower and lower.

So close.

"I want to kiss you so bad." He looks at my lips and licks his before returning his gaze to my eyes.

"So why don't you?"

"Because if I kiss you, I'll want to taste you. And if I taste you, I'll need to fuck you. And when I fuck you, it means you're mine. When I make you mine, I want it to be in *our* bed—not a hotel room . . . Is that okay?"

I'm so turned on, an uncontrollable cry escapes me. Before I know it, his boxers are off and he's flipped me on top of him. I'm straddling him, my wet heat on his hard dick. He's moving us so we're grinding, but he's not inside. It's so intense, I think I'm crying from the pleasure of it.

"God, Kayla. I just want to feel you," he whispers. He reaches one hand for the back of my neck, the other holding my ass. It feels so fucking good, I don't know if I'm making any noise in reality, or if the screams are just in my head.

He leans his head forward and takes my nipple in his mouth. He sucks and licks, then he's pushing up, and I'm moving back and forth, my wetness sleeked over both our parts. His grip, squeezing my ass, hurts in all the good ways.

I don't know if my eyes are closed or if the world has just stopped existing.

The buildup is so powerful, but I'm trying to hold off because I want to feel like this for the rest of my frickin' life. His mouth moves from my breasts to my neck. I lower myself onto him, and he's thrusting up and hitting a spot I didn't know can be hit. Now I know I'm actually saying all the sounds that were in my head, because my throat is scratchy.

"Fuck, Kayla. I'm so fucking close." He starts moving faster on me, and that's all it takes.

"Oh, fuck!" I scream, while he moans the manliest sound I've ever heard. At some point, he has enough respect for the other hotel guests to grab the back of my head and plaster my face into his neck to catch most of my scream. I ride every wave, panting "Holy fuck" the entire time.

Ho. Lee. Shit.

I feel sorry for all the girls in the world who'll never get to experience a Jake Andrews at least once in their lifetime.

When it's over, he starts to chuckle. I sit up and cock my head at him questioningly.

"You are so fucking *loud*, Kayla. Jesus, we need to work on that."

FORTY-FIVE

MIKAYLA

I look at Jake with my nose scrunched, a disgusted look on my face.

"It's not at all what the rap videos make it seem like." He's laughing to himself.

We're having dinner at the hotel restaurant the next day, and we somehow—I don't know how—got to talking about strip clubs.

"So you guys weren't sitting in red-leather booths with stunna shades, making it rain money?"

He laughs out loud, causing other diners to stare at him. "No, Kayla, it most definitely was not like that. More like sticky pleather chairs, making it rain germs." He shivers.

The waitress comes over for our drink order, never once looking at me. Her eyes are glued to Jake.

"I'll have a beer," Jake says calmly. "What about you, baby? Champagne with ice?"

I nod and smile.

"Make it two of each—we're on our honeymoon," he tells the waitress, who then looks at me like she just realized I'm sitting here.

Slutbag.

After more than a couple of beverages each, we head back to our room.

"Oh my God," I say, "That old dude is my lit professor, and that girl is in my class." I watch the couple make their way over to us, fondling each other, not a care in the world.

Jake laughs, and as they come closer he decides to be a smart-ass and stand right in their way, so they have no choice but to stop and look. When they see us, it's awkward as hell.

"Hi, Professor Greene," I say quietly, looking down. I try to smile but can't follow through. Jake is an asshole.

"Oh!" The professor sounds surprised. He lets go of the student and straightens up, running a hand through his hair. "Hi, Ms. Jones." He looks at me then Jake. His eyes widen slightly. "I didn't know that Jake Andrews is your boyfriend."

"Oh, he's not."

Jake tenses next to me then walks away, heading toward our room.

The professor tries to make conversation while the student tries to hide behind him. As quickly as possible, we say our good-byes, and I walk back to the room.

When I open the door, he's coming out of the bathroom. "I'm going to take the floor, so you want to pick what pillows and blankets you want?" he says to the room. He won't look at me.

"What?"

"I said—"

"I know what you said, Jake. But we have a king-sized bed here, and it's not like we haven't slept in the same bed before. Did I do something?"

"Whatever, *Micky*. Just choose so I can get some sleep. I'm tired as fuck."

Micky? "What happened? You never call me Micky."

"Well, maybe I should, since that's what your *friends* call you, right?"

"Jake—"

"Well, if I'm not your boyfriend, and I'm not your friend, then what the fuck am I?" He's yelling at me. "What the fuck am I to you, Mikayla? Tell me, please, because you sure as shit aren't making it clear!"

I look down and shrivel inside, hoping to God this isn't happening. I need him so badly, and he hates me right now.

Jake

"Jake, I can't. I can't be more than this—not now, not yet." Kayla's voice breaks as tears form in her eyes. She won't look at me.

"More than what, Mikayla?" I growl. "More than friends? We're more than friends, and you know it. You can't deny it, either—all the touching and feeling, the *innocent* kisses and hand-holding. You—" I point at her. "You sit on my goddamn lap whenever you get the chance. What about last night, when you rode my dick, and I made you come? Is that what friends do, Mikayla?"

"Jake, that's bullshit! Don't put it all on me. You know damn well you're partly responsible for that, too. It's not just me! It never has been."

"I'm not the one denying anything, *Micky*." I spit out again, just to bring it home. "You're the one who can't decide what the fuck we are."

"I don't know!" she yells. Her voice is hoarse, and tears are leaking from her eyes faster than she can wipe them away. She bites her lip. "I don't know what to say, Jake. You know how I feel about you. You know that I . . ." She trails off.

"Know what, Mikayla?"

"I don't know, okay?" She starts pacing the floor. I watch her. "I just know that we can't be together—not in that way. It's just too

much . . . I'm not ready! It's too soon, and I'm not fucking ready!"
She screams more loudly with every word. Then, calming down,
she looks at me. "But you know how I feel, Jake. I want you—only
you . . ."

MIKAYLA

He instantly rushes over to me and pins me against the wall. He lifts
me up by my ass, and I wrap my legs around his waist. He's kissing
my neck, my collarbone, my face—everywhere but my lips. I grip
his hair and throw my head back so he can better access my neck.
I'm moaning and groaning, so fucking wet I'm sure he can smell it.
God, I want him so bad.

He places me down on the bed, his lips never leaving my skin.
He starts to remove my top, and I sit up to help him pull it off. I'm
not wearing a bra, and my nipples are so hard they could cut glass.
He continues to kiss my neck while gently and passionately cupping
my breasts. I scream quietly. He positions himself between my legs,
and I let out a cry as we start to move together.

He moves his lips lower and lower down my neck until they
reach my chest. He starts to kiss my breasts, one, then the other,
licking the slope in between them. Then his tongue is on my nipple,
and his mouth covers it, sucking gently. He moves to the other and
does the same—licking, sucking, nipping. I'm about to lose control,
my hands gripping the comforter under us and my head thrashing
side to side on the pillow. The pleasure is so amazing, I'm struggling
to keep from crying out loud.

He moves lower, his tongue dipping into my navel. I know
where this is going, and I want to cry in anticipation—I want it so
badly. Holding the band of my pants, he slowly starts to pull them

down. My hands are in his hair as I not-so-subtly push him further down, begging and pleading for a release, the alcohol making me braver.

"What do you want, Kayla?" he asks.

"What?" My brain is too fuzzy from the heat between my legs.

"What do you want?"

I stop to think about what he's asking. "I still don't know, Jake."

He sits up, and my body already misses him. "I can't be what you want," he says, slowly standing up. I whimper internally for him to come back. "I need to be more than this." He points his finger at himself then me. "You need to pick. It's all or nothing."

I can't—I can't pick. I sit and pull my pants up, then I throw my top over my head to cover myself. I start sobbing uncontrollably. I can't lose him, but I can't give him everything yet, either. And he deserves everything. "I can't, Jake."

"What do you mean you can't? You can't choose? Or you can't be with me?"

"Yes."

"So which one?"

"It's been six months, Jake. Six fucking months since my life turned to shit." He flinches at my words, and I know he's taken them the wrong way. It's not about him at all. "Jake, it's not—"

"It can be six months or six fucking years, Mikayla! Your boyfriend will still be an asshole, your best friend will still be a whore, and your family will still be dead!" he spits.

My eyes snap to his, and I see the regret instantly. "Kayla, baby, I'm sorry. I'm a dick. I shouldn't have said—"

"Go to hell, Jake."

"Kayla, please." He's crying now, his voice breaking.

"Get the fuck out, Jake!" I scream.

He flinches but walks out the door, closing it quietly behind him. I don't see him for the rest of the night.

FORTY-SIX

JAKE

I left Kayla alone in the hotel and ended up crashing at Cam's dorm. He asked what happened. I told him to fuck off, so he left me alone.

I'm at the school gym, lifting weights to try to get rid of this angry energy I have. I'm pissed off that I fucked up—that both of us fucked up. Because it's not just me—it's her, too. We both said shit that we can't take back, and I think this is it. This is the point when it's over. I'm so fucking angry, because it never even began. She won't even give me the chance to try.

I'm not concentrating on what I'm doing, and I think I put the wrong weights on the bar. I can't press them, and I'm struggling to get the bar off my chest.

"Whoa," I hear someone say. He spots me and gets the bar back on the rack. *James.* Of course it is. "You all right, man?" he asks.

"I'm fine, asshole," I snap.

He's taken aback for a second. He then removes his earphones and starts winding them around his iPod, like he's ready to have a long conversation.

Great, just what I fucking need.

"I, uh." He clears his throat. This kid's awkward as hell. "I heard you went to Emily's grave on her birthday."

I look at him sideways.

"Micky told me," he says.

I don't care.

He takes a deep breath then sighs out loud.

I don't say anything. I just sit on the bench and wait for him to fuck off.

"You know I asked Micky to marry me, right?"

Oh God, I can*not* have this conversation with him—not now. I stay silent.

He continues, "I asked Kevin, her dad. I asked his permission before I did it."

"So?" I bite out. I don't know where this conversation is going, but I hate that we're having it. "She said no, right?"

"Yeah, she did. That's not the point I'm trying to make, so quit being a jerk and let me finish."

I'm quiet.

"Kevin was a really good guy. He loved his girls more than anything. But my dad's kind of a prick. He's one of those dads you're always trying to impress, you know? Like nothing you do is ever good enough."

I remember his dad from the funeral. I get it.

"Anyway, Kevin was different—he always accepted you. His girls could have been or done anything, and he would have always loved and encouraged them."

I wait for him to go on.

"What I'm trying to say is, when I asked him for permission, he kind of just looked at me strange for a few seconds, and I swear I thought he was going to say no. Then he clapped me on the shoulder and said, 'James, she's eighteen, so I can't stop you. I think it's a little young, but I was eighteen when I met Denise, so I can't talk. I'm sure you will both make the right decision, and she'll learn to love you as a husband.'"

He clears his throat. "I was so happy he was okay with it, I didn't even think about what he said until later—that she would 'learn' to love me as a husband." He pauses for a bit, thinking about his next words. "I get it now, Jake. I know what he meant. She shouldn't have to *learn* to love me like that—she just *should*. Somehow, Kevin knew that she didn't. And now I see the way she is with *you*, the way she looks at *you*, and that's how it should have been. Like you're the only one. You're it, Jake—you're all of it. Her forever."

FORTY-SEVEN

MIKAYLA

I call Lucy to pick me up from the hotel and take me home. I didn't hear from Jake. I even made sure my phone was fully charged. Nothing.

I think we're done.

When we pull into our driveway, Logan's leaning against his car.

"Asshole," Lucy greets him with a nod.

"Kinky hornbag," he replies, but she's already reversing out the driveway. He turns to me. "Where were you?" he asks.

"Long story. How is he?"

"Who?"

"Jake."

"What? I don't know."

"Oh." I thought for sure Jake would be with him.

"What about Jake?" he asks, eyeing me curiously.

"Nothing. What's up? What are you doing here?" I'm not looking at him, but I can feel him watching me. It's awkward and uncomfortable, so after a few seconds I look up.

He's still watching me.

So we stand there for a few seconds—minutes? Who knows. We wait for one of us to talk first. Finally, he breaks the silence.

"My friend's mom is selling her car. It's in your budget. I thought I'd take you to look at it now?" He says this like a question.

"Okay," I say quietly.

I bring my and Jake's overnight bags into the house and drop them just inside the front door. Then I get into Logan's car.

He drives us about ten minutes away to look at the car. It's perfectly fine for what I need and in my budget. I tell her I'll take it but won't be able to get the money until Wednesday.

On the ride back home, Logan asks, "So I'll pick you up on Wednesday, yeah?"

"Thanks." I still haven't said much, and he hasn't asked about Jake again.

Awkward silence.

Then a tear falls down my cheek, and I wipe it away quickly. I turn to look at him. "I love him, Logan," I say. Because if I can't tell Jake, then somebody needs to know.

He looks at me before turning back to the road. "No shit," he deadpans.

"But I think we're done."

He shakes his head, still looking straight ahead. "You guys will never be done."

"He's the one for me—was the one. He was my happily-ever-after."

"So what's the problem?"

"I can't give myself to him."

"What do you mean?"

"I'm not who I want to be yet. I'm not ready to give him everything. I'm still broken, and I need to pick up the pieces of myself and put them back together. If I give myself to him, I have to be complete. I can't be half the person I want to be."

He pulls over to the side of the road and turns the car off. Then he looks at me for what seems like a lifetime. "I'm sorry, Micky," he says. I look down, because I am, too. I'm *so* fucking sorry. "I'm sorry, but I think you're wrong," he continues.

My eyes dart to his.

"Jake saw you at your worst. He was there when your life changed and your heart shattered. He was there to help you piece some of it back together. He's seen it all, Micky. He's seen you at your worst, and he still fell in love with you—like, truly the *forever* kind of love with you. And I'm sorry, because I think you're making a mistake. Maybe you don't need to be a complete person, or maybe you do. But maybe he's it—maybe he's the other half of you."

Forty-Eight

Mikayla

When Logan drops me off, I see Jake's truck in the driveway. I fumble to open the car door before Logan even brings it to a complete stop. I rush to open the front door, because I really, really need to see him. I need to tell him that I love him and that I need to be with him—like, *be* with him.

"Jake!" I call out.

"In here!"

"Where?" I stop just inside the front door, trying to hear where he's calling from.

"Here!"

I walk down the hallway and look in the study. He's not there. Then I look into my room.

He's there.

And the world around me goes black.

I know why it's called "heartbreak," because my heart really does feel like it's physically breaking. I feel every single excruciating bit of pain that comes with it. I feel like I've died.

But I haven't. I'm still breathing. I just haven't opened my eyes. For what could have been seconds, I stand in the doorway, eyes closed, for what feels like a lifetime. When I open my eyes, I'll see the one thing I never, ever wanted to see. I take two deep breaths, in and out, and count to ten in my head. Then I open my eyes.

I see my room. The bed has been stripped, my comforter and baby blanket gone. Cardboard boxes are scattered around the room—some empty, some filled with my belongings. Jake has my dresser drawer open, and he's packing one of the boxes with my clothes.

It's over.

He wants me out.

Gone.

From his house *and* his life.

We're done.

My legs start to give out, so I gather all the energy I have left and sit on the edge of the bed.

I don't look at him. I can't see him.

I sit there and cry silent tears, my head bent, shoulders slouched, and my hands gripping the side of the mattress.

I *can't* face him.

I hear him pack more of my things—my life. Everything I have left in this world is packed up in a few boxes.

I cry.

He shuffles in and out of the room, taking boxes and bags with him.

And I cry.

Because it's all I can do. When your heart breaks, and you lose absolutely everything you have left in your life, the only thing you can do is cry.

I don't wail.

I don't sob.

I just sit in silence and let the tears fall.

All the regrets I've ever had play like a movie in my mind. Every moment when I should have told him that he was it. He was my Prince Charming, my knight in shining armor, my happily-ever-after.

Then I sense him in front of me, but I'm too scared to open my eyes. His warm hands reach for mine and place them around his neck. I know what this is—a sad good-bye. I can't take it, so I do nothing.

Then he lifts me in the air, holding me under my thighs. I tighten my grip around his neck and wrap my legs around his waist. He's walking, one hand on my back and the other behind my head, like I'm a baby. I hold on to him tightly, like I want to climb him and never let go.

Suddenly I'm lying on something soft, and something warm covers me. It feels so familiar, but I can't comprehend what it is. I still don't want to open my eyes and face reality.

Then I'm on my side, and he's next to me, his arms wrapped around me so tightly, it's hard to breathe. But I breathe through it, because I want to feel alive in this moment. I want to remember every single piece of him in the last few moments we have together. So I open my eyes, and he's there.

We're in *his* bed.

Under *my* comforter.

Surrounded by boxes of *my* things.

He kisses away the tears that have fallen on my wet face. He looks at me—really looks at me. Then his lips are on mine, and I close my eyes because the sensation is so overpowering. At first his lips don't move, like we're just connected at the mouth, waiting for the sparks to sizzle away. But after a few moments, he opens them slightly, and our lips start moving together in perfect synchrony. His arms around me, I grip his T-shirt. His tongue brushes against my lips, and I moan in pleasure. Then our tongues touch for the first time, and I see white behind my eyes. We hold each other, kissing with our lips and tongues and so much passion that I don't know if either of us is actually breathing. I get it. My mom was so frickin' right about this moment.

And Jake Andrews was so wrong. He didn't need to kiss me to make me his. I was his the moment he asked me to move here with him and the moment he held my hand at the funeral. I was his when I had nowhere else to go, and he took me into his home. I was his the moment he held me while I cried in the back of that ambulance. He was my strength when I had none. I knew it when he cleared his throat, and I looked up at him with tears in my eyes in that tiny hallway by the restrooms at Bistro's. And I knew I was his when I fixed his tie at Walmart. That instant, intense feeling was the exact second I knew I was standing in front of my forever.

—

We kiss for so long our lips begin to ache. When we finally pull away, we look into each other's eyes.

Talking without speaking.

But something needs to be said, because I never want to go another day without his knowing. "Jake, I am so much more-than-a-lot in love with you."

He kisses me again, but this time it's different—less intimate and more passionate. He dips his tongue further in as he positions himself on top of me, holding himself up on his forearms. He kisses me with so much passion, I almost forget that this is going to be our first time. He presses his body against mine, grinding his hardness into me. His kisses move from my mouth to my jaw then down my neck to my chest. I try to take his shirt off, because I need to feel all of him. He sits up to remove his T-shirt and takes mine off, too.

"I want you so bad, Kayla," he whispers into my neck.

"I'm all yours," I tell him.

Because I am.

And he reciprocates—three times in a row.

It feels so frickin' good, I don't know if I'm dreaming. After the second time, I beg him to stop, but he just keeps going with his mouth and tongue and his fingers. Everything before must have been done so wrong, because Jake Andrews knows. He knows how to do things so *goddamn* right.

Once he's finally inside me, I work out why I never felt like this before. If I compare my feelings for Jake to my feelings for James, then I know I've never loved anyone before. Not even a little bit. Not even at all.

FORTY-NINE

MIKAYLA, AGE 8

"What story would you like to read, sweetheart?"

"I want you to tell me a story, Mommy. My own story, please."

My mom smiles at me, her brown eyes softening when she sees my pleading face. "Okay, I'll tell you a very special story. It's a fairy tale about kissing a prince."

"Yuck, Mommy! Kissing is gross."

She laughs a little. I don't know why, because I don't think it's funny. "This is about a special kiss. Are you ready?"

"Yep." I nod.

"One day in the future, Kayla, you'll meet a handsome prince— a prince so handsome, he will make your heart skip a beat." I giggle, which makes her laugh, too. "Every princess has one prince to share the loves and joys of life with. Do you know how that princess knows which prince is hers?"

"How, Mommy?"

"From a kiss."

"But how?"

"Your very first kiss with your prince will change your life. When your lips touch for the first time, the earth will feel like it has stopped moving, but at the same time the world around you spins. It'll feel like fireworks in the night sky—a bright light in the darkness. You'll feel your heart beat fast in your ears, but silence will surround you. When you pull apart and open your eyes and really *see* each other, you'll know in *that* moment from *that* kiss that you've just let someone own a piece of your heart, and you'll live happily ever after."

FIFTY

MIKAYLA

"Jesus Christ, Kayla. Where the fuck have you been? Where is your phone?" Jake puts out his hand, asking me to hand it to him. I get it out of my purse. It's dead.

I've just walked into the house after picking up my new car with Logan. Everyone else is here—Lucy, Cam, Heidi, and Dylan.

Jake takes the phone from me and sees that it's dead. He walks off to the bedroom in a huff, presumably to charge it. When he comes back, he still seems pissed. "Start charging your fucking phone, Kayla. I'm sick of this shit," he growls.

"Jake," Cam says. It's a warning.

I look at Jake, confused. He's never acted like this before . . . Except that one time when he thought Logan and I were messing around.

Jake looks at Cam then at me, and his features even out. Something else takes over. He walks up to me and takes my hands. I'm wary, because I don't know what the hell is going on. "I'm sorry, baby. We've just been trying to call you. Has no one contacted you today?"

I look at him, brows furrowed in confusion. I glance at everyone. They're watching me, waiting.

Waiting for what?

I slowly shake my head. "I'm scared, Jake. What's going on?"

Still holding me by the hand, he walks me to our bedroom, sits me on the edge of the bed, and starts pacing. He keeps looking up at me nervously, like he's trying to find the right words to say next. It's as though the conversation is playing out in his head, and he keeps restarting it. He's opened his mouth three or four times already but keeps snapping it shut, changing his mind.

What the fuck is going on?

"Just say it already. You're scaring me. Is it your parents? Did something happen? Julie?"

"Shit!" he says. "No, baby. I'm sorry, I didn't mean to scare you. No, they're all good. It's not that. Sorry, babe."

"Then what is it? Just tell me. Please?"

He sits on his heels in front of me, his head bowed. He holds both my hands, playing with the rings on my fingers—my mom's and dad's wedding and engagement rings.

It's about them.

When he looks up, there are tears brimming in his eyes. "They caught him, Kayla. They found the asshole who killed your family."

—

I didn't leave the bedroom for three days, and the whole time Jake was beside me, leaving only when absolutely necessary.

I hate this stupid, broken me.

I hate that Jake is back to being the guy who has to save me.

And I hate *him*.

I hate him so fucking much.

Christopher Leon.

That's the asshole's name.

The murderer.

The one who took everything.

It shouldn't matter that they caught him. I mean, it shouldn't make me this upset, because whether they have him or not, it's not going to bring back my family.

Apparently, he was busted for breaking into another house, and the fingerprint DNA matched. Nathan keeps Jake up-to-date on the situation. He's been keeping a close eye on the case to make sure the asshole doesn't find any loopholes in the system and get less than what he fucking deserves.

He's a murderer.

Our friends came around to check on me a few times, but I asked Jake to tell them that I wasn't up for visitors. Even James came by once. I heard him and Jake having a proper, decent conversation—no name-calling or punching.

Nothing like a fucked-up girl to bring peace between two enemies.

For three days I cried, sulked, and went through the stages of grief all over again, like I was reliving their deaths. Denial. Anger. Bargaining. Depression. And today I woke up and reached the final stage. Acceptance.

I was not going to let this asshole ruin me—not again.

I just don't think you should let bad people dictate whether you have a good *life*.

Jake walks into the bedroom and pauses briefly when he sees me up and dressed. He's been super wary of me, not wanting to suffocate me or push me far away.

He has been perfect.

My perfect boyfriend.

He eyes me sideways, a little confused. I would be, too. I'm wearing yoga pants and one of his baseball jerseys and holding his bat. "Hey, baby." I saunter over to him and kiss him—really kiss him.

He kisses me back and cups my ass lightly. "Jesus, Kayla. I've missed you," he says. He deepens the kiss, leading me toward the bed.

I laugh into his mouth. "Jake, it's been three days, not three years."

"I know, but it's been hard . . . I was going to say it's been hard keeping my hands off you, and I think I'll leave it there. Yep, it's just . . . hard." He smirks, thrusting into me. I laugh out loud.

"It's so good to hear you laughing again." He takes my face in his hands and looks into my eyes. "I so much more-than-a-lot love you, you know that, right?"

I nod. I do know. And I so much more-than-a-lot love him, too.

"So what's with the outfit?" he asks. "Not that I don't love it. Your wearing my jersey is hot, but why?"

"I want you to pitch to me." I throw him a baseball.

"What?"

"You've never pitched to me. I want to see if I can hit one. Please?"

"You want me to go easy on you, or you want me to challenge you?"

"Challenge me."

I drive us in *my* car, which I've only driven once before when I brought it home, over to the field near *our* house, and for an hour or so we take my mind off Christopher Leon. Pitch, hit, chase, repeat.

"Hey, um, Mikayla?" Jake says. He barely ever calls me Mikayla, so I'm paying attention to whatever he's about to say.

"Yeah?" I answer warily.

"I know that, uh . . ." He clears his throat, takes his cap off, runs his hand through his hair, then puts it on backwards. "I know that you're wearing your mom's engagement ring, but, um . . . What if a guy wants to propose?"

Where is this coming from? "What are you saying, Jake?"

His eyes go big. "Oh, shit, Kayla! No! I'm not asking you. I was just, um . . . I was just wondering." He waves his hands frantically, trying to get his point across. I laugh at him, because he's trying to backtrack, and it's funny as hell.

—

We order Chinese for dinner again and eat on the sofa, watching TV.

"I would want my own ring," I say.

"Huh?"

"When said guy, hopefully you, proposes, I would want my own ring. Just so you know." I look down at my food for a second then back up at him. A blush is creeping to his cheeks. "I love these rings, but they belong to them, you know? They represent their story. I would want my own to represent *my* fairy tale—my prince and my happily-ever-after."

He smiles. "I'll let that guy know," he says and goes back to his food.

—

We're lying in bed that night after making love. I've learned to tone down the noise level, but it's hard, because Jake's learned my body inside out. He knows me—like, *really* knows me.

"Do you want to go to the hearing, Kayla?"

"Do you think I should?"

"Dad says it's an open-and-shut case. I don't think you *need* to be there."

"Then I don't want to."

"Are you sure?"

"I think I'm done with the past, Jake. I think I just want my future." I look at him, and he gets it. He knows what I mean. I just want *him*.

FIFTY-ONE

MIKAYLA

It's been one year since my life changed—since the people I thought I loved betrayed me, and the people I did love were taken from me.

And it's been one year since I stood in front of my forever.

Jake and I stayed at his parents' house over the weekend. Now we're at the cemetery. Jake got red tulips for Mom's birthday tomorrow. It's one of the reasons why I love him—so much more-than-a-lot.

We walk, hand in hand, toward my family's headstones. There's a lone figure standing by them, dressed in black with sunglasses on, looking down. I don't recognize her from this far. I'm not really in the mood to share the space with anyone, so we wait.

When she finally turns around, I see her. But it's not really her—it's like a shadow of who she once was. Her long blond hair, cut to a bob just below her chin, is now a shade of straw. She's lost weight everywhere but around her belly, which is huge—pregnant, about-to-give-birth huge.

I squeeze Jake's hand, and he looks down at me. "It's Megan," I say, nodding in her direction.

He understands. "I'll be in the truck," he says. He kisses my temple and walks away.

As I walk toward Megan, she must sense my coming, because she looks up at me, then straight back down. I think maybe she wants to leave but doesn't know if she should, so she waits. Either way, I'd know she was here, which has to mean something, right?

I stand next to her, not looking at her. She doesn't look at me. We stare at the headstones. "You're pregnant?" I ask, because I feel like we should talk if we're going to stand here.

"Yeah," she whispers. Her voice is hoarse, like she's been crying or taken up smoking two packs a day.

"Where's the dad?"

"Don't know."

"He bailed on you, huh?"

"No, Mick, I mean I don't know who the dad is."

I clear my throat. "What are you doing here?" I still don't look at her.

Megan stares straight ahead. "The adoptive parents live in town. I'm here until I have the baby, then I'm gone."

It's silent for a moment.

"I meant, what are you doing here at the cemetery?"

"Oh," she says quietly. "I can go." She turns to leave.

"Where were you, Megan?" I say more loudly, because I need to know why my best friend in the whole world never bothered to contact me in the entire year my family's been dead. "It's been a year. Where the fuck have you been?"

"I didn't think you wanted to see me."

"Shit, Megan! What happened here"—I wave at the headstones—"was bigger than you and me. It was bigger than high school drama, and your cheating with James. My family was murdered, and I needed my *best friend*. Where the *fuck* were you?" I spit out each word so she knows that I'm so frickin' mad at her. Tears start to fall down my cheeks, and I don't bother to wipe them.

"I couldn't," she says, so quietly I almost miss it.

"You couldn't? What the hell does that mean?"

"It means I couldn't face you, Mick. I just couldn't."

"Why?" I yell. I don't care about hiding my feelings anymore.

"Because, Mick . . ." Then she breaks down and falls to her knees, pregnant belly and all. I stay standing . . . and wait. "Because," she continues, "it's my fault they're dead."

My eyes dart to hers, and my breathing accelerates. "What does that mean, Megan?" I say through clenched teeth.

"It means I called him. I told him to do it. I called Chris— Christopher—that night, and I asked him to steal that necklace James gave you for your eighteenth birthday."

"What?" I can't believe this.

"He wasn't supposed to kill them! No one was supposed to be home. I told him not to hurt anybody. Mick, you have to believe me. He wasn't supposed to hurt anybody!"

I stare straight ahead, tears falling fast. My hands are balled into fists. There are so many questions and emotions running through my mind, I don't know what to say or ask. I want to kill her.

"I fooled around with Chris a few times, so I knew he would do it for me. I just . . . When you caught me and James at the restaurant, and he told you he loved you, he then discarded me like a piece of trash. He didn't even care how I felt. I'm sorry, Mick, for all of it. I was in love with James, and he didn't even care. I was so fucking angry! I saw him first. You remember that day we met him—*I* wanted him! You didn't even want a boyfriend, but you got the best one. You didn't even want him. I did."

She's talking like we're fourteen years old. I'm so consumed with anger, hurt, and every other emotion, I can't see straight. I have to close my eyes so I can keep my breathing calm. I think of Jake.

"I went home after you caught us. I was expecting James to come after me, but he didn't. He didn't even call to see if I was okay. Nothing. And then I saw you," Megan says, her tone almost angry—like she has the right to be upset. "I saw you doing that shit to James's truck, laughing and smiling. You were with these people who I've never even seen before, and they were laughing with you, helping you through your pain. They don't even know you, and they like you already. And you were in Jake Andrews's arms . . ."

I speak up, because she shouldn't even breathe his name. "Jake has nothing to do with this! You didn't even know who he was when you saw us at James's house."

"That's bullshit, Mick. Everyone knows Jake and Logan! They were the hottest two guys out of fifteen schools. Only you—perfect little Mikayla, so loyal to her perfect boyfriend—only you didn't bother to notice anyone else. Only *you* didn't know who he was."

I want to punch her. If she brings up Jake's name again, I will.

"And that's when I called him, Mick. I called Chris because I wanted to take something away from you, like you had from me, but he wasn't supposed to kill them. I loved them, too!"

"Don't you fucking *dare*!" I snap at her. "Don't you dare talk about my family or my boyfriend like you give a shit! You have no fucking right to speak their names or even think about them for the rest of your fucking life. Do you understand?" I breathe in, trying to compose myself, because I really don't want to punch a pregnant girl. In the distance, I see Jake get out of the truck, but he pauses and waits.

"Are you going to turn me in?" Megan asks, actually looking concerned.

And that's when I see her—truly see her.

"Look at you," I spit out. "Who the fuck *are* you, Megan? What the fuck happened to you?" I look at her and scrunch my nose, disgusted. "You sleep around so much, you don't even know who the father of that baby is. You think opening your legs and having some random guy pound into you is going to make him love you? It didn't make James love you.

"You'll have to look at yourself in the mirror every fucking day. Every day, you'll have to live with the guilt of what you did. You killed my parents, who genuinely loved you. You killed my nine-year-old sister, who looked up to you. She'll never grow up and experience life. Every day, you'll have to wake up and be the person you are, and you'll have to live with it. And that, Megan, is punishment enough."

Then I walk away from her—from all of this.

I run to Jake.

He's waiting for me with arms wide open.

Like always.

My prince.

My knight in shining armor.

My happily-ever-after.

EPILOGUE

MIKAYLA

It's been six months since Megan's confession. I only told Jake about it, and that was because he forced it out of me. I guess it's hard to hide your emotions when you find out that your best friend played a role in your family's death.

Luckily for me, Jake was my rock, as always. He knew not to push me, and he knew not to be distant. He knew exactly what I needed. I guess that's why fate brought us together.

Logan was right—Jake *is* the other half of me.

I never did move out of the house, and Jake and I have begun our happily-ever-after.

This year we started a new tradition—we made our own birthday shoe boxes. We decided to make them on the anniversary of my family's death. Mine is already full. I see him writing things constantly and stuffing them in there. I love that he does it—that he unknowingly gives me a part of them every day.

I love Jake Andrews, my very own prince.

I more-than-a-lot love him.

And I can't wait to tell our children our very own fairy tale and happily-ever-after.

Logan

If you knew about my past, you'd understand why I don't let people get too close to me. The people who are supposed to love you don't always love you back. Sometimes they hurt you, physically and emotionally. Sometimes they just check out completely.

In my nineteen years, I've only loved one person—my dad, or Dr. Matthews, as most people know him. He saved my life. I've come close to loving only one other person—or at least I thought it *could* be love. But I had to kill that idea really fast, because you're not supposed to fall in love with your best friend's girl.

ABOUT THE AUTHOR

 Jay McLean is an avid reader, writer, and, most of all, procrastinator. She writes what she loves to read—books that can make her laugh, make her smile, make her hurt, and make her feel. She currently lives in Australia with her fiancé, two sons, and two dogs.

Follow Jay on Instagram and Twitter @jaymcleanauthor. For more information, visit her blog at www.jaymcleanauthor.com.